The Covert Messiah

A NOVEL

J R Lankford

Great Reads Books

Published by Great Reads Books LLC
P. O. Box 2112
Bellaire, TX 77402
http://www.novelpro.com/Great_Reads_Books/

ISBN 9780971869486
LCCN 2013938727

Manufactured in the United States of America

To my family…

There are people in the world who do more good than all the statesmen and philanthropists put together. They radiate light and peace with no intention or knowledge. When others tell them about the miracles they worked, they also are wonderstruck. Yet, taking nothing as their own, they are neither proud, nor do they crave for reputation. They are just unable to desire anything for themselves, not even the joy of helping others. Knowing that God is good they are at peace.

I Am That by Sri Nisargadatta Maharaj

Chapter 1

I didn't expect to run into my son eight years after he died.

In the brightness and the crowds I almost missed Jess. The sunrise had just turned Lake Lugano into liquid diamonds. I was at the *mercato del sabato*, the market in Porlezza, held every Saturday on the lakefront. By now I was used to Italy's northern lakes—their extravagant aura, the surrounding green of Alpine hills, the markets held in shore side medieval towns, each on its own special day.

When he was hours old, I'd brought Jess to Lake Maggiore, the large lake to the west of Lugano. *Brought* isn't exactly the right word. It was an escape. Then a year after he died at the age of ten, I took his infant brother, Peter, to live on Lake Como to the east of here. *Took* isn't the right word, either. Peter and I and Adamo, the man I married, live in hiding in a village there.

Since transportation between Lake Como and Lake Lugano is easy, I'd taken the 6:20 am ferry, caught a taxi and come to Porlezza alone, leaving Peter and Adamo to fish and myself to spend a day pretending we were a regular family.

Today would have been Jess's eighteenth birthday.

He stood beneath a hanging hand-lettered sign that advertised *Ricotta di Mucca*, cow cheese. Did I glimpse a crescent birthmark on his chin, identical to the one on mine? Light filtering through an adjoining stall's white curtain made details hard to see. Nearby an old man played an accordion. A woman in an apron scooped olives from a clay bowl. Naturally, my logical mind kicked in and told me that, at the age of fifty-four, my eyes had decided to lie to me.

"*Ciao, mia cara madre,*" he said in a voice that belonged to no one but Jess, even eight years older.

I must have dropped my market tote and passed out, because

the next thing I knew I was on the ground, staring at people's legs, my head resting on what smelled like squashed oranges and my precious Jess bending over me.

A small crowd stared, mostly at Jess.

"*Mia madre è bene,*" my mother is well, he said, helping me stand. This caused furtive glances between Jess's brown sausage curls, his olive skin and me—dark sienna Maggie Duffy Morelli—African, at least via my ancestors. Someone retrieved the unsquashed former contents of my tote and handed them to Jess. A few followed as he took me to a lakeside bench, eased me down, and then sat beside me.

Still dazed, I hadn't spoken.

I knew it was Jess. I knew he was here. I knew he was dead.

"Are you real this time?" I whispered, finding my voice. Jess had appeared to me in a vivid dream after Peter's birth seven years ago.

Now he put a hand on my back and replied, "I am real in the way you mean."

I had a thousand anxious questions—starting with *how did he get here, how long would he stay?*—but for a moment I just sat there, marveling that his hand was on my back.

"*Siete tutta la destra, signora?*" Are you all right, ma'am, a man in a grey shirt and brown felt hat asked. All the while he stared at Jess. So did the woman in the apron from the olive stand; and a younger one in glasses and long pink dress, auburn hair gathered at the nape of her neck; also an older woman I recognized by the big red flowers on her blouse. She'd been tending the shoe stall and had left it to come here. All I could see of the cheese stand now was half of an orange wheel of Rigatello because people had stopped their shopping and crowded near.

They all stared at Jess and now I saw why.

Like the diamond surface of the lake, he gleamed. It was an aura I could feel, more than see, as if happiness had arrived in the Porlezza market and taken the shape of a boy. He had on tan pants and a blue polo shirt, but it was the blue in rainbows, the tan in the sky after a storm. A closer look and his skin seemed as iridescent as my mother of pearl combs.

"It's really you, Jess?" I asked.

He gazed at me, peace and power behind his eyes. I'd never been looked on with such love.

The girl in the glasses must have felt it, too, because her eyes brimmed with tears. People murmured, breaking the silence. The man in the felt hat frowned, as if expecting an explanation.

Jess didn't seem to notice.

I had to do something, so I leaned toward him. "Jess, sweetheart. People are staring—"

"Who are you? What do you want here?" demanded the man in the felt hat.

Jess glanced up and the girl in the glasses began to weep. So did the woman who owned the shoe stall. Their tears only upset the man.

"I asked who you are!"

Around us the murmuring grew louder. There was a gasp of joy.

"Sweetheart," I repeated.

Jess said, "Oh!" As if he turned off a light switch, the blue in his shirt and the tan of his pants became normal colors. He stopped gleaming. He was just an eighteen-year old boy.

"Are you all right, Mother?" He brushed orange bits out of my hair.

"Yes," I said, though I was not.

"*Vien.*" Come. He took my hand and the tote. Smiling in delight, nodding with confidence, he led me from the stunned crowds of Porlezza's Saturday market.

Eagerly I followed, desperate to hug him, but when we reached the street, everyone was either still looking or coming our way. I caught the eye of the woman in the flowered blouse. My expression must have pleaded because she shouted to the market crowd, "Why are you bothering a boy and his mother? They have done nothing to you!"

Those who'd followed us paused, suddenly come to their senses. Eyes cast down in embarrassment, they returned to the market and their shopping—all but the felt hat man, who glared as Jess got us a cab.

"Go anywhere, please," Jess said to the driver.

The car pulled away from the Lungolago and at last I cried out in jubilation and threw my arms around him. Jess put his head on my shoulder, as if he were still ten years old.

The cab driver smiled. In Italy, family affection is cherished. As for me, my heart almost burst as I held my long lost son, filled my fingers with his curls, touched his arms, to prove he was a person and not a ghost.

Tears wet my face, his face, as we hugged.

"Jess, you're here! Oh, sweetheart, how I've missed you!"

"Dear Madre. I wasn't gone. I was always here."

Wiping away his own tear at witnessing a joyful family reunion, the driver sped away from Lake Lugano as I hugged the clone of Jesus of Nazareth, who'd died and now returned.

Chapter 2

Zach Dunlop weaved his way through Wall Street's lunchtime crowds, heading for Bowling Green Park. Nearly everyone's trades had gone badly today and he wanted to eat his lunch in the park's tear-shaped patch of green. From there he could watch tourists molest the famous charging bull. It would lift his spirits to see them rub for good luck the testicles of the symbol of the stock market—an angry, massive animal swerving in mid-charge that couldn't protect its private parts from being fondled daily.

There'd been another earthquake.

He had a friend at the U.S. Geological Survey who liked to say earth movements were so common there was a hundred percent chance of an earthquake every day, but a Magnitude 6.0 in Connecticut? He imagined fallen plaster being hauled away tonight by hedge fund managers in Greenwich, one of Wall Street's bedroom communities.

To Zach, the earthquake was yet another signal to start preparing for what he couldn't discuss—the end of the world. The Stock Exchange couldn't picture the opening bell not ringing. Yet with people acting crazier and weird disasters popping up, Zach felt a new vibration in the air. He planned to call his geologist friend this afternoon. Then he'd Google what landmasses the psychics predicted would be safe and which would disappear.

His cell phone buzzed the arrival of a text. It informed him that the stock of AmerCan, the Canadian mining company he'd been watching, had jumped in price again. Usually trading below 2800 a share, the stock had broken its resistance level and was now and then trading up to and beyond 3000. Since there'd been nothing about AmerCan in the news, Zach had nosed around and concluded inside traders were quietly taking advantage of something they knew. Who were they? Maybe AmerCan execs, looking to make a secret killing before a big announcement. Alert brokers like Zach had noticed and were joining in. He called his CEO's private line.

"Blankman here," the CEO answered. Behind his back, everyone called him Da Gawdfadda.

"It's Zach. Buy AmerCan."

"You're sure, Zach?"

"Absolutely."

"AmerCan, $2 million position," Blankman said to his assistant. To Zach he said, "Well, it's about time you gave us something. Now, watch the stock."

"Don't worry. If anyone takes it on the chin for AmerCan, it won't be Silverman Alden Investments, sir," Zach said. Not that the firm operated under the fiduciary standard, which put the client's best interests first. It didn't. Silverman operated under the suitability standard, which—requiring only reasonable disclosure—let it further its own interests at the client's expense.

He knew better than to say this or ask how Da Gawdfadda would allocate gains from AmerCan. Zach hoped it would be fair, but he only had control of the portfolios he personally managed.

To his surprise, Da Gawdfadda continued, "I do worry, Zach. You know what they're calling you?"

Zach knew. "The grandma broker."

"Help me understand why you're focusing on these widows' portfolios."

"Yeah, I know. They were just average guys who held jobs, saved and invested wisely so after they died the house would be paid for, the grandchildren would have college funds, and the wife could go on a world cruise as soon as she stopped crying because he was dead."

"You admire that kind of guy."

"I would have *been* that kind of guy if I wasn't rich before I was thirty."

"Ah, I see. It's not a crime to be a genius with stocks, Zach."

"I'll have the last laugh. I parked my widows' portfolios in solid municipals. I'm poised for the next upturn, not the next fall."

"Zach, being right about dozens of small portfolios isn't as good for the firm as being right about a single massive one."

"I know, but this is a dangerous time to be making big moves."

"So you say. Let's hope you're right." Da Gawdfadda hung up without saying goodbye.

Zach looked at his cell, shook his head, then smiled as he approached the marauding bull. Tourists obscured all but the muscled back and raised tail. It was an apt symbol. The market still hadn't recovered from the bull's last big mania. Billions invested in worthless mortgages brought the world economy down. Not that such bubbles were new. From the South Seas one of 1720—all of England investing in a company with no products or customers; to the dot.com one of the 1990s—millions thrown at companies that were nothing but a website—bubbles arose and inflated when the unscrupulous and the stupid joined forces. Then as now, governments had to save the banks when the bubbles popped.

Zach's cell phone rang. It was his wife—the chief person he had to prepare for the end of the world without actually using those words.

"Hi, Zach. Having a good day?"

"Trying to keep my widows from losing what their husbands worked a lifetime for." He didn't add: *in case the world doesn't end.* "How about you, Zenia?"

"Stop moping. You'll fix it. You always do."

He didn't say, *That was when the stock market made sense.*

Most of their neighbors in Hewlett Bay Park Village thought like Zenia. One of sixty-four villages in ultra-prosperous Nassau County, it was on Long Island's South Shore, just across the Sound from Greenwich. His and Zenia's side was the richer one and apparently immune to earthquakes. Because it was an hour away by train, he and other financial district execs preferred the charters at the Downtown Manhattan/Wall Street heliport, which reduced their Long Island, commute to minutes. Zach shared his daily roundtrip with five other guys at a grand a pop. Zenia worried until he pointed out the U.S. President used the same heliport, so it was safe.

"I've just learned something exciting," she said.

He shifted the phone to his other ear to wave at a coworker, Ahmed Bourguiba, a Tunisian American who would deservedly take over the mantel of genius of the firm if Zach kept focusing on the widows. "Hey, Ahmed," he said as they passed.

"Hey, Zach! Bad morning?"

Zach nodded. Ahmed was the only one who knew where Zach went on bad days. He liked Ahmed, but could never shake the feeling that his friend was hiding something important. Zach hoped it was something good, like being a secret revolutionary in the Arab Spring. Once he'd come upon Ahmed reading an article with jihad in the title. Just in case, Zach used their talks to up the idea that killing people was way too twentieth century.

"Whereya been?" Zach asked.

"Nowhere much." Was Ahmed lying?

"Sure, right." Zach grinned.

Ahmed grinned back. "See ya later," he said without breaking his stride.

"Oh, you aren't alone?" Zenia asked over the phone.

"Yeah, I am. It was just Ahmed."

"Humph," she said. "I can't fathom why you chose to befriend him, after what happened here in New York."

Zach knew Zenia didn't really hate Ahmed because he was Muslim. She just hated a lot of things. Zach hadn't seen it until months after they married. Fortunately, his view of life made it easy to put up with other people's likes and dislikes, however misguided. At an early age, Zach noticed he wasn't God. Besides, Zenia made up for it by being hot and a great cook. She was loyal, too, which meant a lot to Zach. He'd learned long ago from his congressman father that loyalty was for sale.

Now, given the tumult going on the world over, Zach concluded he might not have time to bring her around. For days he'd been planning a romantic weekend getaway replete with Biblical predictions, psychic predictions, news clips about earthquakes, melting ice, the world's increasing violence and its strange weather—all while extolling the virtues of non-coastal states, say, Ohio.

"So you learned something exciting?" he asked, entering the park and heading for the benches nearest the bull.

"It's more than exciting, Zach." He could hear her take a breath. "Paul Joseph is holding a special service tonight. Now don't roll your eyes."

Too late. Zach was already rolling them. "I thought the good pastor was on some mysterious out-of-town mission."

"He is!" Her voice rose. "He'll be back tonight and I think he'll have something important to share!"

"Good for him." Zach had reached the far benches under the trees. He sat and with one hand fished a health drink out of the paper bag he'd brought.

"Will you come this time, Zach? I so wish you could just listen to him again. You're a Christian. Why won't you give a prominent clergyman like him more of a chance?"

Zach looked skyward and silently mouthed, *Because he's a phony, Zenia.* For two months, Zach had listened to Paul Joseph preach to his rich congregation's egos and pocketbooks, Solomon being a favorite: *In the day of prosperity be joyful.* Never: *Except the Lord build the house, they labor in vain that build it.* Scratch Paul Joseph's pious surface and Zach was sure they'd find a ginormous ego, but no real faith.

"Plus…"

"Plus?" he said, teasing.

"I'm going to help with his mission in Africa. I'm going over there."

"You are? Hmmm." Zach decided to speed up their weekend getaway. "Well, okay, if that's what you want." Still, he saw no reason to suffer through a Paul Joseph yawnologue. "Um, listen. You go ahead. Ahmed and I made plans to hang out tonight. I don't want to cancel. I think he wants to talk about work."

If there was anything that could trump God for Zenia, Zach knew it was the business of raking in cash, preferably indecent amounts.

"Oh! I'm sorry," she said. "Why didn't you tell me? Yes, tend to work tonight, of course. I'll be fine. I'll leave something in the

fridge for you in case I'm not home when you get here—
something delicious."

He knew it would be.

"Love you, Zenia. Enjoy Paul Joseph."

"Love you," she said and clicked off.

Zach downed his drink. A meal in a bottle, it was one of those
green super foods. It always got him through the afternoon. He
returned the empty bottle to the bag and stared at the tourists. As
a result of their good-luck fondling, the bull's balls gleamed. To
Zach, Paul Joseph had about as much chance of communing with
God as that bull had of protecting its cojones.

Zach knew because he'd had a genuine religious encounter. It
kept him on the straight and narrow as he made money, if less than
those with no morals. Zenia hoped for hundreds of millions, like
their top Wall Street peers, but tens of millions was good enough
for Zach.

Of course, no one had believed his religious experience back
then, nor would they now.

His cell phone buzzed the arrival of a new text. The DOW had
dropped 300 points. The firm's traders would be making a mad
dash back to the office. Sure enough, Ahmed zipped by,
telephoning instructions Zach couldn't guess. Everyone on Wall
Street knew big interests were secretly manipulating the market to
forestall a collapse. Nowadays, DOW graphs bounced around like
seismic charts. You had to be psychic to know what to do. Or
smart.

He texted Blankman. *DOW drop good for AmerCan. Buy more.*
They'd make a fortune.

On impulse, Zach rose, tossed the bag in a trash bin and lifted
his arm at a passing cab. The taxi halted then came to the curb.

"Central Park," he said to the driver. "Boy's Gate." Zach got in
and slammed the door. "It's just north of 96th on Central Park
West."

"You got it."

As the cab pulled off, Zach didn't see city streets speed by. In his
mind, he was a teenager again on a dark night eighteen years

ago. At the behest of a powerful man, his congressman father had been trying to outlaw the rumored cloning that was all over the news. The DNA source? The Shroud of Turin. In defiance, Zach had used the web to form a worldwide organization called OLIVE—Our Lord in Vitro Emerging. He'd caused a big ruckus by holding prayer vigils all over the world.

The cab stopped and Zach paid the driver, got out and made his way into the park. For years, there'd been long lines because of rumors the Jesus clone was born here, but the city got tired of it and chased the people away. Now it was impossible to light candles, leave baby Jesus statues, flowers, prayers or letters, leave pictures of your dead children, sing hymns, make speeches, congregate in groups, or form long lines to Glen Span Arch without being harassed by the police. Anyone carrying an OLIVE sign was arrested on the spot for creating a public nuisance.

Those who came knew to come alone and make no religious display.

He'd met Zenia at an OLIVE rally, but since she liked being on the winning side she never came anymore. She wouldn't have been on the Mount of Olives when Jesus was crucified, either. Zach, lucky all his life, didn't have her need to win.

He walked casually past a mounted park policeman and nonchalantly whistled as he descended the path to Glen Span Arch. There he gazed left to the waterfall, down to the stream, up at the brooding gray stones then walked into the hallowed shadows beneath the arch. It felt like a small cathedral.

Zach thought of how he'd helped the clone and its mother escape pursuers. Briefly he'd seen the newborn's face, a sight he'd never forget. The news said they'd died. Zach doubted it. Sure enough, ten years later, the woman surfaced in New York, supposedly carrying a second clone.

Zach didn't believe in a second clone or that the first one was dead.

No one had seen or heard of the woman since.

If the clone ever showed up, Zach would readily resurrect OLIVE—what with people slaughtering each other, Connecticut shaking, and honey bees dying off.

Only rarely did he risk a visit here, saying a prayer and meditating as he remembered the baby's face. The office definitely wouldn't like it if they knew—much less that he'd founded OLIVE—but with the market plunging there was no chance he'd run into anyone employed by Silverman Alden Investments.

He'd never seen a Paul Joseph type at Glen Span Arch. Such men didn't believe it could really be the birthplace of the most important child in over two thousand years.

Chapter 3

At first Jess and I hugged in the cab then hugged again, spilling over with excitement. Eventually we sat straight and tried to act normal.

"Is there a place here where we could stay?" Jess whispered.

I knew of a perfect place.

"*Vorremmo andare all'hotel Parco San Marco,*" I said to the driver. *We'd like to go to the Hotel Parco San Marco.* Whenever I came to Porlezza's Saturday market, that's where I had lunch. A family hotel, it was always full of laughing children who made me think of Jess.

"Sì, signora," the driver said. He took the SS340 away from the Menaggio ferry and along the lake toward Cima, where the hotel was.

Since we couldn't really talk, we sat quietly, squeezing each other's hands, me humming *Go Tell It On the Mountain* and Jess grinning at my choice of song as we drove toward Lake Lugano's Swiss side. It's hard to describe the beauty of the place, kind of like the Garden of Eden with a lake in the middle, surrounded by steep pre-Alpine hills, except there was no snow now because it was early fall. Red clay-roofed towns sprinkle the lakeshore. The deepest lushest greens on the most perfect trees, the most gorgeous flowers cover the hills and towns. Let the sun kiss the water in which white boats bob, put a rainbow in the sky and you've got Lake Lugano on almost any day.

To make conversation that wouldn't scare the driver to death, I said, "Once I looked up the lake's name, Lugano. It comes from the Latin word, *lucus*, which means sacred forest."

"It is ancient. I'm glad you come here."

I nodded, too addled to think what else to say.

Minutes later we pulled off the lake road into the Hotel Parco

San Marco's grounds. Rising in tiers against the hill, the sunny walls of its multiple buildings made it resemble an untidy lemon cake, the layers iced in orange roof tiles. I almost forgot to pay the driver, I got out so fast. We went to reception, which had glass walls to keep from rudely blocking a guest's view of the heaven outdoors. Otherwise, the place was all stone, clay pots, glass tables and comfy chairs.

We said our Buon giorno signores and signoras, the man and woman at the desk staring politely but quizzically at us. I hoped they weren't feeling what the market people had. Surely it wasn't every day that bliss walked into their lobby on two legs.

"*Come posso aiutarvi?*" the female desk clerk asked very pleasantly. Everyone usually smiled at Hotel Parco San Marco and spoke in such a voice.

I replied in Italian.

"You have a family suite with two bedrooms?"

Just then two young children ran into reception, laughing. A girl and a boy, they were obviously sister and brother given their identical brown eyes, button noses, and impish grins. In mid-run they stopped and stared at Jess with awed expressions. Their dog ran in behind them. Jess bent to the children as they came near. The dog cocked its head, emitted a few whines then, his tail wagging fast, pounced on Jess, licking his face. They tumbled to the floor—Jess, children and dog, rolling in happiness. Was this how it would be?

"*Per quante notti?*" For how many nights?

I had no idea. I looked down at Jess.

"One, two at most," he called from the floor, the children tickling him.

I tried not to panic. Would he be gone in two days?

Both of the desk clerks gaped at Jess and the children.

I spoke faster, unsure of what each new moment might hold. "*Due notti.*" I took out the credit card I never used. It didn't say Maggie Duffy Morelli. It had the name on the fake ID I'd had since Jess's birth. I'd kept the false records updated. "I'm Mrs. … Hetta Price and this is my son, Jess."

"Sì, grazie, signora."

She typed on her computer and instead of saying, *Would you please hurry up!* I glanced up at the lobby TV monitor in an effort at nonchalance. There'd been an earthquake in Connecticut, of all places.

"Eh, sì signora. Le Lake View Family Suite." She gave directions. "*Ed i vostri bagagli?*" And your luggage?

"*Non abbiamo bagagli.*" We have no luggage.

The desk clerks stared, if politely.

I grabbed our room key cards, the map and Jess before anyone else could fall in love with him. Ignoring the children's calls, the dog followed as we hurried outside, but thankfully a hotel maid scooped him up and returned him to the children. By the time we found our room, an entire flock of birds had alit in the near treetops and a half dozen squirrels were scampering along beside us, to say nothing of the duck that waddled our way as Jess passed by, like the swans on Lake Maggiore did when he was a boy.

I opened the door, shaking a warning finger at the duck. We stepped in. The door closed. I held out my arms. Jess came into them.

"Jess! Oh, my goodness. Where did you come from? I can't believe it." My heart pounded, my head spun, unable to take this in.

"Mother, I'm here."

"Look at you! Look at you!" I said, holding his face. "How you've grown! My goodness, you almost have a beard!" I hugged him tight. "You're back. My beautiful boy! How long will you stay?"

"I'm not sure. You're more beautiful, too, Madre." It was the Italian word for mother. Always before he'd called me Mamma, but I didn't care. He was here.

I laughed. "Don't lie."

He stroked my hair. It had grayed since he died. "I never do."

I remembered my husband, Adamo, my son Peter. "Oh, my goodness! I've got to call home and tell them." I reached for my cell.

Gently, Jess took it. "Not yet."

"Not call? Why, Jess?"

He led me to the beige couch. I hadn't even noticed it, or the matching stuffed chair, the tiled floor, the rose and aqua rug, the brown drapes and white orchids and through the glass doors a terrace and the wonderful landscape.

Jess gave me his *vast eternity* look as he sat beside me. "It will be all right. You must leave your life right now."

"But, Jess, they'll worry."

"No, I've taken care of that."

That's when I first wondered if this was a dream. Had I fallen asleep on the boat to Porlezza or was I still in my bed back home and dreaming this whole thing?

"We have important things to do. Thank you for being my—" he searched the air, "my voice crying in the wilderness. No one believed in me this time but you, not even Felix, though he cloned me."

Overcome, I pulled Jess to my side, put my arm around him and nestled my face against his head. Understanding nothing, I'd do anything he said. He wrapped his arms around me, too, and we must have hugged forever, like we used to in Arona on the deck of our lakefront cottage, hidden away from the world. If people had seen us, they wouldn't have understood, but it was easy to explain. If God was love, Jess God's son was, too. Mix in the normal mother-child bond and the result was Jess and me. Once Jess said we were like twins separated by a generation and, emotionally, it was true. In a way, he was the other half of me. I was the other half of him. I wanted to die, too, when he died. Crazy with grief, I'd wanted to kill those who'd caused it. It took month to come to my senses.

"You were so lonely," Jess said.

"Yes, I was." Reluctantly, I released him.

"Can we call Felix?"

Though he was the one who stole DNA from the Shroud of Turin...though he was the one who implanted Jess in my womb.... Felix finally doubted Jess's identity. He tried to make me believe Jess was an ordinary boy.

"No, we can't yet."

"All right, but I wish he could see this. You've risen from the dead just like Jesus because that's who you are, like I told him!"

He smiled at me. "In your terms that's who I am, though … well, almost no one's who they think they are, Madre." He leaned back against the sofa with the same physical grace he'd always had, pure kindness beaming from his face. Girls would fall in love with him on sight—like the dog and duck had.

"Can I ask you questions?" I said.

"Of course."

"Why did you pick the Saturday market? Didn't you know I'd faint in public?"

"I apologize, but Mother there are always people around you. Adamo walked you to the ferry, then on the ferry you talked to everyone."

I saw his point. "Are you physically here?"

"Yes."

"But how?"

"Our bodies aren't just physical."

I clapped my hands. "Yes, that's right! In 1 Corinthians 15:44 Paul said, *there is a natural body and there is a spiritual body*."

He gestured like he'd learned to from the Italians. "Another way of saying it is this. Imagine that everything is energycsunlight, the air, this table …" he patted the glass then his chest … "our bodies. When the physical body dies, the energy of its pattern remains at a higher frequency. Normally, human eyes can't see this energy."

I must have looked confused because he added, "You know there is sound that humans can't hear, but dogs can? Well, there is energy that most people and most instruments can't detect; yet it exists. What I did was focus my … I think *intention* is the best word and, to simplify, slowed my frequency down until my body became physical matter again."

"If that's not a miracle, I don't know what is."

"Yes, Madre, but everything is. You could do it, too, if you tried."

I rolled my eyes.

"If you have the faith of a mustard seed—"

"Oh, sure. I could move mountains. Jess, I've got more faith than most people, and there's no way on earth I'm moving any mountains." I laughed.

He sat back. "You don't believe the words of Jesus."

I hadn't thought of it that way. "Well, if you mean those particular words applying to me, specifically, well…"

He looked solemn. "Yes, applying to you, to everyone. What if I tell you it's vital that you believe this now?"

What was happening? I felt like I was failing a surprise test or had suddenly lost my way. Here I was contradicting the reincarnated Jesus about things he'd said in a book I'd claimed to believe in all my life. Yet all I wanted was to look at him, hold him, hear his voice, cook some pasta and feed him. Instead I rose and went to the orchids.

"Don't be upset with me, Jess. Most Christians don't believe people can move mountains, because they've never done it or seen it done."

Jess grinned. "You want me to turn a staff into a snake for you, Mamma Pilate?"

That hurt. I turned around. "Mamma Pilate? Don't be smart-mouthed, young man!"

He chuckled. "I don't think I'm really a young man."

Quietly we looked left and right then cracked up laughing at ourselves, me collapsing into a chair. For ten years we'd laughed happily at life in our yellow villa in Arona.

Jess rose and sat on my chair arm. "What do you want of me, Mother? Shall I command the wind, the sea? Shall I turn water to wine to prove that you should believe me? I can do anything unless my Father forbids it."

Excited, I pointed across the room. "Do something with the flowers."

"I have a better idea." Jess stood, shimmering, a human rainbow in the room. The sight filled me with such joy.

"Remember the withered fig tree? You do something with the flowers. Trade belief for knowledge."

"Me?"

I quoted the fig tree passage, Matthew 21:21-22, "*Assuredly, I say to you, if you have faith and do not doubt, you will not only do what was done to the fig tree, but also if you say to this mountain, 'Be removed and be cast into the sea,' it will be done. And whatever things you ask in prayer, believing, you will receive.*"

"Did you know I was not the first to say that, Madre. Many did, inspired by God. In the sixteenth century, Paracelsus did."

I said nothing. I'd never thought of praying for the impossible. Who would?

"You must not doubt. You must have faith."

What I had to do was stall. "Okay, sure, but—Jess, you go first, okay?"

I heard a knock at the door and almost jumped out of my skin. Jess jumped too.

I wagged my finger at him. "Nothing strange in front of people. Okay?"

Jess smiled. "So you want me to be a covert messiah?"

I shushed him and opened the door.

It was the maid who'd rescued the children's dog for them. She pushed in a tray of delicious-looking cheese, fruit, pasta and drinks, but we hadn't ordered anything.

She must have seen surprise on my face. "Compliments of the hotel," she said in English.

I stood back so she could roll it in, Jess back to normal and nodding at her.

She took the food out to the terrace, raised our umbrella, and set our table fast. Then, like the children and the dog, she came in and went to Jess. Before I knew it, she'd knelt beside him, clasped her hands and put her face on the couch.

"Oh, child," I said.

"You are what they call a psychic?" Jess asked.

She nodded.

No holier moment had I felt, not in prayer, not in church.

"What is it that you want of me?"

She looked up from a timid face with wide-set eyes, ears elfin under a short pixie haircut. "I'm not worthy, but if you will only heal me."

I looked anxiously at Jess.

"What is wrong?" he asked her.

I noticed a grotesque twist under her loose blouse.

"My spine. The doctor says I'll never be well."

"You believe I can heal you?"

"Yes, yes. I know you can."

"It must be a secret. Will you tell no one? Will you leave this place until it's safe to return? You will know when that is."

Had healing this girl been part of his plan? If not, should he be taking risks before he even got started? "Jess maybe you should think this over."

"Yes," she cried. "Oh, yes! I'll leave today."

Jess put his hand on the girl's spine. For a moment—an hour?—nothing seeming to exist but Jess, the girl and me. Finally he took his hand away and helped her stand, the two of them bathed in soft light.

With calm eyes, he smiled at her. "Your faith has healed you."

What else would he say?

The girl gasped, moved her shoulders, stretched her back. Gleefully she spun about the room then ran to the door, bowed to Jess, and left. Out on the terrace I saw her leap in joy then run from the hotel grounds, her spine straight.

"You really healed her."

He pointed to the table the girl set. "You must eat. We have a lot to do."

We went outside. Two squirrels joined us on the terrace, standing on hind legs to look at Jess. A bird landed and hopped near.

"Do you eat, Jess?"

"While I am physical, I must or my body will die." He pulled out my chair.

As if girls were healed in front of me every day, I sat and drank some juice. Ate pasta. Watched Jess eat. I drank water, swallowed it.

I set the glass quietly down, facing the problem. My fear. I'd have to control it. I didn't doubt Jess, I doubted myself. Would I fail him? I didn't want him to prove my faith was nonexistent—only words mouthed as I read the Bible. I didn't want him to see I was unworthy.

"You can tell me now, sweetheart. What have you come for? Is it the end of the world?"

"I hope it isn't."

"You don't know? Aren't you omniscient now?"

He looked off toward the lake. "On earth, omniscience doesn't mean consciously knowing everything all the time, just what we need to know when we need to know it."

My fear returned. He was still saying *we*. There wasn't the smallest chance I could do what he just did.

I took a last sip of water and gave my full attention to the boy I'd risked my life to bring into the world. Before his birth I'd felt worthless. An old maid, no education, church and God were all I had. With Jess's arrival, I became the virgin preserved by God to mother his second son. From the first, I knew he was my life's great work. From the first, I knew he'd save us. His death had made no sense to me. When it happened, I grieved for him, but in the intervening years I'd grieved for his lost purpose, too.

"What have you come to do, Jess?"

"To remind the earth."

"Of what?"

"A message that has been shared throughout the ages. Now it must be understood and lived for humanity to survive."

"Is it in the Bible?"

"Yes, and in every religion in some form. It's also in many non-religious teachings."

Now this I could handle. "Okay, don't tell me. Then it must be in the Ten Commandments, right? Thou shalt not kill?"

Jess grinned. "No, but it's a good idea." Absently, he stuck a finger in one of his sausage curls, dangled it down his face and let it snap back, a teenager again.

"Okay, then what? Oh, the Golden Rule. Do unto others as you would have them do unto you. Luke 6:31. Matthew 7:12. That's got to be it, right?"

"No and you surprise me, Madre," he said, teasing. "You of all people know your Bible."

Exasperated, I tried again. "Okay, then it's to love God with our whole hearts, right? Mark 12:30, and other places."

Jess chuckled. "Eat your fruit." He was enjoying the game.

The breeze ruffled our umbrella. We looked down on the glorious lake, the thrilling mountains.

I picked up an apple and put it down, anxious because whatever Jess wanted me to do, I was failing. "I can't guess. I can't. If it's not loving God or loving each other or not killing, what is it? What's more important?"

Jess smiled. "It has been overlooked, misinterpreted, but the words mean exactly what they say. More important than all to humanity now is Luke 17:21."

Amazed, I said, "First there's some lo and beholds then it ends: *The kingdom of God is within you?*"

"Yes, and I can prove it. Put your hands on the table like this." He rested them, palms up, on the cloth the girl laid.

Rattled, I followed suit.

"Now, close your eyes and breathe calmly for a moment."

I did.

"Now, focus on your hands. Can you feel the energy in them, a kind of tingling or vibration?"

At first I couldn't. Then I could. I nodded.

"Without that, your hands could not open, close, move or live."

"Uh, okay."

"I sympathize, Madre. Words, words! They are insufficient, but this energy animates your entire body, beats your heart. Focus and you can feel it in every cell. It is immortal. It is all-powerful. It is spirit. It is the kingdom."

I'd been trying to hold it together, but what he said was so scary, I jerked my hands off the table, grimaced an apology, and shook my head.

He kept talking, rising to pat my back in reassurance. "Mother, it is time for humanity to shake off its blindness, its ignorance. Life on earth will survive if enough do. Now the journey, the path, and the destination are one and it is this: *the kingdom of God is within you.*"

Chapter 4

The Reverend Paul Joseph lived in the village of Plandome, the poorest of Nassau County New York's richest towns and privately he resented it. He hadn't grown up like the famous Rick Warren, who had a respected Baptist minister for a father, an admired school librarian for a mother. Paul Joseph's father preached across the South in dusty tents that his mother got drunk behind, after spiking her lemonade and sweet tea. Paul Joseph's road hadn't been paved with divinity degrees and bestselling books, like Warren's had. He hadn't been invited to speak at the U.N. Paul Joseph had simply worked hard and feared God.

Now his reward was here. He stood beside his Volvo outside what their real estate agent had called a charming colonial, his wife at the front door, wobbly waving goodbye. Blonde and blowzy, she was just like his mother, except in one respect; his wife drank liquor openly and made no pretense. It was a relief that she skipped church. For a moment he imagined she was the admirable Zenia Dunlop, his foremost parishioner in spite of her husband, Zach, who never came to church. Too busy making millions on Wall Street.

He watched a Cadillac limousine pull up to their driveway and stop. No doubt decorum would dictate he wait in the house for the driver to come to the door and ring the bell, but Paul Joseph didn't want to miss a moment of today.

The black-suited driver got out and called to him. "Pastor Joseph?"

"Yes, I am."

"Good morning, sir." Paul Joseph returned the greeting while the man came around to open the limo door. "Watch your head, sir."

Paul Joseph got in, nothing but a Bible in his hand, and took one last look at the low-ceilinged, clapboard-roofed, picket-fenced mediocrity he hoped they wouldn't call home for long. Suddenly he caught himself. Rather than feeling gratitude for the home God gave them, he was scorning it. He'd passed judgment on his wife, wishing she were someone else, when Jesus said *Judge not, that ye be not judged*. Fearing God's punishment, Paul Joseph lowered his head and asked forgiveness.

When he felt the limo pull away, he ended his prayer and said, "I assume you know where we're headed."

"Yes, of course, sir."

No one in Plandome but Paul Joseph and his wife knew about the momentous event unfolding. Tonight, he'd share the news with his congregation. In the ten-mile drive to Garden City Island Heliport, he contained his excitement. He boarded the waiting chopper as if he rode one every day. He thrilled when it swooped into the sky and hugged the shoreline, the pilot talking on his headset as the chopper was handed off to the next airspace. They flew inland, crossing New Jersey, the mighty Atlantic to the left, Delaware Bay below, and entered Maryland over the Chesapeake Bay. Shortly afterward, Paul Joseph's helicopter landed at Bolling Air Force Base where an unmarked limo waited. It drove him off the base and into traffic on a highway called I-295 then across a river.

"Is that the powerful Potomac?" he asked.

"No, sir, it's the Anacostia. We're on the 11th Street Bridge. I could detour to the Potomac, if you like."

Horrified by thought of delay, Paul said, "No, no, keep going."

Moments later, they exited beneath a sign that said, *Washington/Navy-Yard/Downtown*, went about a mile and a half on another highway, then got off, making a series of turns that took them across the three-block-wide, many-blocks-long National Mall to D.C.'s Constitution Avenue.

They turned left, the driver informing him that the marble building taking up the entire massive block was the Smithsonian's National Museum of American History and the one taking up the entire block behind was the National Museum of Natural History.

Paul said, "Mmm-hmmm," intent on their destination. Quickly it was in sight, though not swiftly reached, the limo waved down by guards at three locations for inspection.

Finally, the limo stopped. Paul Joseph's heart hammered as he got out under the famous cupola he'd fantasized about for years. It felt like a dream that two marines opened white-paned doors beneath the Presidential Seal.

Somehow his feet moved and Paul Joseph went through, only to be inspected by a new set of guards who ultimately ushered him to a desk where a woman advised him to wait on a couch in the lobby of the West Wing of the White House.

Though his watch said an hour passed, time stood still, important people coming and going. He tried to guess who they were—senators, members of Congress, lobbyists, agency officials, campaign donors? Finally, someone came and led him toward the most famous office in the world. He was shocked to find the West Wing cramped, crowded, staff swarming all over each other in the low-ceilinged yellow halls—an old and elegant beehive. History and power were its honey and Paul Joseph could almost taste them in the air.

Could he really have been summoned here? As they approached the renowned door and the guard outside, Paul Joseph half expected to be stopped, his fraud discovered—he was not Rick Warren. Yet suddenly he was in the Oval Office, being introduced to the President of the United States who came from behind his desk and invited Paul Joseph to sit with him on the famous sofas.

The President said, "Thank you for coming, Reverend Joseph. That was a remarkable article you wrote."

An Op-ed for the New York Times, it was entitled, *Is God's Economy Conservative or Liberal?* He wrote it with the intention of catching influential eyes, never guessing they'd be this important. He wished he could take photographs of the Resolute Desk, the painting of George Washington over the fireplace, the tall paned windows in the curved wall and the Rose Garden beyond, but he'd been told it wasn't allowed. For half an hour Paul Joseph, pastor of Christ Baptist Church, Plandome, Nassau County, discussed economics and faith with the head of the free world.

"You have a mission in Africa?" the President finally asked.

"Yes, for five years. I'm leaving to visit it tomorrow. We're helping them deal with the drought."

"So I've heard. And something about AmerCan?"

How did he know that? "Yes, they're interested in local mineral resources."

The President rose. "May I ask a personal favor?"

"Yes, anything, Mr. President."

"Would you come with me to the East Wing and pray with me and the first family for a moment?"

Paul Joseph only nodded, for fear of blubbering in gratitude all over this man. He had advised a President. Now he would pray with him and his family.

Humbly he followed the President from the Oval Office to the Rose Garden's colonnades, surprised to learn Presidents had to walk outside to reach the Residence. They entered through the Palm Room, passing its white-latticed walls, benches and greenery. Next was the grand Center Hall vaulted—ceilings, chandeliers, paintings and busts and statues. He noticed white-shirted guards strategically positioned at every juncture.

Soon the President motioned left and said, "The family elevator." It had laurels carved into the frame. They rode it to the second floor and entered a private living space with bookcases, a piano, cozy chairs and an amazing Chinese screen. The First Lady and the First Offspring rose from their seats to greet him. Moments later, he led the nation's First Family in prayer.

Even as it happened, Paul Joseph couldn't believe it. He barely realized what prayer he said, only that when it was over the President shook his hand and invited him back for a formal service.

Paul Joseph's life had permanently changed. No one who entered the White House by invitation left as a nobody, even if they'd been one before.

Now he only had to take things one step at a time.

The limo returned him to the helicopter, which returned him to Plandome, where the same driver delivered him back to his home.

Too excited to try communicating through his wife's alcoholic haze, he got into his Volvo and drove toward the imposing church edifice his prosperous parishioners had taken out a mortgage to build. Having suffered hits themselves on the stock market—one couple having lost everything to Bernie Madoff—the parishioners had been in no mood to pay the huge mortgage off.

Paul Joseph knew this would change in about an hour.

He pulled into the driveway of the stone, glass and steel Christ Baptist Church. Zenia Dunlop's SSC Ultimate Aero sat in the parking lot. She was a patriot and refused to drive a foreign car, so she'd forked out almost $700,000 for the fastest American car made and painted it violet. Zenia was already attractive, but whenever she snaked her legs out of that car, he had to fight his lust for her. He entered by a side door and was surprised to find her waiting in his office. Impeccably dressed, long black hair perfectly coifed, not blonde and blowzy in the least, she never drank. She ran sober eyes over him in distaste. He knew why.

She was a married woman. He was a married man and her pastor.

They'd vowed not to succumb to the flesh again and he tried hard to forget the two times they had—once at a church picnic against a fallen tree trunk after getting lost in the woods and two days later in his private bathroom at Christ Baptist, the need to be absolutely quiet only intensifying the experience.

That was more than a year ago.

"How are you, Zenia?" he said, sitting at the desk.

"Fine, Paul, and you?"

For a while they gazed at each other, saying nothing.

She cleared her throat and opened her purse. "Zach and I want to make a large contribution to the church mortgage fund."

Paul Joseph held his breath.

She took out her checkbook and started writing then stopped, frowning as she saw a smudge of fingerprints on the desk. "Has the Ladies Circle decided to stop cleaning?"

Zenia fulfilled her member service covenant with Christ Baptist by organizing the social events. She didn't view cleaning as a personal duty.

"How was it at the White House, Paul?"

So she'd heard. Good, because he couldn't hold back anymore. "Amazing. Unbelievable. Such an honor. Such a responsibility."

"I am so proud of you." She signed her name to the check, stood and handed it to him. It was for a million dollars.

"Zenia! Are you sure? Does Zach know about this?"

Stubbornly she wrinkled her nose and frowned. The power of her disapproving look brought the other ladies in line when disputes arose and it fascinated Paul. "It should be more," she said. "One-tenth, remember? Don't worry. I'll handle Zach."

"Thank you, Zenia. I won't disappoint you. I'm trying hard to follow where God is leading me."

"Back to the White House, of course. Remember me if you go again?" She said it with displeasure, as if she didn't like that he'd met the President first.

He nodded. "I'll try, Zenia. I'm sure the President and First Lady would love to meet someone like you."

She knelt at his prie-dieu. "Would you pray with me, Paul?"

He hesitated. That's how they'd ended up in the bathroom a year ago. She'd kneeled. He stood in front of her, but prayer never happened.

She glared at him. "I mean pray from your desk, Paul."

Oh, he thought. "Heavenly Father, I know that I have sinned and that I deserve to burn in hell."

Zenia recited the Sinner's Prayer with him.

"I am sorry. Please forgive me. I believe that your Son, Jesus Christ, died on the cross for my sins, that He was raised from the dead, is alive, and hears my prayer. I receive Him as my personal Lord and Savior. Please save me. In Jesus' name I pray, Amen."

"Amen."

Zenia stood and Paul recognized her expression—shame mixed with zeal to do good works to compensate. She'd been thinking about what they'd done a year ago, too.

"Paul, I want to go with you to Africa tomorrow."

Paul Joseph couldn't have been more shocked. "You want to go to a poverty-stricken African village full of dirt?"

He'd worked unstintingly there every summer for the past five years, determined to save souls from hell and bodies from droughts. He'd taught the village to repent of its heathen beliefs and accept Jesus. He was teaching them to fear God's punishment if they did not. Also important for their long-term survival, he had lined up western mining interest in the village's untapped mineral reserves. Why it interested the President he couldn't guess, but AmerCan had responded to his request and was sending a survey crew there.

"Are you sure, Zenia?"

She stood. "You need money, but most of all you need publicity and I'm the best fundraiser and promoter in Nassau County. You need some shots of me over there for the society pages."

Paul Joseph clapped his hands. In five years he'd never been able to interest Zenia in Africa. She didn't even know about AmerCan.

"Notice in the society pages would help a great deal. It could bring in millions. Thank you for offering. Let's see, we'll need to make arrangements—"

"I've already talked to your secretary and booked the same flight you're on. I'll be in business class, of course—they don't have first class; imagine that. I took the liberty of upgrading you."

Paul Joseph's budget didn't permit a business class ticket. "Thank you," he said. He pictured a maid busily packing for her. Zenia did what Zenia wanted, but this was a surprise.

She smiled. "Can't wait to hear your sermon tonight."

Through the door he watched her walk toward the sanctuary. Single-handedly, she'd just saved the church mortgage fund. If she fulfilled her promise about Africa, she might very well save the church's entire mission. In a way, it disturbed him. As minister, his personal efforts should be successful without outside intervention though, of course, Zenia wasn't an outsider. She was a believer, a member of the *ekklesia*. Jesus could certainly work directly through her, as well as through him. Even so, it felt unseemly. He'd imagined the triumph of a deal with AmerCan—a feat on the Rick Warren global scale—but it would have taken time, perhaps a long time. Zenia's solution could immediately bathe everyone in cash.

Paul Joseph picked up his Bible and walked slowly toward the sanctuary, opening his heart to commune with the triune God and minister to the People of the Book.

Word must have spread about this special service, because the pews were full. He chose the lectern, rather than the pulpit. Tonight's message concerned the earthly versus the heavenly realm.

The nave quieted as he put his notes on the lectern.

"Good evening, everyone, and thank you for coming. I'd like to begin with an announcement. Good news for Christ Baptist. Today, a limousine came to my home in secret and took me to a local heliport."

He paused, knowing the effect this would have. Silence fell.

"I landed at Bolling Air Force Base..."

The anticipation was palpable now.

"Another limo took me to the White House."

Gasps and excited murmurs rose from his wealthy, hard-to-impress congregation.

"Believe me, I was as surprised as you are. I'm sure you're wondering how this happened. I certainly did."

Eager eyes. Nodding heads.

When Paul Joseph explained about the Op-ed article, the church erupted in applause.

Hands up, he quieted them.

"Furthermore—"

He saw Zenia become alert. Not even she could know there was a furthermore.

"The President is sending an observer to our African mission. The result could be recognition of our efforts on a national, even a global scale."

Take that, Rick Warren, Paul Joseph thought, as the People of the Book rose to their feet in wild applause.

All he and Zenia had to do was keep the covenants of Christ Baptist and their hands off each other for the duration.

Chapter 5

Felix wondered how sixteen-year-old daughters could talk so much. He'd been waiting a good five minutes at the front door of his Roxbury, Connecticut home for her to hang up and come downstairs. He called, "Ariel, your mother's ready!"

No response. Just faint, high laughter.

As he waited, he took pleasure in their home's sprawl of stone and wood, white-paned windows, porches and columns. His wife, Adeline, had asked him to redesign the exterior and he was proud of its handsome details, especially the new French mansard roof of blue-black slate from the Pyrenees.

Footsteps padded on the stairs then Ariel raced into the foyer, her cell phone still to her ear, her hand out. Dutifully he deposited a credit card in it. She kissed his cheek as she flew by. Adeline waved from her Mercedes and when Ariel got in, guided the car from their circular drive to the country road beyond. They'd visit his sister and her husband, then shop for school clothes. Ariel was entering Sixth Form at Choate, an hour away in Wallingsford, and registration had started today. This year she wanted to stay on campus, and Felix and Adeline had agreed.

Living in a house full of females being the challenge that it was, he relished the temporary solitude. He sat on one of two couches in front of the stone fireplace that extended to the ceiling in the living room. An earthquake centered in Greenwich had opened a tiny crack in it, but that seemed the only damage his property had sustained, pending a visit from the inspector he'd called. Felix had phoned within an hour of the quake, but nervous homeowners had already booked the firm solid. He flicked through local channels, each still reporting on the quake.

One anchor asked the station's meteorologist, "How rare was today's earthquake?"

"New England doesn't have many to begin with. Connecticut's last noticeable earthquake was in 1791."

"I understand it violated plate tectonic models."

"Yes. New England is on the interior of the North American Plate. There isn't another plate anywhere near for it to rub against."

Weird, Felix thought.

Through tall windows on either side of the fireplace, he could see fall leaves rustle over the now multihued New England landscape.

"Pardon, Monsieur Fubini?" It was the maid, calling him by the last name he'd adopted in place of Rossi to create a sane life.

The maid put down the glass of kir he'd requested—an old-fashioned drink, but he liked it. Michelle was French, like the roof and the drink. Felix had quite enough of Italy and American maids, especially black ones from Harlem, their best friends, and the utter chaos that resulted. For eight years now, his life had been his own again—no reporters outside his door, no one following his wife to her charity events, or his daughter to school. Incredible those paparazzi would harass a child like that. Never again.

"Merci, Michelle," he said and picked up the glass as she left.

True, he'd started it all by stealing DNA from the Shroud of Turin and producing a clone from it. Maggie's son, Jess, had been the result. While she was pregnant, they'd hidden away in his and Frances's Cliffs Landing cottage. An incongruous grouping if ever there was one: he and Frances members of New York's wealthy elite—its Jewish elite, by blood, as they'd discovered—Maggie their black maid and Sam, the Irish doorman from their 5th Avenue condo. It couldn't be helped. Maggie had volunteered to carry the cloned embryo and with press closing in Felix had no option but to accept, vanish with her, and get on with it. Sam had physically protected Maggie for the duration. Felix had seen to her and the baby's medical and financial needs. However, that responsibility ended when Jess died. What Maggie and Sharmina did next was unforgivable.

He heard the doorbell and Michelle answering it. A man's voice. Felix stood and went to the foyer as a workman stepped in and took off his hat.

"Mr. Fubini?" he said.

"Yes."

"I'm the inspector."

That was quick. "Yes, follow me," Felix said. "Thank you, Michelle."

The man followed Felix to the living room and the crack in the fireplace. He kneeled and poked at it then swiftly ran a tape measure up its jagged height. As the tape zipped back, he looked at Felix, a question in his eyes.

"Twelve foot ceilings?" he asked.

"Yes, well it vaults here and there."

"Mmmm," the man said, his expression curious. "Don't I know you?"

Felix stiffened. Only rarely did he encounter someone who remembered him from all the TV coverage. "I don't believe we've met."

The man stood and scratched his head. "Okay, I need to do an outside and inside inspection then take elevations in each room."

"Certainly," Felix said, turning his back and calling, "Michelle!"

When she appeared he said, "Please show this gentleman what he wants to see."

Felix kept his head turned as they left, thinking of Maggie and what she did after Jess died.

Pregnant by Sam, she returned to New York from Italy. Then Maggie allowed all of Harlem, then all of New York, to believe she was carrying Clone II.

That was the last straw.

Felix had cut all ties with her, and with her friend Sharmina who'd been his maid at the time. He fled with his family from New York City to Connecticut, changing their last name from Rossi to Fubini—his parents' real name when they escaped Nazi Italy during World War II.

Felix sat down, taking a breath, resolving not to engage the workman's firm and risk renewed exposure. It had taken years for his sister, Frances, to decide the ongoing clone crises were finally over and she could have her own life. She married a man she'd dated off and on. They lived close enough for frequent visits and that's where his wife and daughter were going now, so Ariel could say goodbye before she left for school.

As the taste of cassis and white burgundy slid down his throat, Felix had a disturbing thought. He put down the glass. Was it coincidence that the inspector might have recognized Felix, or had something surfaced in the news? He picked up the remote and flicked through the TV news channels. Finding nothing, he turned to the Religion Channel, just in case. Long ago Felix accepted that he was Jewish by blood and Christian by faith. His belief in Jesus had not changed.

There was some sort of interview.

He turned the volume up. Somewhere in Italy a man was talking to a reporter. Ignoring the bad translation, Felix listened to the man's angry, scoffing words. This morning there had been a commotion at the Porlezza market. A strange young man had appeared and gotten everyone excited. Later, the man's own wife claimed she saw a neighbor afflicted with scoliosis of the spine run to the train station, her back perfectly straight. People were saying Jesus had returned and performed a miracle healing.

Oh, for crying out loud.

At least this rumor didn't involve him.

Reassured, Felix switched off the TV. He downed his kir, stood, and gazed out at the autumn landscape, shaking his head. It bothered him to still feel guilt that Jess had died after Felix left him and Maggie alone in Italy. Ariel had been kidnapped. What else could he do?

He took out his wallet and from a compartment withdrew the last photograph he'd taken of Jess—ten years old, healthy, smiling, filled with a joyful love that beamed from his eyes. He'd be eighteen now if he hadn't died.

Felix flicked the TV back on, curiosity having gotten the better of him. The man was still being interviewed. He said the young man who appeared in Porlezza this morning had so disturbed the market crowds that a woman fainted, a black woman. The boy claimed she was his mother but they'd looked nothing alike.

Felix's knees jerked him up from the sofa, his mind reeling, his pulse racing. Had the workman's near-recognition been a portent? "Dear God, no!" he said aloud, desperately hoping the woman's name wasn't Maggie and that the greatest nightmare of his family's life hadn't resumed.

Chapter 6

Jess and I sat on the terrace, watching boats go by. Given where the sun was, I knew it was mid-afternoon, but I'd had no sense of passing time. We hadn't eaten since the maid brought us food, but I wasn't hungry. Seeing Jess perform a miracle, I'd grown afraid. If he kept doing them, would it upset people, like it had 2000 years ago? Would he be killed?

Fear made me content to sit beside him, talking less and less. I could pretend our side-by-side lounge chairs were at our villa in Arona and the terrace was our former deck over Lake Maggiore. We grew so quiet, it surprised me when Jess spoke.

"You feel better now, Madre?"

I nodded, though calm left at his question.

"Then we must begin."

I didn't ask, *begin what?*

Jess unfurled himself from the lounge chair and only then did it strike me he was nearly six feet.

"How tall are you now, honey?"

"Five eleven."

"How much do you weigh?"

"About 160 USA pounds."

I'd read all of Felix's research on the Shroud of Turin. He'd estimated the image was of a man five foot eleven, weighing 170 pounds. Did Jess's face resemble the face on the shroud? I felt awed, deathly afraid and ashamed of my cowardly reaction as the similarity sank in.

His back to me, Jess casually asked, "Mamma, will you be my disciple?"

The question made my head swim. "Me? Your disciple? Mary wasn't Jesus' disciple."

Jess turned around. "She knew who he was before anyone else."

I got out of the lounge chair, my self-confidence at zero. "What do you want me to do?"

"Find the kingdom of God within you."

"Okay, but how?"

"Remember that mustard seed?"

Weakly I laughed. "Not that again."

Jess came and took my hands. "Have faith, Mother. Believe my words."

"Okay. Which ones?"

"*Ask, and it shall be given you; seek, and ye shall find; knock, and it shall be opened unto you: For every one that asketh receiveth; and he that seeketh findeth; and to him that knocketh it shall be opened.*" Nothing in your Bible is truer than these words, Madre, if you do not doubt. The degree of your faith determines how much this promise comes true."

I remembered Jess said he came to earth because Felix and I asked, believing. It wasn't the cloning, but how could that be?

"Why does it matter what I believe?"

"You know the Mayans predicted the world would end on December 21, 2012?"

"Well, it didn't."

"In a way, it did. Earth energies rose. Change is underway. For some, chaos will rein, for others greater joy. If all goes well, humanity won't destroy itself and the earth. Eventually, all must come on this journey. If my own mother won't, perhaps humanity is lost."

A tear slid down my cheek and bitterness I didn't know I had exploded. I let go of his hands so I could wring mine.

"You think I didn't ask, Jess? Asked God on my knees every day of your life to protect you?" I raised my hands. "I asked and it most certainly was *not* given to me. God allowed you to die in my arms at the age of ten, innocent and full of love."

He fixed me with that soulful stare again. I shut my eyes, determined to get this off my chest.

"You think I didn't seek, Jess?"

I felt his hand on my shoulder.

"I sought you day and night—on the lakeshore, in your room, in the garden, in your boat out on Lake Maggiore in the middle of the night. I sought and didn't find you, Jess!"

"Mamma—"

"You think I didn't knock? I banged on heaven's door with every beat of my heart. 'Open and bring him back to me!' I begged. I knocked and it *didn't* open. You didn't come back."

"Don't you see? It *has* been given, you *have* found, it *has* been opened. I did not die. I am here."

Stunned to silence I paced the room. It was true, my prayers had been answered.

"By the way, must I continue quoting the Bible, Madre?"

Jess had strayed from the Bible in his youth. I thought I'd nipped that in the bud. "It's Christianity's book and you're the reincarnation of Christ. What else would you quote, Jess Johnson?"

He grinned. "*The science of uniting one's individual consciousness with the Ultimate Consciousness attains the state of self-realization.*"

"Huh?"

"It is the Hindu way of saying the kingdom of God is within you. It's from the *Bhagavad-Gita*, the book you made me throw into the lake, remember?"

I put my hands to my forehead, because I was getting a headache. "You're serious? You, Jesus, are quoting Hinduism?"

"Not just Hinduism. Truth is written everywhere. You've heard of Kabbalah? Much truth is there. As the Upanishads say, *Truth is one; seers express it in many ways.* Franz Kafka, a novelist said, *You do not need to leave your room. Remain sitting at your table and listen. Do not even listen, simply wait. Do not even wait, be still and quite solitary. The world will freely offer itself to you to be unmasked, it has no choice, it will roll in ecstasy at your feet.* The Bible shortens this to *Be still, and know that I am God.* Gurus call it meditation."

"But Christianity—"

"Isn't something I started."

I gaped at him.

"Well, yes, technically Paul and Peter did, but—"

"My message on religion is contained in the parable of the Good Samaritan. A Samaritan was an infidel and a mortal enemy to the Jews of that time…very like a member of Al Qaeda is to Christians of today. When thieves left a Jewish man for dead, the representatives of his religion passed him by, a priest and a Levite. Only a Samaritan helped him—a man of the wrong religion and wrong tribe."

"You're saying religion means nothing?"

"Unless beliefs are lived, religion means nothing."

"I choose to be a Christian and I try to live those beliefs."

Something happened when I said that. His physical body stayed the same, but Jess's presence grew larger, his eyes kind, but penetrating.

"Madre, you are not a Christian."

He might as well have hit me. "Why would you say that to me? Of course I am! All my life I've prayed and gone to church, read my Bible. All my life, Jess!"

"You don't believe Christ's words and you never have."

"I'm offended by that, Jess."

"You accept the interpretations of men and reject the actual words of Christ."

"I don't. I…"

"What could be plainer than, *ask and you will receive?* What could be plainer than, *love your enemies?* What could be plainer than *Do not worry about tomorrow?* Yet you and others who claim to be Christian, refuse to act on these powerful things because you don't believe them."

"We're supposed to love our enemies, people who're trying to hurt us? Don't we have to protect ourselves?"

"Only because you worry, you hold grudges, and don't ask God to solve your problems. If you believed and practiced Christ's words, you would have no enemies."

"Well, like you said, nobody's perfect."

"Madre, hundreds of thousands on this earth are fully practicing these things and living entirely different lives than most—lives of joy overflowing."

"Hundreds of thousands?"

"I have come to change that number to hundreds—to thousands—of millions. Will you help? Will you be my first?"

Sweat had soaked my blouse, my heart banged against my ribs. The dead son I adored was alive. Mercilessly, he was tearing my beliefs—or lack of them—to shreds and demanding that I change on the spot. It was true. I didn't believe. I would fail at what he asked.

His voice grew deeper still. "As if your life depended on it, Madre, ask God to deliver new towels to the room."

"What?"

"New towels."

"Now?"

"Yes."

"As if my life depends on it?"

"It does, though you don't see."

Trembling, crying, I sank to my knees and clasped my hands. "Lord, I don't know why, but please, please, send us some new towels like Jess wants!"

As I kneeled there mumbling *please, please* Jess went to the door and opened it. A maid stood there, about to knock, her arms full of towels.

Jess took them, said thank you and closed the door.

Then it struck me. The sun was setting. "Jess, that's just the evening turndown service."

"For you that is true, because you don't believe."

How much longer would Jess torture me?

He put the towels down, came and grasped my shoulders. "Do you need to eat?"

I couldn't have eaten if I tried. "No."

"Follow me," he said and went out to the terrace. When we got there, I could see outdoor diners below, candles flickering on their tables, waiters moving among them taking orders and bringing food. Faint music floated above their conversations and laughter. Intensely I longed to be at those tables, having a normal dinner with my Jess. Instead, he stepped up on a chair and held out his hand to me.

"If you have faith as a mustard seed, you will say to this mountain, 'Move from here to there,' and it will move; and nothing will be impossible for you."

It was a direct quote from Matthew 17:20. Jesus himself said it.

Jess added, "Including flying. Mother, take my hand."

Terrified, I stepped back, shaking my head. "Jess, don't do this to your poor mamma! Don't do this! You want me to hurt myself? I can't fly, for Christ's sake!"

Jess smiled, "But I am Christ."

Overcome with anxiety, I ran inside, found a bedroom and fell onto the mattress, not trying to hold back sobs. Either this was all a delusion or my faith was a fraud, as Jess had so clearly revealed. It was impossible to move mountains. I couldn't fly without a plane. No one could. I hadn't summoned towels. They'd come by coincidence. Most of all, I was ashamed of failing my son who'd come back to life to save us. At least, I thought he was my son. I sat up, full of dread, remembering Matthew 24:24: *For there shall arise false Christs, and false prophets.* Had a demon come, disguised as Jess?

Terrified, I stared as Jess came in the room, sat beside me and gave me a hug. My fear vanished. My heart knew who he was.

"Let's try a different way. Trust me. It will be all right."

I nodded, wiped my face and followed him back to the living room, twilight gone, a gibbous moon hanging gorgeous in the sky. He turned on the lights and sat crossed-legged on the rose and aqua rug like a swami.

"Let's meditate," he said.

"I don't know how."

"Remember, *Be still and know that I am God?* That's all it is."

I sat cross-legged beside him.

"It helps to follow your breath. Pay attention as it goes in and out, but don't change it. Or you can focus on your body's energy field. Pay attention to the vibration."

At first I was so awkwardly aware of inhaling and exhaling that my breath became ragged. Then I noticed how calm and shallow Jess's breath was, how peaceful. I tried to remember how it felt not to interfere with my breath and soon a more natural rhythm came. I closed my eyes and followed. Breath in, breath out. Soon I felt a kind of warmth in my chest. My breath became shallower and for no reason I felt calmer than I had all day, felt light.

"Do you know what you are feeling, Madre?"

I shook my head, no.

"A glimmer of what Christians call the Holy Ghost."

That made sense. Whenever I prayed I felt it. I stayed in peace with my breath and the Holy Ghost.

"Now open your eyes, Madre."

I did.

Jess was beaming at me and I guess I was beaming at him, too, because smiles spread across our faces like the afternoon sun on glass skyscrapers. "Keep following your breath," he said.

I could hear the music from the outdoor restaurant. Instead of disturbing my meditation, it became a part of it—breath, music, Jess's smile, the happy energy we shared.

"Look at the orchids, Madre."

They sat in their pot on a shelf across the room beside the TV, four graceful stems, heavy with white blooms.

"Can you trust me, just for a moment?" he asked.

I nodded.

"Then trust in yourself equally."

Suddenly my doubt was gone. I could move mountains if he asked.

He grinned. "Wouldn't it be nice if the flowers danced?"

I looked at the orchids, and knew I couldn't do it.

Avoiding his gaze, I stood. "Sweetheart, I do need to eat. Let's talk about this later."

Jess rose. "You mean talk about the fact you don't believe in Jesus, much less in God?"

"I do so—"

"What you believe in is nature, Mother, like almost all Christians on this earth. They give lip service to the things Jesus said, nothing more. Nature, not spirit, is their God. They dismiss whatever violates their perception of natural law, ignoring that all of nature is itself miraculous."

"But the laws of nature are—"

"Far beyond the grasp of today's science. They are not laws but loose patterns sustained by cooperation between God and human beings, who ignore clear proof of this. What happened one second before the Big Bang? What motive force causes an assembly of inert matter to live? You were a nursing assistant. What is the placebo effect, but absolute proof that humanity can create miracles when it believes?"

"Stop, Jess!" I said. "Please! I can't take this in. I can't. I'm sorry, sweetheart. I know you're disappointed in me, but you'll just have to carry out your mission on your own."

Jess gazed at me with perfect love, though this was the worst disagreement we'd ever had. "What if I can't proceed without you?"

"Can't?"

"What if I can't? What if the fate of the world depends on Maggie Clarissa Johnson Duffy Morelli—on you, Madre?"

"But that doesn't make sense."

"In reality, there is no you; there is no me. We are one. There is no separation. Remember? *I am in my Father, and ye in me, and I in you.* Together our souls abide in God's perfect love. That is why I say nothing is impossible for you. Remember? *He that believeth on me, the works that I do shall he do also; and greater works than these shall he do.*"

"Why can't you do like you did before?"

"Two thousand years ago, I said and did what I needed to. My words have been preserved; though surrounded by untruths, they are there. Those who read them with open hearts know they're true."

"But you're the Messiah!"

"I have not come to lead the way this time. I have already led. If anything, I am the Comforter. I come only to remind. Now the teaching of old must take root in humanity. You must put it into practice. You must, Madre. If my own mother won't do it, who will? Salvation can't be found by keeping the Sabbath, by going to the right church, by kneeling to mouth prescribed prayers, by reading, but not believing, sacred truth. It is time. The kingdom comes. It is within you."

"Oh, Jess!" I lowered my head but he didn't stop. He was certain, resolute, determined.

"Humanity must wake up to who you are—holy creatures in a holy universe God created just for you. It responds to your every thought. But unbelieving, unknowing, you create Hell on your earth. Yet within you is the power. Uncreate your sorrow; uncreate your pain and fear. Trust God by whatever name you use—all the names are wrong. The power that you call God predates earth languages. Call God what you will. The kingdom comes. Take my hand."

"But what must I do?"

"Have the courage to abandon fear."

All I knew was that I was exhausted. Even if the whole world depended on it, I couldn't think another thought. "Can I sleep, Jess?"

Jess came and put his arms around me, spoke kindly. "Yes, sleep, Mother. Tomorrow is an important day."

No way I was asking why.

In one of the suite's bedrooms we found cartoon drawings on the wall and two twin beds side-by-side for children. Without speaking, we lay on them and looked out at the gorgeous moon. Jess beamed at me. I smiled back and slept.

Chapter 7

Ahmed Bourguiba wasn't Tunisian as his friend, Zach, and their coworkers at Silverman Alden thought. To prevent anyone's looking up his past, he'd bought himself a new identity when he came to the U.S. Since Tunisians weren't terrorists he'd picked that nationality and adopted the last name of the country's first President. He was actually Egyptian, a Muslim who'd been raised in East Africa. His father was a militant Islamist, one of the four still at large for the 1998 bombings of two American Embassies there. Ahmed and his mother had accepted that his father could be martyred one day because almost half of the seventeen indicted for the bombings had been killed, including Osama bin Laden. The rest were imprisoned for life.

He was at the former hangout of the defunct Lehman Brothers—Emmett O'Lunney's Irish Pub. It was one of the bars on Stone Street, the first one paved in New York. As in European walking streets, the bars and restaurants along Stone Street spilled onto the sidewalk, attracting Wall Streeters and tourists alike to the tables and umbrellas outside. Rarely frequented by Silverman Aldenites, it was *Cheers* for the Wall Street crowd. Emmett knew everyone's name.

Even though he was thought to be an easy-going Tunisian, Ahmed didn't like breaking *shari'a* law in public. For privacy, he preferred the booths inside, each with bench seats upholstered in green leather. Frosted glass panels separated the booths along with wooden lampposts, topped by globe lights. In these booths, fewer people could see him not being a true Muslim and taking a drink, which was *haraam*, forbidden. They couldn't hear what he and Zach said. Fortunately, he wouldn't have to worry about taking out his prayer rug and performing the rituals of *salat* again until *al-'isha* at 10:36. It could be later, as long as he completed it before dawn. Prayer was something Ahmed would always perform. He didn't want to slip so far from his Islamic duty that he became one of the growing numbers in America who were merely culturally, rather than religiously, Muslim.

However, Ahmed was doing a second forbidden thing, according to conservative Islam, anyway—listening to Taarab on his iPod. It was a genre of music unique to the Swahili people of East Africa. He remembered how his dad used to sing it, though Islam taught that singing and music and instruments were all *haraam*. But his dad and all of Egypt had revered their legendary singer, Ummu Kulthoum, and thought her music was *halaal*, allowed. At worst it was only *marouh*, blameworthy but not a sin. When they moved to Tanzania, in the days before his *jihad*, his dad had learned Taarab, even though he wasn't Swahili. From the Arab word meaning *having joy with music*, Taarab had influences from Asia, Africa, Europe and the Middle East. Originally the singers were male, but Ahmed was listening to a *waswahili* women's group. Dressed in lovely clothes, they faced the audience in a line and swayed to the music—their facial expressions and movements subdued as they sang. This lyric was a poem that would have scandalized his father, a new form called *mipasho*—openly sensual, vulgar and bad mannered. His father would hate it. Ahmed didn't. He was in love with one of the singers, beautiful Ajia, one of the few non-family members who knew both him and his father because of their mutual interest in Taarab. He sensed she liked him, but he knew Ajia was wary of getting closer to him. He wasn't Swahili. Also, she knew his father was a terrorist.

It was true. Almost the entire Muslim *ummah*, both Shi`a and Sunni, Arab speakers and not, had condemned the embassy attacks as violations of shari'a law because so many non-combatant civilians were killed. Yet he understood why his father thrilled at bin Laden's declaration of war, even though bin Laden had no authority, no *bay`ah* from the ummah, the community, to declare one. All in the ummah agreed with bin Laden's grievances: foreign troops on sacred Saudi soil, the suffering of the Palestinian people under Israel, and of the Iraqi people under foreign sanctions. Even so, Ahmed himself wouldn't have done what his father did; at least he hadn't thought so. Until recently, he had considered himself part of the Egyptian revisionist jihadi movement, which renounced violence. Meeting Ajia had complicated things. In sleepless nights, yearning for her, he had realized what he must do.

Sitting with his eyes closed nursing his beer, Ahmed didn't see Zach approach, only felt someone tug on his earphone and then heard, "As-Salamu `alaykum," Peace be upon you. Ahmed didn't have to open his eyes to know it was Zach. No one else greeted him that way. The Americans he knew said hello and his Arabic friends said, *kif halak*, how are you, when they met.

He replied, "*aleikum-salam*," turned and exchanged a handshake with Zach Dunlop, great guy and infidel.

As Zach slid into the booth, his usual Lionshead arrived, sent by Emmett.

Ahmed grinned and raised his bottle.

Instead of taking a swig, Zach slid his hand across the table, and then lifted it, a grin on his face. There was the BuckyCube Ahmed had admired in a store window when they were last out at lunch. Encased in green plastic, it was a cube of tiny magnetized squares that could be rearranged in thousands of ways, and then if you were lucky, returned to the shape of a square. Ahmed had started to buy it, but they had to get back to the office.

"Get out of here, Zach, dude," Ahmed said, picking it up.

Zach's eyebrows were up, his face a question. Was Ahmed pleased?

Ahmed was. "Thanks, man."

"No problem, dude."

Zach was always doing things like that and acting like it was nothing. He seemed to take pleasure in giving things and money away—though not like his wife, Zenia, who organized elaborate charity events that made the news. All the beggars knew Zach. He had a fiver for whoever held out a hand, even the guy with a dog who got arrested for peddling drugs from his begging bowl. If asked, Zach gave—also if unasked. His co-workers knew to be careful what they said around Zach. Admire something in his hearing and it was likely to show up. Yet nobody felt Zach was a show-off. He didn't seek praise. He was just so lucky, it seemed to overflow onto anyone he met. More than once a tale of woe from a local business having trouble or someone about to lose their home had ended happily in an anonymous donation and Ahmed suspected it was Zach. He could have had a giant ego because the luck hadn't missed his face, but Zach didn't. He seemed to like and want to help whoever came into his path. Ahmed was sure Zach gave away more than the two and a half percent required of Muslims.

Once Ahmed came upon Zach mumbling to himself and Zach revealed he had a running conversation with God, whom he called Dude One. Zach would make a perfect Muslim and Ahmed dreamed of teaching him the Shahadah, Islam's testimony of faith, *La ilaha illa Allah, Muhammadur rasoolu Allah.* There is no true god but God and Muhammad is the Messenger of God. To convert, Zach must only recite it, sincerely believing. Then together they could study the Holy Qur'ān.

Ahmed eyed Zach's beer. "Still not ready to branch out from college? You can afford it now, you know, Praise Allah." Knocking each other's beers was one of their pastimes.

Zach took a swig, a look of bliss on his face, and then gave the beer drinker's satisfied gasp. "Lionshead and I are never getting a divorce. This is the best pilsner in the world."

"Maybe the cheapest pilsner, but…"

Zach ignored him and turned over the Lionshead cap to see if it had a rebus to solve. Apparently it did, because he raised his eyebrows, said, "Got it!" and handed it to Ahmed, who sighed, looked at the drawing of a cinnamon roll, an exit arrow, the word *the*, a barrel and said, "Ready?"

Zach nodded and together they said, "Roll Out the Barrel," then laughed. He and Zach had been doing Lionshead rebuses off and on throughout the ten years they'd been at Silverman—as had anyone else who drank with Zach.

Ahmed took a sip of his Ninkasi I.P.A., a French beer that an ex-pat Tunisian might drink. "We are too old for bottle caps," he said.

Zach grinned. "Probably right, but at least I'm not drinking French piss. Hey, did you see AmerCan take off again today?"

Ahmed pretended ignorance, his face blank. He had seen it and knew why it was happening.

"I wonder what's up with them," Zach said.

Ahmed could have told him because he was keeping a close eye on the African doings of western firms. AmerCan was about to descend on another beleaguered village, destroy its ground water, if it had any, cut down the trees, and pollute its earth until it wasn't livable anymore. They called it mining. Ajia called it robbery and murder and Ahmed had come to agree with her.

When she first said the world used sub-Saharan Africa as its combination mugging victim and dumping ground, it had opened Ahmed's eyes. Now he saw. Where did drugs banned in others countries go? Africa. Food that didn't pass inspection? Africa. Toys with lead in them, unsafe medical equipment, commercial refuse of every kind? Africa. If an African region was found to have valuable mineral resources, the flow of goods changed direction. Systematically, local governments would be bought off, overthrown or marginalized if they didn't offer favorable terms for extraction. If necessary, civil wars would be started. Ajia made him see that anything of value Africa owned was taken from it—its minerals, its forests, its wildlife—and it was tricked into buying trash on offer from the outside world. Just recently, a Catholic news outlet had called for an end to the plunder of Sierra Leone's forests before they were gone forever.

Now, AmerCan had its eye on a large tract of western Tanzania where Ajia was from and seemed to be targeting a particular village—one just emerging from a long drought and that didn't have the resources to take on AmerCan. Ahmed had decided to do something about it.

Unlike his father, he'd never been personally involved in jihads, except of course the "great jihad"—the spiritual struggle within oneself toward perfection. Ahmed simply oversaw the holdings of people who were Islamists, whether violent or non-violent he didn't know—their money hidden away in disguised accounts. His job at Silverman Alden was a perfect cover.

Ajia said she didn't trust him because Arabs were the first African slavers and he was no better than the rest of the world that was destroying her continent and its people. He would prove her wrong.

"Maybe it's just a fluke," Ahmed said.

Zach belched. "Hope not. I talked Da Gawdfadda into buying a piece of them."

"It'll pay off in the short term anyway," Ahmed said.

Zach eyed him. "You know something."

It couldn't hurt to tell Zach. "Yeah, they're about to get control of a big piece of land in East Africa."

Zach slapped the table. "I knew it! Where?"

"Around a village called Udugu. It means brotherhood, but that's not what's about to happen."

Zach slid from the center of his side of the booth to the wall and raised his legs to the seat, swigging his Lionshead. "I guess it's not the agri thing then, right?"

He was referring to the land grab going on in which foreign concerns purchased whole tracts of Africa for almost nothing to produce food, all of which left the continent as export. Instead of thriving, locals labored in the new foreign farms at low wages, suffering from exposure to pesticides. Some of the western companies who first exploited Africa had since grown a conscience. Not most. East Africa had formed a Common Market, hoping to deal with emerging markets now emulating the west. Substandard and dangerous goods still flooded Africa.

"No, it's mining. They've found something valuable. Not sure exactly what. They've been working on it quietly and now they've persuaded a missionary to talk the locals into signing over the land. Can't remember his name. Joseph something."

Zach sat up. "Paul Joseph?"

"Yeah, that's the guy."

"Hey, he's my wife's pastor."

Ahmed frowned. The truth was that he'd learned about AmerCan through spyware he'd installed on Zach's computer. Zach never failed to sniff out new trends. If the firm had an

African connection, Ahmed added his own research. He'd never guessed there'd be a personal connection between AmerCan and Zach.

"Well, tell her to stay away from there."

"Wow, she said she wants to go there, Ahmed. What's going on?"

Ahmed delayed by drinking his Ninkasi I.P.A. He'd always known that, sooner or later, his friendship with Zach could come in conflict with his duty. He should have avoided getting so close to anyone at Silverman Alden, but as soon as he met Zach he'd liked him. He felt like a brother. Ahmed couldn't tell him what was about to befall Paul Joseph and his AmerCan friends. It would stop any mining ventures near Udugu forever, or at least for a very long time. Ahmed would prove to Ajia that he cared about the exploitation of Africa.

"I just..." Ahmed leaned forward, hating to lie to his friend. "I traveled there a lot when I was young, so I kind of know. When a mining concern targets a new area, there could be trouble." Unfortunately, that usually wasn't true, but he hoped it sounded convincing. The last place Zach's wife should be anytime soon was Udugu, God willing.

Zach searched his face. Did he suspect something? "Okay, Ahmed," is all he said. "Thanks. I'll tell her."

Chapter 8

Zach awoke, only a slight hangover from his night of beer with Ahmed. They'd made the rounds of the Stone Street bars then ended up at a place he didn't want Zenia to know about. Ahmed didn't want anyone to know, either. He said a true Muslim shouldn't watch strange women disrobe. Nevertheless, they'd both enjoyed it. Like other western Muslims Zach had met, Ahmed prayed five times a day and believed firmly in Islam, without feeling the need to do all it said. Not that he blamed him. Christians were like that, too. Actually, Zach wasn't sure whether it was the religion or the culture that forbid Muslims so many things.

He yawned and opened his eyes, looking over towards Zenia's bed, but found it empty. Zach was relieved to have a delay. Should he tell her about the strip club or not? He and Ahmed hadn't planned to go. They saw it and went in, pretty drunk. Neither of them had lap dances, just looked. That's as far as Zach would ever go toward infidelity. It wasn't his thing.

What he needed was to find Zenia and plan their, "break the news about the end of the world," weekend away. The idea didn't upset Zach. Everyone would die one day and be with God. He knew it would upset Zenia, though.

He heard heels, which meant Zenia was already up and about to leave. Where was she going?

Tying his pajamas, he rolled out of his queen bed, identical to hers. "Zenia?"

He padded toward the sound of her heels. "Zenia?"

Why wasn't she answering?

He pushed open the door to surely one of the largest dressing rooms in Nassau County. Zenia had designed and decorated it herself in shades of violet, her favorite color, with coordinating grays, blues and pinks. It had a window seat, a chaise lounge, an easy chair and dressing table, a chandelier, and what seemed miles of clothes on movable racks. Push a button for her summer wardrobe, push again for fall, spring, winter. Her shoes rested on a movable belt that extended behind wood paneling. She could summon casual or evening, a certain heel height, a specific color. He suspected more engineering went into getting his wife dressed than existed in some department stores. Twice a year, she donated much of it to charity, making room for the latest styles.

"Zenia?"

Zach rubbed his eyes, surprised to see the Henks packed. Zach had indulged her in the most expensive luggage in the world. Zenia sometimes dashed off on little notice for charity events or jaunts with girlfriends. Had he forgotten something?

"Oh, you're up," he heard and there she was, dressed in khakis as if she were off for a safari, Ginger the maid in her wake. Ginger had ginger hair, the source of her nickname. She was actually a non-spicy matron who took excellent care of them. Zach hired her when they were still in Manhattan and he made his first million.

"Good morning, Mr. Zach," Ginger said.

'Good morning, Ginger."

"Did I forget something?" he asked as Zenia came to kiss him.

"I told you I was going to Africa."

"Africa? Today?"

She stepped back, adjusting her earrings, which was what she did when she wanted to avoid something. "Yes."

"You never said you were going to Africa today, Zenia. I would have come home last night if you had."

She stopped fiddling and folded her arms. "Well, perhaps I didn't want to be talked out of it."

Zach slumped, flabbergasted, onto the chaise lounge. "May I ask where in Africa you'll be?"

"A village called Udugu."

Where had he heard that name? Then he remembered Ahmed's warning. "Zenia, I don't want you going there."

She delivered a severe frown. "I'm going, Zach. I don't need your approval. It's important."

"Why?"

"Because Paul Joseph needs my help there."

"He's needed help there for five years, Zenia. Why are you suddenly going now?"

She blew out air. "You should have come to church last night."

"Did I miss something?"

She smirked. "Just Paul Joseph's description of his visit to the White House!"

"Whoa! Well, he's always wanted to go there."

She fixed him with her eyes. "So have I."

"That's what this is about? You're campaigning for a White House invitation by helping Joseph?"

She looked in a full-length mirror, adjusting her clothes. "I wouldn't call it campaigning."

He stood. "Well, you can't go! I'm not kidding. I heard there might be some trouble because of what AmerCan is up to there."

She turned to him in surprise. "You know about AmerCan?"

"I know Paul Joseph's got himself involved in something he might not be able to handle."

She gave him an indulgent smile, came and patted his cheek. "Darling, how many times have you been to Africa?"

"Once, when we went to the pyramids."

She nodded. "Paul Joseph has been going there bi-annually for five years." She raised her eyebrows pointedly. "I do think he knows a tad more about it than you?"

"But—"

That seemed to be the end of the conversation because Zenia picked up her purse and headed out, Ginger rolling suitcases behind her. "I've got to hurry," she called. "The limo's here."

He ran behind her and grabbed her arm. "Zenia, you need to listen to me!"

Sarcastically, she said, "Zach, the President's sending someone. Believe me, there won't be any problems."

"This is crazy! You hate Africa. You could barely stand the luxury hotel where we stayed in Cairo. Can going to the White House be so important? Why, Zenia? What's eating you? Isn't what we have enough?"

She became sweetness and light. "You give me everything and I'm so grateful to you, Zach, but *you're* the money-maker. I'm just a nobody."

He wrapped her in his arms. "My wife is no nobody. How could you say that?"

She sighed, rubbing his back. "Your wife. Is that who I am? Thanks for clearing that up. Have you thought of stitching your name tag on me so, in case I get lost, I don't get confused with other men's wives?"

He stood back. "Well what do you want to be?"

She looked off. "Nancy Reagan?"

"Seriously? For that to happen, I'd have to be Ronald. You can't want that."

She sighed and looked so wistful he kissed her. She responded, dutifully kissing back until he stopped. Pulling away, she smiled and started down the stairs. He couldn't believe it. She was actually leaving.

"Zenia. Good grief! How long will you be gone? What are your flights? Where are you staying?"

"I left it all in a note on your bed table. Paul Joseph needs money for the village. A few photos in the society pages and a few phone calls from me will do the trick."

Desperately Zach tried to remember exactly what Ahmed had said. All he could conjure up was the warning that she should stay away from Udugu.

They reached the ground floor and in the columned marble foyer, he grabbed her arm again. "Zenia, stop! Listen to me!"

Angrily, she turned. "What?"

"There's something going on over there. I'm telling you it's not safe! Besides, I wanted to talk to you about something very important. It's about…about changes in the world."

She responded with a withering glare. "Are you going to let go of me, Zach Dunlop?"

He couldn't shout, *the world might be ending, Zenia*! Unable to think of what else to say, he asked, "When will you be back?"

"Before you know it."

She kissed his cheek and opened the iron front door, its bars masquerading as decorative grillwork. Zenia bought it to feel safe. He followed her out to the steps and stood barefoot on the 100% natural coir sunburst doormat, which she'd selected to keep dirt from being tracked onto the marble. This same woman was going to a village in Africa? For a moment she paused, regarding the trees and flowers of their expensive wooded portion of Hewlett Bay Park Village, the life of luxury he'd given her suddenly not enough to keep her here. She waved at him, got in the waiting limo, and was gone.

Full of worry, Zach waited until the limo was out of sight. He looked at his watch. He had to hurry if he was going to get to the heliport and catch the charter to work.

Back in the house, he showered and dressed in the clothes Ginger laid out for him, then grabbed a bite of the eggless omelette she made him each morning, took a sip of fresh orange juice and fresh latte made in their espresso machine. He paused to message Zenia, *Text me ur ok when u board and when u land,* then Zach hopped in his Porsche and was off to work.

During his short flight to the Wall Street heliport, Zach ignored the amazing views of rivers and skyscrapers. He didn't chat as usual with his charter chopper companions because he was worrying about Zenia. As soon as they landed, Zach rushed from the heliport to Silverman Alden's massive building. If Big Brother existed, he'd work in a place like this, its proportions and artwork massive, dwarfing the people who came and went and worked here. In a silent silver elevator, which managed to sweep up and down vast distances without causing stomachs to lurch, he rode to the executive floor. As soon as he alit, Zach hurried down windowed halls toward Ahmed's office—the view not meant for those with altophobia. He opened the door. Ahmed wasn't there and neither was his assistant. She'd taken the day off. Zach was about to call Ahmed's cell, when the exec in the next office arrived.

"Hey, Zach,"

"Hey, John."

"If you're looking for Ahmed, he said he's taking two weeks off."

Zach stared at John, apprehension overwhelming him.

"I am, too," Zach declared.

"Oh. Well, good," John said. "Where are you off to?"

Zach didn't reply. He was rushing to tell Da Gawdfadda he'd be gone.

Chapter 9

Ariel Fubini sat on a white horse at the Danbury Fair Mall's Venetian carousel, sunlight streaming in from the glass dome roof and glass walls, calliope music playing as she rode. She was sixteen and too old for carousels, but couldn't resist one last ride before leaving home. *Choate isn't far, besides you've been going there for three years*, her mother Adeline had said, but for Ariel the difference between being a Day Student at Choate and a Boarder were monumental. Since the age of eight, she hadn't lived a single day without her dad always around. He drove her to school. He picked her up. He drove her to the movies and picked her up—took her to her hair salon, her nail salon. If she went out with friends he drove them, waiting patiently outside parties, restaurants, theaters, swimming pools, inside malls until they were done. Her friends accepted him as part of the furniture of their lives. *It's just Ariel's dad*, they'd say or if they didn't have a ride somewhere, *Ariel's dad will take us*, because he was always there—except on the few occasions, like today, when she was out with only her mom.

Ariel barely remembered being kidnapped when she was eight. At the time, she hadn't felt any danger. Only later when she overheard her parent's hushed conversation did she realize what had happened, which caused her nightmares for a while.

Her dad had personally guarded her ever since. Technically, boarding at Choate this year would give her only a slight increase in freedom. It was actually called Choate Rosemary Hall, because of the 1971 joining of Choate, an exclusive boys' prep school and Rosemary Hall, an exclusive girls' prep school. Average SAT score? High. Vibe? Way beyond conservative. Other schools might not act *in loco parentis*, but Choate did—sheltering its charges, guiding their every step. What she'd be free from was the constant company of one Dr. Felix Fubini, her dad.

Not that she didn't love and appreciate him or understand his concern, a tad obsessive-compulsive though it was, in her opinion. If anyone asked why Ariel's dad was always around, her friends would just say, *She was kidnapped when she was eight* and that was that. Everyone understood, but that didn't mean it was easy to take. Desperate to avoid her dad's surveillance, she and her friends mounted conspiracies a few times—all perfectly innocent in intent, anyway. Sometimes Ariel feared she'd never get to walk down a public street alone, or grow up, or fall in love.

The carousel stopped and, waving to her mom, Ariel stayed on the white horse for a second ride. Sipping coffee with other shoppers, her mom waved back from the tables outside the carousel's low fence. Ariel wondered if she'd ever know the truth about who kidnapped her and why. Her parents treated it like their own personal secret—something so dangerous or so huge it was unthinkable to share it with her. Rude, to say the least, in her opinion.

When the ride ended, she hopped off the horse and joined her mom at the table. Strangers never guessed they were mother and daughter. Ariel had her dad's dark looks, which couldn't have been more different than her mother's gray eyes, pale skin and blonde hair.

"Hungry?" her mom asked.

"Nope," Ariel said. "Let's get this over with."

Her mom laughed. "So that's how you regard shopping for new clothes?"

Ariel grinned. She knew she was lucky.

Her mother stood, ready to head for *Abercrombie* on the Lower Level. It had the largest selection of clothes they were likely to agree on.

"Mom, wait," Ariel said.

Adeline sat down again and put her hand over Ariel's, her grey eyes all attention. Ariel knew she was the most important person on earth to both her parents.

"Mom, I just…"

"Yes, honey?"

"I just don't feel right going off by myself to Choate without knowing…"

"Knowing what, darling?"

Ariel blurted out, "Knowing the whole story about the kidnapping, that's what."

For a moment there was only the music from the carousel and murmurs from nearby conversations. Adeline looked trapped, as if it wasn't fair for Ariel to corner her with such a question when her dad wasn't around.

"Okay, Mom, never mind," Ariel said and rose. "I know I'm lucky to be the only child of Felix and Adeline Fubini of Roxbury, Connecticut, wealthy and urbane CIA operatives, Russian spies, assassins, or whoever you really are." Ariel started to walk past, but her mom grabbed her hand.

"Wait, Ariel," Adeline said. "Is something bothering you?"

"No, it's just—well, if I don't know who did it and why, how can I be sure they won't come after me at Choate?" She didn't like to admit that this thought had crossed her mind.

Her mother sighed. "You do have a right to know, but you should hear it from your dad, from both of us."

Ariel couldn't believe it. "You mean you're really going to tell me?"

"Yes, I think it's time."

"In that case, forget the clothes."

Thirty-five minutes later when the Mercedes pulled up to the house, Ariel jumped out, ran to the door, used her key and went in. Hearing the TV playing, she rushed toward the living room, calling, "Dad, we're home. Dad?"

"In here."

"Hi, Dad."

"Well, that was quick."

She plopped onto the opposite couch and sat cross-legged. "Mom said it's time you told me."

He looked up quizzically at Adeline as she entered the room. "Told her what?"

Adeline sat next to him and patted his hand. "About the kidnapping. Ariel's right. She should know before she leaves."

Her dad looked at her mom as if she'd betrayed him.

"It's time, Felix," Adeline said. "Tell her."

Seeing her father's stricken face, Ariel wasn't so sure she wanted to know anymore.

Adeline said, "She's afraid she'll be kidnapped at Choate."

"Oh, is that it? You won't, I promise," her dad said.

"Tell her, Felix," her mom insisted.

He hesitated, his forehead in his hand. Then he looked up at her. "Ariel, what I'm about to say will sound ... well, strange. Very, I think."

She wanted to reassure him. "I could have guessed that by myself."

"Two, almost three years before you were born—" He paused again, shaking his head. "Sometimes I still don't believe this actually happened. Well, I removed DNA from the Shroud of Turin and produced a clone from it."

Ariel blinked. Had she heard right? A clone? From the Shroud of Turin? Wasn't that supposed to be Jesus' burial cloth? "You did what?"

"I cloned what I hoped was the DNA of Jesus of Nazareth."

Ariel flopped back on the couch, her hands to her face; she waved her arms wildly. "Gee, Dad! And you worry about me? Gee, Dad! I mean! That's totally unbelievable, dude! ... oh, sorry, I didn't mean to call you that."

"It's all right. We know you're surprised," Adeline said. She looked at Felix. "So was I."

"Well, holy Moses ... what in the world happened?" Ariel said.

"I succeeded."

Ariel shot to her feet. "OMG! You mean, like, a clone of Jesus Christ is alive!"

"No." He looked at the TV screen. "At least I'm 99% certain that he isn't. Sit down, Ariel, if you please."

She sat down. "You mean he died?"

"Yes, when he was ten. You were eight. That's where the kidnapping came in. His name was Jess. A powerful man located him in Italy. The man's dead now, but he kidnapped you to get me out of the way so he could destroy Jess."

"Oh, wow! A modern Herod! You mean Jess was murdered?"

"Yes, I mean…well, not by that man. By someone else. When you were kidnapped, I came back to New York to find you. While I was gone, a neighbor threw stones at Jess and killed him—at least—" Felix looked at Adeline as if he were making a decision. "You both should know that something might be going on."

Adeline said. "Goodness, Felix, what is it?"

Felix flicked on the TV and selected something he'd recorded. Ariel watched, her mouth open, as an Italian man reported on the commotion at the Saturday market in some place called Porlezza. When he described a black woman fainting, her dad switched off the TV.

"You don't think—," Adeline said.

"Think what?" Ariel asked, trying to process what she'd heard in the past ten minutes.

"The woman who carried the clone was black," he said. "She was our maid and she volunteered."

"You can't mean Sharmina, Dad? You don't mean Sharmina!"

"You remember her?" Felix asked.

"Of course I remember her."

"It was Sharmina's best friend, Maggie. She was our maid before Sharmina was. Maggie Johnson. At least that's what her name was then. She married Sam Duffy, our doorman, but he's dead."

"The doorman? God, Dad, did somebody kill the doorman?"

"Yes, but a different person did it, and for another reason, I think."

"Dad, I was right! You're a secret agent! A mad scientist, secret agent!"

Adeline frowned. "Darling, please try to take this seriously."

"Seriously? You've gotta be kidding." Then Ariel remembered what the man said on the TV interview. "OhmiGod, Dad! You think there's a chance Jesus is here—you think that's who was in the Porlezza market and the black woman who fainted was Maggie, his mother. Don't you?"

"I certainly hope not. Our lives were almost destroyed by this."

Ariel stood. "Dad, you've got to go find out."

"I certainly won't. I've only told you a fraction of what happened. There's much more."

"Dad, you've got to go! If you don't, I will! This could be Jesus, Dad. You might have started the Second Coming, Dad! You've, like, absolutely got to go."

Her mom and dad stared, horror on their faces.

"What do you mean, if you don't I will?" Adeline said.

"Mom, wake up! This could be the most important thing happening on earth!"

Her dad stood. "Give me your credit card, Ariel."

"What? Why?"

"Give it to me," he said. "You're going overboard. The clone wasn't Jesus, for goodness sake. How could it be?"

Angrily she searched her wallet and handed it to him. "Why did you bother telling me if you're just going to keep treating me like a baby?"

Before they could answer, Ariel left the room, stormed upstairs, slammed her door and threw herself onto her bed, crying so hard that before long she ran to the bathroom to throw up.

———

"What do you mean the flight is booked?" Zach yelled into his cell phone.

"Apologies, sir. South African Airways Flight 204 to Johannesburg is overbooked. Even the standby list is full. However, if you can fly tomorrow—"

Zach clicked off. How could an Airbus be fully booked? Then he realized there probably weren't that many direct flights to Johannesburg. Maybe this was the only one. It left JFK at 10:40 am, less than two hours from now. Zenia was on it with Paul Joseph and God knows who else, all of them crazily flying off into some unknown danger. Repeatedly he'd tried phoning her cell, but she apparently had switched it off. To keep him from changing her mind? In Johannesburg, she'd connect with a flight to Dar es Salaam, Tanzania on Africa's east coast. Zach had hoped to grab a helicopter to JFK and make the flight—no luggage, but he didn't care.

He decided to try his travel agent.

"I need to get to Dar es Salaam ASAP. What's available?"

As he waited, he silently prayed, *God, get me a flight.*

He listened to her confirm that the 10:40 am Airbus was full. The best flight would put him in Dar es Salaam at 10:25 pm day after tomorrow because he was crossing the International Date Line. That was almost eight hours after Zenia would arrive. The flight left from Newark this evening at 5:50 pm. Total travel time, twenty hours and thirty-five minutes.

Then he remembered. "Do I need a visa?"

"Yes, but you can get it at the airport there."

"Thanks. Book it," Zach said.

He hung up, feeling discouraged and uneasy, but at least he'd get to pack.

Chapter 10

Ahmed Bourguiba looked with envy on the Business Class passengers boarding SAA 204 for Johannesburg. South African Airways didn't exactly have a reputation for being king of the skies in terms of service, making business class almost a necessity on this 16-hour flight—one of the world's longest, save for non-stops to Singapore—but today he couldn't risk calling attention to himself. He'd booked an economy seat under his real name, Hanif Hassan, and was traveling under his real passport.

Still, with some dejection, he watched the business class passengers board. A woman with black hair caught his eye. She looked familiar, but Ahmed couldn't place who she was. She wore khakis like a tourist and was traveling with an older man—not old enough to be her father, but for her too old, given how attractive she was.

Ahmed wondered where he'd seen her before. Who was she? Not remembering made him uncomfortable. Was he on the same flight with someone who knew him? He studied the woman and her companion. They didn't have the easy nonchalance of long-established relationships, nor were they exactly formal with each other. They weren't giddy like new lovers. The man was attentive to her, though, and courteous—taking her carry-on bag, handing her ticket and passport to the attendant, letting her board first. She smiled an acknowledgment of each action, as if she wanted to please him. Surreptitiously Ahmed photographed them, watched them until they disappeared, then returned to his cell phone, sending final instructions to his dad's friends who awaited him.

He'd booked an aisle seat in the second row of coach. First row seats were narrower because the tray table and TV were in the armrest. Still he could see into business class when the curtains weren't closed.

The woman and her companion sat next to each other in the middle of row 6, another row and a galley between him and them. They'd probably booked too late to get two seats at the window. When the AirBus took off and soared into the clouds, Ahmed whispered *Bismillah*, with the guidance of God, as he always did during takeoffs and landings. Flights this long had their own reality. He lived in New York, would land in Africa, but in between was his life on the plane. Usually he talked to people, learning things. On this flight he watched the unknown couple as best he could, trying to place who the woman was. It helped that they both used the lavatories in back of Business Class, just a few feet from his seat. The man was older, something of a sad sack, Ahmed thought. The woman was younger and close to spectacular, but for a vacant dissatisfaction in her eyes.

Ahmed gave up and turned his attention to photos of Udugu village and the map by which he'd find his way there, pretending to be on safari.

He ate dinner—a too spicy curried chicken—terrible, compared to business class where at least the food was edible and the menus frequently changed. Ahmed knew because he flew home to Africa every other month.

He watched half a movie, dozed, and then woke in the darkened plane. Not wanting to disturb his seatmates, he went to the galley to look at Ajia's photo. When a flight attendant asked if he wanted something to drink, he said he was only stretching his legs.

He leaned against the bulkhead, Ajia's photo smiling from his hand. A long-limbed mix of African, Persian and Arab, she was a classic Swahili beauty. Wearing a shawl and full-length gown, she wore beads and a white flower in her braids. He was intoxicated by the vibrant *joi de vivre* shining from her, the innocent sensuality of her songs, the confidence with which she denounced depredations of her continent and its resources by the outside world. Technically, it was his continent, too, though sub-Saharan Africa was viewed as real Africa and northern Africa as part of Europe.

Ahmed had adored her on sight and now intended to be her warrior. He would attack whatever hurt her. He took pride in the brilliant plan underway, Praise Allah.

Remembering the couple in business class, he looked up. The flight attendants were gossiping and paying no attention to him so Ahmed moved toward the partially closed curtain. In the dim light from TV screens he could see that most had lowered their seats to the full-recline position, including the couple. Perhaps they were sleeping.

Ahmed thought otherwise when he saw the woman's body move. He peered through the darkness at the shape quivering beneath the blanket. Perhaps she was just stretching. Yawning, he casually walked to the other side of the galley, hoping the curtain was open and he could see the man. Ahmed looked out at the night through the porthole before turning toward Business Class. Except for a small slit, the curtain was closed. Ahmed persisted, pretending to be gazing at Ajia's photo, but peering through the slit. Finally he saw the man. The slightest telltale movement under his blanket told Ahmed what was happening.

They were quietly giving each other hand jobs.

Wondering who they were, Ahmed chuckled and returned to the other side. Apparently there was more than one way to join the mile high club. Just then the woman rose and headed toward the lavatory, giving him a glimpse of her face. It was less distracted now. He smelled a whiff of expensive perfume. Where had he smelled it? Where had he seen her before? As she opened the lavatory door, her eye caught his through the curtain.

Ahmed froze, remembering. It was Zenia Dunlop, Zach's wife. He'd met her at the last office party. She appeared not to recognize him. More importantly, she'd just been unfaithful to Zach, his best friend. Last night Zach mentioned she was going to Africa. He hadn't said she was going today. She would walk into the middle of his plan. She would learn his real name was Hanif Hassan. She was probably on the plane with Paul Joseph, the minister AmerCan had convinced to help them—minister and apparent scoundrel—happy to use his position to lead a woman astray, rather than save her soul. Happy to dupe villagers he claimed were his Christian brothers.

Though Ahmed was abandoning his non-violence for Ajia, he would take pleasure in killing this man. Would he have to kill Zenia Dunlop, too? If he didn't, one day she'd be able to make a link between the Tunisian Ahmed Bourguiba, her husband's friend who worked at Silverman Alden, and Hanif Hassan, the Egyptian who'd been in Udugu when all the dying started.

If she were Muslim and there had been one other witness—actually, four witnesses since it was a sex crime—she could be accused of *zina* under shari'a law. It was a *hudud* crime against God—stoning to death the penalty, laid down by the Hadith, the sayings of Prophet Muhammad that supplement the Qur'ān. Stoning rarely happened in modern Islam anymore, but Ahmed wished it could apply to Zenia Dunlop.

He listened to the lavatory water rinse away the evidence of her infidelity to a husband who would surely do anything for her. He should kill her along with the rest. Would it break Zach's heart if she died?

Angrily, he started back to his seat but was stopped by the sound of muffled crying. Puzzled, Ahmed paused to listen to the faint tears of Zach's whore. They didn't soften his anger. If Zenia Dunlop had a heart, she wouldn't have jerked off another man and allowed him to pleasure her. Curious, though, he waited until she emerged. In the dimness, he saw her rest her hand above her breast—in regret, or because she wanted more?

Ahmed stood back, watching until she reached her seat, lay quietly down, and turned once more to the man.

Chapter 11

I awoke at Hotel Parco San Marco, the sun shining through the window where last night the moon had hung. Jess lay on the other twin bed, smiling at me, his skin luminous against the pine wood paneling. Was I dreaming?

"Buon giorno, Madre."

Apparently not. How long before that inner light consumed him and he was no longer here with me?

"Did you sleep, sweetheart?" I asked.

"Yes, some. I had work to do, so I meditated. Mostly I rested in the kingdom."

"What does it feel like? Is it the same as being saved?"

"It's the same."

"How will I know I'm there?"

"No one will have to tell you. You won't need to read the Bible again or any spiritual teaching because you'll know God directly. All your problems will fall away. It's like being in heaven while you're alive."

"That can happen?"

"In your case, you must only take my hand."

I knew he didn't mean that literally. I'd held his hand repeatedly since he returned. I thought of bathing, brushing my teeth, a change of clothes. Jess nodded, as if he'd read my mind. Then I realized his slacks were no longer tan, but tree trunk brown; his shirt wasn't blue but grass green. Without doing anything, he'd changed.

"Today we need every moment," he said.

I went to the master bathroom and showered. In the suite's bedroom I found a new skirt, blouse and jacket in my size. Given yesterday, I wasn't astonished.

As I put on the clothes, which were just what I'd buy, fear

wrapped me in knots again. Was I ready to be in heaven while I was alive? I said a silent prayer: *Lord, if it's your will that I accept Jess's teaching, help me do it without fear.*

When I returned to the living room, Jess rose. "What about breakfast down on the terrace? I think they're still serving."

I watched as he became less luminous, more physically real.

I took his hand, my overly logical mind still warring against the reports of my eyes and ears. *You're dreaming this, Maggie.* No, I'm not. *What's happening is impossible.*

Down on the terrace, the waiter was full of typically Italian exuberance. "Buon giorno, signore di signora!" Promptly he led us to what I knew they considered their best table. He pulled out my chair and seated me as if I were royalty. Quietly he seated Jess, handing him the small menu, pouring water into his glass.

So many days I'd had a bite to eat under the pale, square umbrellas on this terrace, listening to the children laugh and thinking of Jess. It was a gift to be here with him.

Juice and coffee arrived and we opted for the buffet's boiled eggs, fruit, yogurt, hams, cheeses and breads—the breakfast Adamo made every day, adding sausages and American grits sometimes for me.

The waiter hovered nearby, though he had half a dozen tables. Fortunately, he didn't act like the children, the animals and the maid did yesterday, but more like a chameleon that, finding a warm, sunny spot, blends into the background to enjoy it.

Halfway through our meal, Jess said, *"Per piacere?"* and motioned to the waiter whose attention other diners had been less able to quickly get.

"Si, Signore." Swiftly he was there, bending to hear Jess's request.

"C'è una piccola radio?" Is there a small radio? *"Vorremmo sentire le notizie."* We would like to hear the news.

"Naturalmente! Con piacere!"

Naturally there was a radio and he'd bring it with pleasure, but I'm ashamed to say I wasn't pleased. I didn't ask what Jess expected to hear on the news. I felt zero curiosity.

Though dead, Jess was in front of me. We were sharing a meal. Surely the kingdom was coming, like he said. Why else was he here? Whether Maggie Clarissa Johnson Duffy Morelli upchucked her breakfast from nerves in the process was surely beside the point.

———

uganga - healing
waganga - those who heal
mganga - a healer

When speaking of traditional health care in Tanzania, one speaks in Kiswahili. According to the government, a third of the country is Christian, a third Muslim, a third subscribe to indigenous belief, the goal not a census, but peaceful coexistence. Besides, all in both city and countryside believe in *pepo*, the inner force given by God. Any *mganga* will tell you:

A sick *pepo* is the source of illness or harm.
It's cause? Disharmony in the family or tribe; failing the ancestors.
Music and dance are gateways between *pepo* and the physical senses.
In trance we cross the door.

The waganga wa pepo are spirit healers, certified by the government's Department of Traditional Medicine to minister to the physical, mental, and social ailments of the people, and to their hearts, free of charge. Long before colonialism called them witchdoctors, they healed. They counter spells and cure African illnesses western medicine cannot.

Simeon Mbeya stood outside his mud and thatched-roof compound at the edge of Udugu. No one came to sit in sacred circle beneath the ancient, spreading fig tree. The orange sunset outlined the limbs where the spirits who guided him dwelled. Years ago his uganga-family had called him Babu, grandfather, but no more. The trouble for him and all Tanzania's waganga began in 2007 with the albino killings.

White like the sun, which brought drought and death, albinos had always been discriminated against by those dark like clouds that brought rain and life.

Then somewhere in Nigeria in 2007, or perhaps earlier, those practicing *uchawi*, the bad medicine called witchcraft, began to seek albino body parts for good luck potions. BBC journalists exposed the murders and, embarrassed, the Tanzanian government lifted the licenses of all traditional healers. Fortunately, this only lasted eighteen months. As a new election approached, the politicians ended the ban, knowing they could not win without support of the waganga wa pepo, who so heavily influenced Tanzanian life.

In trance Babu was warned to heed the ban and stop his spirit practice—not to bring rain or cure ills. He'd been told not to resume when the ban was over. As a result, drought had fallen upon Udugu, illness and death. Of course, any mganga who could not maintain prosperity for his uganga family was abandoned, at best. No one had listened to him or sought his help for years. Being male made it easier to be ignored. Most waganga were female since they usually had stronger pepos. But Babu had to listen to the spirits who guided him.

He continued sweeping debris from the packed clay walkway to his compound of thatched mud huts, bending to reposition one of the rocks that lined the path. Two women with babies on their backs stopped and discussed Babu's unusual activity.

"Babu," one called. "Why you sweep? Long time no one comes to you. No one is coming now."

Time had only two dimensions in traditional Africa: now and the past. Babu smiled and didn't answer as he prepared for a new now.

"Babu, no one comes," called the other.

He beckoned the two women toward the fig tree, where his unused *ngoma* drum hung, suspended from a large branch, but they laughed at him and walked on, hiking their babies higher on their backs.

Babu did not feel hurt. He had too much to do.

As the sun approached the horizon, he put away his sweeping branches, picked up the fly whisk he'd made from the tail of a cow, his *nsanza*—called an *mbira* in other places—went to the ancient fig tree and sat with his back against it. It hugged him in embrace. Often waganga on the coast used the ngoma drum to heal. The nsanza was used more in the interior. Some used only singing. Babu had learned to use them all. Music in any form was medicine. It stopped the worry and the thoughts, which block pepo cures. Like most waganga, Babu was also an herbalist and knew how to counter witchcraft as well, but he was primarily an *mganga wa kuoua*, able to receive messages directly from the spirit realm. Born with an angel, he'd had pepo illness until he accepted God's intention that he become a healer. For weeks, now, his pepo, had been receiving messages on the wind.

If he had been one of the coastal Swahili healers, he would have invoked Allah first, seeking protection from the evil *jinn*, but the jinn did not venture into Africa's interior. They stayed on the coast where the Arabs first came. If he had been a Christian, he would have addressed the Jesus of the missionaries. But Babu had not adopted foreign religions, though he pretended to. He was Bantu and had stayed with Mungu, the one God, keeping faith with the spirits of ancestors, fire, earth, water and wind.

To open the door between himself and the will of Mungu, be played his nsanza with his thumbs. Its high, sweet notes accompanied his pepo song: *Kulitetesya kumwanya, kulitetesya*—in heaven there is peace, peace. The words and the music sent Babu into trance where he saw Paul Joseph the missionary would return, saw the Arab coming, saw blood spilling on the ground.

Babu did not tremble in fear. He kept playing his nsanza to make a bridge for a Great One to cross.

Chapter 12

A blast of Africa's heat penetrated the jet way as they stepped from the plane, but Paul Joseph couldn't resist taking Zenia Dunlop's hand until they entered Dar es Salaam International Airport. It was the last time he could touch her without risking his credibility as a man of God. As soon as they left the jet way, they'd be in the company of important people. A scandal now would ruin him, just when his dreams were coming true. Until they reached the terminal, though, Paul Joseph would take advantage of being next to this remarkable woman who made love to him on both their long flights. He hadn't *known* her in the Biblical sense this time—only their hands touched each other, eagerly caressing under the blankets. The need for stealth and silence had caused Paul Joseph acute bliss, but their worst sin was in the past.

"Oh, God, what heat!" Zenia complained. Shaking off his hand, she forged up the ramp toward the terminal, dragging her aquamarine Henk carry-on—the ultimate in luggage, as she'd informed him—glaring at the slow-moving people. Paul Joseph kept pace with her, eager to be among these Africans who astonished with their smiles. During greetings and when they were happy, the light of the soul shone in their eyes. Seeing it had made him yearn to bring them the true God. He gazed on the powerfully built Bantu men in those brown and olive business suits peculiar to Africa, the graceful-eyed and graceful-bodied Swahili men and women in colorful traditional and western clothes. Whites bobbed among them like marshmallows in hot chocolate.

He was home again.

"No one rushes in Africa," he bent and whispered to Zenia. "When you get in the sun, you'll see why." Still he wanted to rush. They were among the first off the plane and immigration and customs would normally take less than half an hour, but Zenia needed to get her visa. That could take forever if they didn't quickly get in line.

The man in front of her stopped abruptly. Caught off balance, she swayed toward Paul, her free arm flailing, making one of the snaps on her safari shirt come undone, revealing what he longed for. That he should desire her against his will was something Paul Joseph held against God, the creator of men's ungovernable libidos. He had to make the effort, though.

"Get a good enough look?" she said in an unfriendly way, when he caught her.

He had and it was delightful. Her tone perplexed him, though. How could she give herself to him one minute and hate him the next? No doubt, it was the guilt.

When they reached the terminal, he heard her gasp and say, "Where in the world am I?"

"Tanzania," he said. "Full of lovely people."

"Who apparently don't use deodorant or know how to turn on the air-conditioning, much less build, repair or clean anything." Fortunately, she'd lowered her voice.

She scoffed at the rudimentary terminal, partly open to the air, and, on the level below, the two immigration kiosks, which would handle all three hundred or so passengers and those on any other international flights that might arrive.

"It's a poor country," he said. "The air-conditioning's probably broken. Things often are, here."

As they descended to the kiosks, Zenia said, "Shoot!" and smacked her arm.

"Sorry. Mosquitoes," he said as if he were responsible for them.

She smacked her neck, bent and scratched her leg, muttering, "Ouch!"

Paul Joseph faced what a bad idea bringing Zenia to Africa probably was. At least she looked rested, having slept in their flatbed seats when they weren't otherwise involved. She had energy to complain. He was too tired. He'd stayed awake convincing himself they hadn't sinned very much.

"Who's Julius Nyerere?" she asked, looking at a sign.

"A revolutionary and their first President who helped them gain independence from England. They honored him by calling him *Mwalimu*, teacher. He was a socialist, though."

"Some honor to name this mosquito trap after him." She scrutinized the passengers filling the terminal. "Why do they wear gold, but no wristwatches?"

"They have a different concept of time."

"Backward people."

Paul Joseph sighed. "Not so backward. They invented steel production over two thousand years ago."

"Oh? Well, a lot of good it did them."

At the bottom of the stairs, two women in traditional dress and importantly large matching head wraps approached the kiosks. The immigration official took their pictures on a computer, took their documents, and disappeared. They'd been in business class, too, and had slid calm eyes toward him and Zenia more than once. Had they seen anything? He didn't recognize them, thank goodness.

He saw someone, probably an Arab, scrutinizing them. Paul Joseph didn't recognize him, either. Was he from Africa, the Middle East, America, somewhere else? Impossible to tell. In his expensive western attire, the man had that *lived-all-over-the-world* look.

Paul decided he was just being paranoid from a guilty conscience and no one was paying attention to them. Mumbling *mmm-hmm* to Zenia's gripes, he allowed himself to daydream about what awaited them and the resultant boost to his career. He was bringing investment to the village and helping AmerCan, a firm the President cared about. When he succeeded, he'd be invited back to the White House. Word would spread. Donations would rise. He'd buy a more suitable house. He'd be invited to the kind of places Rick Warren was invited to. Paul Joseph welcomed fame because it was useful. Not even Jesus could have accomplished much if no one in ancient Jerusalem had heard of him.

They inched their way toward the two kiosks and Paul

maneuvered Zenia to the queue on the right where he knew visas were issued.

"This is where you'll need that hundred dollar bill I mentioned," he said. "They don't take credit cards."

Zenia fished one out of her stylish purse and handed it to an official who was taking money and passports from the *wazungu*, the whites, and taking their pictures. To Paul's surprise, they didn't have to wait like the other westerners, all of them visibly sweltering in their clothes. Had someone paved their way? The official returned, stamped their passports—which included Zenia's visa now—and escorted them out, pointing them toward a space in the hallway where luggage from their flight was being placed. First came the large rollaway that Henk had made in aquamarine at Zenia's request, she'd told him—a gift from Zach. In her usual sensibleness, it was all she'd checked. That, her large shoulder bag, and the Henk carry-on she'd dragged off the plane could still accommodate a sizable wardrobe. His twenty-inch nondescript black canvas came next. Pulling the bags behind him, he led the way to the terminal, expecting to be mobbed.

Instead of the usual crush of cabbies and tour operators, two photographers barred the way, snapping photos. A BBC film crew began filming. Paul Joseph glanced around to locate the object of this attention, but a young black man in a smart business suit reached out from behind the barrier railings. He wasn't soaked in sweat like the other foreigners, but to Paul, he didn't look African.

"Paul Joseph, I presume?" East Coast American accent. Who was he?

"Yes?"

"*Hujambo, Mzee* and welcome to Tanzania. My name is Steve Harris. Call me Steve. I'm with the embassy."

It had begun.

Paul Joseph stepped forward, putting extra daylight between himself and Zenia. He tried to look equally humble and urbane, like Rick Warren.

"I've been asked to accompany you to your mission," Steve continued.

Ignoring that he didn't consider himself old enough to be addressed as *Mzee*, Paul Joseph shook his hand, shocked and pleased. Could the observer the President sent be an embassy official?

"Jambo, Steve Harris. Who sent you?"

"The White House." Steve was speaking to the cameras instead of to Paul. "Allow me to introduce the Honorable Bahari Mahfuru, an MP and member of the Parliamentary Committee for Land, Natural Resources and Environment."

A man dressed in an African-style brown suit offered his hand. In spite of his westernized garb, he exuded the self-possession of a tribal chief, yet even his restrained smile would warm an iceberg. "Hujambo, Pastor Joseph. We are grateful for your services to our people and for the help you are bringing to Udugu."

"Jambo, Honorable Mahfuru," Paul replied, happy to hear the fluid Tanzanian accent in which i's were pronounced like e's.

They held their handshake, allowing obligatory photos.

Zenia joined them and presented her hand. "I'm Zenia Dunlop. You don't know me, Honorable Mahfuru, but I'm a parishioner of Pastor Joseph and I've come to help him raise … well, to be frank—lots and lots of nice money for you."

The Hon. Bahari Mahfuru allowed the trace of a different sort of smile to cross his face, and only fleetingly glanced at Zenia's partially unsnapped shirt. Tanzania's Union Parliament, locally called the *Bunge*, had chronic budget shortfalls. Zenia managed not to slap at mosquitoes the whole time she was shaking his hand.

Then she fixed Steve Harris with a glittering grin. "And I'm sure you're indispensable, Steve." They also presented their handshake to the cameras.

"Gentlemen," she said to the photographers, "I'm going to need a copy of your shots of us."

The men lowered their cameras and pulled them close.

"Don't worry. Your competitors won't get them. I need them for society pages back home to help raise money for the mission. It's for Africa." She reached into her purse and pulled out two cards. "Email them, okay?"

The photographers looked at each other, at Mahfuru, Harris and Paul Joseph for confirmation then nodded agreement.

Paul Joseph could see her irritation that her word wasn't enough. "Thank you very much." She turned away from them to Steve. "Where may I exchange money, Mr. Harris? Steve?"

Paul Joseph said, "You won't really need it. We'll be at the village."

"I don't go anywhere without money, Paul." Zenia looked expectantly at Steve, who offered his arm to escort her. "Only change a little here. The best rates are in town."

While she was gone, the BBC Crew interviewed Paul Joseph and Honorable Mahfuru about the drought in Udugu and how Paul Joseph had come to help. When she returned, Zenia seemed more interested in Steve Harris than in the BBC, no doubt because of his White House connection.

When the BBC crew finished, two men took possession of their luggage. Paul Joseph followed them to a white van parked at the curb. As always, the first things that struck him when he emerged from this airport were the slim, tall fir trees lining the curb and the parking lot's islands in front. Once again he reminded himself to ask the name of these trees. Before, he'd always forgotten. Their feathery, needled branches hugged the trunks, making them look like green popsicles. They actually resembled the Italian cypress he'd seen in Cypress, California when the church went to Disneyland in 2005—except these needles pointed down, not up. Perhaps they were relics of vanished forests, felled for colonial use. The airport's tall pillars resembled trees, its sectioned roof a jungle canopy. Long ago he'd had an argument with Udugu's local spirit healer about preserving trees and shrubs to make medicines. Superstitious nonsense. Trees gave shade, anchored soil, served as home and sometimes food for wildlife, but sick people needed doctors, not trees.

Paul walked toward Hon. Mahfuru climbing in the front seat. "Honorable Mahfuru, may I ask a question—"

A white man with a handlebar mustache, sitting in the van's middle row of seats, interrupted him. The man held up a finger then gazed at the olive land vehicle until the photographers and press had climbed in. Did he want to talk out of their earshot? "Pastor Joseph, I am Kevin van der Linden with AmerCan, pleased to meet you. Call me Kevin."

Kevin van der Linden had the accent of a Boer—the original Dutch settlers of South Africa. His words sounded like: Bés-dor Joseph, *oy am Givn ven' der Lndn wiTH ÉmerGén. Gall me Givn.*

Paul had heard the Boer accent before. Even so, he had to listen carefully to *Givn.*

"Pleased to finally meet you, too, Kevin, after all the conversations we've had. Call me Paul."

Givn patted the seat beside him, indicating Paul should sit. Grateful for the van's air-conditioning, Paul did.

"I'm glad we have a chance to speak alone," Givn said as Hon. Mahfuru turned to them, nodding.

"Everything has been arranged," Hon. Mahfuru added. "We've designated Udugu as a Planning Area and issued Mr. van der Linden a GCRO. He's been discretely exploring in the area around Udugu."

"Yes," van der Linden said. "Very promising. Of course it's best that you present the plan to the village because they trust you, Bés-dor Joseph."

Paul raised his eyebrows. He didn't know what a GCRO was. "Shouldn't Honorable Mahfuru do the talking?"

Mahfuru touched his arm. "I will simply introduce Mr. van der Linden so they know he has our support. You inform the villagers that we are digging them a new well and installing irrigation. I'll say we'll send food until they have new crops. The changing climate has devastated them, as you know—not as badly as some, but they need help."

Paul Joseph's eyes watered. He really cared about the village. "That's wonderful. Wonderful. I'll be delighted to announce that."

Just then Zenia and Steve Harris arrived and climbed in the back seat, Zenia exclaiming, "Air-conditioning! At last!" She was introduced to Givn. Then Steve said slowly, "*Sasa sisi kwenda,*" and translated, "Now we go."

Zenia vamped in Steve's direction. "He's teaching me Swahili." She hadn't re-snapped her shirt yet.

An unexpected pang of jealousy shot through Paul Joseph as he assessed Steve Harris, who gazed back in perfect innocence, all polite embassy official.

Paul nodded and turned to the front, berating himself as the van drove from the landscaped airport. Soon they were on paved highway bordered by Dar es Salaam's trash-strewn drainage ditches and packed dirt roads, shanties on either side, goods being sold from ramshackle stalls. Despite the poverty, Paul knew there'd be no argument or disharmony here. He pointed out the *mama ntilie* to Zenia, women selling prepared food on the street.

"At least everyone seems to be in a good mood," Zenia observed, with less than overwhelming tact.

"Yes," Steve Harris replied. "Tanzanians are agreeable people."

"It is kind of you to say so," Hon. Mahfuru interjected, "and for the most part it is true, but beware of a small crime wave that targets tourists now. It is best not to go anywhere alone."

"I certainly hadn't planned to," Zenia said, tactless again.

Paul Joseph noticed they'd taken a wrong turn. "Our hotel's in the other direction."

Givn spoke up. "I 'ope you don't mind, but I've tlken the liberty of moving you and Ms. Dunlop to the Oyster Bay."

"An upgrade?" Zenia asked.

Givn nodded.

Paul Joseph wanted to tell Zenia this meant oceanfront luxury digs while they recuperated from their flight. Instead, let her discover it for herself. They drove out to a beautifully landscaped peninsula and along an ocean road, arriving at a pristine white four-story building with forest green shutters. It sat on a rise overlooking Dar es Salaam Bay. Zenia sighed with relief when through white-curtained arches they entered the Oyster Bay's luxurious white lobby full of art, palms and rattan furniture in shades of brown. The very blond and very gracious middle-aged hotel manager greeted them. An equally friendly barman handed everyone a Pimm's Cup or a lemonade. She invited them to the hotel dinner underway, family style, but Zenia said she was too tired. The woman offered to send lobster salads to their rooms.

As Givn van der Linden checked them in, Zenia relaxed in a chair framed by greenery and against his will Paul Joseph thought, *hot woman in a foreign jungle.* How he wanted her.

A man walked by on his way to reception. He and Paul Joseph recognized each other at the same time and nodded. It was the smartly dressed Arab he'd seen in the immigration area. Waiting for Givn to finish checking them in, the Arab stopped near Paul.

"You were on the flight from Johannesburg, too?" he asked in a friendly way.

"Yes, yes we were," Paul replied.

The man reached out his hand. "Hanif Hassan here."

"I'm Paul Joseph, a Baptist minister."

Hanif grinned as they shook hands. "You must be a rich minister to be staying at Oyster Bay."

Paul nodded to Zenia. "My parishioner, not me."

"Ah! Beautiful woman."

He eyed her warily, as if in fear, contempt or both. To Paul Joseph, Hanif Hassan didn't look or sound like he considered Zenia beautiful. Paul felt uncomfortable. Why had he told a stranger Zenia was rich? It must be the jet lag. "We're going to my mission in Mbeya. She plans to contribute."

"With so much money, she should." Before Paul Joseph could reply, Ahmed added, "Mbeya, you say? I'll be on safari there. Where is your mission?"

Paul felt caught. Why was he talking so much? "In Udugu."

Hanif seemed delighted. "What a coincidence. I will be in the area. I'll make camp nearby and come for a visit. Perhaps I should contribute to your mission, too."

"On safari in Mbeya?" Paul Joseph asked. It wasn't the usual safari destination.

"I hear there are marvels off the beaten track."

Paul Joseph nodded. He'd heard as much. He just hadn't seen them for himself.

"All beautiful," Givn said, returning. It came out as, *All bee-oo-*

ti-fool. "We'll be back to pick you up at 7:30 a.m." He handed them their room keys.

Paul didn't introduce Hanif and Kevin. He nodded goodbye to Hanif, went to get Zenia and followed the porter to their rooms—white walls, white bed drapes billowing, braided rugs, artifacts, modern African luxury. An adjoining door offered a second chance for intimacy. He could hear the Indian Ocean beyond the green shutters at his balcony door.

Zenia came in his room, but before he could speak she entered her own room through the shared door then, waving, closed and locked it.

"Goodnight, Zenia," he called.

She didn't reply. She was like that.

Paul Joseph bowed his head, folded his hands, and asked God to forgive his trespasses. Someone knocked and he rose to let in a warmly smiling African man carrying lobster salad and champagne. It was sinfully delicious, like Zenia. Paul sighed, ate the salad and drank the champagne, looking out his balcony door. Then he undressed, ran a tub in the pristine bathroom and got in while the water rose, wishing Zenia were in the tub with him. He forced himself not to think of her and be grateful that tomorrow they'd take a puddle hopper to Mbeya, sumptuously refreshed.

Chapter 13

Ahmed was not in his suite. He had persuaded Ajia to try to meet him. This involved slipping away from strict Islamic parents who meant to protect her until she was married, even though she was twenty-four. Ahmed had heard a rumor that a Swahili man had been to her house, visiting with her and her parents. He needed to find out if that was true. If it was, he had no intention of performing any jihads for her—not when she had a serious suitor.

Agitated, he waited impatiently in the Oyster Bay Hotel lounge beneath a large and beautiful photograph of white cattle or oxen. Perhaps a cow and a double-horned bull, they were probably one of East Africa's Zebu breeds, named after the tribe that bred them, their eyes doe-like, their faces noble. Listening for approaching taxis on Toure Drive, Ahmed imagined seeing Ajia. This exclusive western hotel, more like the home of a friend who intended to pamper guests, was one of the few places it was safe for her to come alone. Lost in his daydream, he was surprised when she appeared, the archway's white curtains framing her dark beauty. She was colorfully dressed in a traditional East African *doti*. It consisted of two rectangular cloths called *kangas*, one wrapped tightly around her lower half from waist to ankles, an identical one draped over her shoulders and head. Across her forehead a golden headband restrained twists of hair that fell around her face and down her graceful neck. Her skin was the color of copper, only a shade darker than his own. Yet her dusky gray eyes outshone the stars. Ajia looked like a descendant of both Cleopatra and Nefertiti. The barman who'd treated him like a long lost brother seemed transfixed by her, too.

Ahmed rose, feeling hopeful again, but as he got closer to Ajia his heart fell. Kangas were more than the most popular East African clothing for men and women alike, they were cultural masterworks, used to send messages, especially in Kenya where Ajia and her friends had attended private school. He recognized the coconut tree on the green, brown and yellow background of the rectangular cloth and below it the message called a *jina* printed in upper case letters. He didn't have to read it to know the Swahili saying there: "*It's strange for a dry coconut to want to break a stone.*" She was the stone and he the dry coconut. It was a rebuke. She was giving him no hope. Yet why had she come? By its fruitfulness, the coconut tree also implied she was well brought up—never mind that she was meeting him in the middle of the night at a hotel.

When he reached her, she bowed and he nodded. Since they were Muslim, a handshake was inappropriate. He knew Ajia preferred secular greetings to Islamic ones. To honor the African side of her, they spoke in Swahili.

"*Habari gani*, dada Ajia."

"*Nzuri*, ndugu Hanif."

Ajia had never heard the name Ahmed Bourguiba. They called each other brother and sister because in Tanzania men were addressed as either brother, *ndugu*; father, *baba*; *mzee*, old man; or *bwana*, sir; and women as *dada*, sister; *mama*, mother; or *bibi*, grandmother or madam.

"You had no trouble coming here?"

She shook her head. "*Hakuna matata?*" You are well?

"*Nimefurahi, dada.*"

Greetings could not be brief here, as in America.

"*Jinsi ni mama yako?*" How is your mother?

"*Yeye ni vizuri.*"

"*Na yako?*" And yours?

"*Ni vizuri san.*" Very well.

Keeping a respectful distance, he escorted her to the windows that overlooked the ocean. They sat, side by side, on rattan seats. Unobtrusively, the barman appeared and asked what she'd like to drink. No British Pimms for her, or alcohol of any kind. Ajia ordered a Stoney Tangawizi, strong ginger ale.

"You look beautiful," he ventured.

"*Asante.*"

"*Asante kushukuru*. What do your strict parents say about you wearing the kanga instead of the Muslim *buibui* and *hijabu*?"

A slow smile parted her sweet lips like a crescent moon in twilight. "They worry that an evil jinn has possessed me or that a witch has cast a spell."

Who could think anything evil possessed someone so lovely? To show respect, he didn't laugh. In Africa, witchcraft was real. "Has one?"

Her smile turned mischievous. "I just don't like to be shrouded in black."

Then Ahmed remembered the meaning of her outfit. It wasn't good. "Your kanga is … interesting."

"I put it on earlier and couldn't change."

So that was it. Yo-yo-like, he felt hopeful again. "What would you have worn if you could have changed?"

She lowered her eyes. "Another kanga that says, '*Hate me, but I won't stop telling you the truth.*'"

"I certainly don't hate you, Ajia. I hear there is another man who doesn't hate you as well."

She didn't look up. "He is Swahili and a friend of my family."

"And a friend of yours?"

She said nothing.

Ahmed's heart swiftly sank. He had to risk it. "Please be truthful with me. I actually care for you a great deal, Ajia."

She raised her eyes. "Then why are you hiding things?"

Ahmed couldn't have been more shocked. Had she heard he'd organized a special safari? "What do you mean?"

"Why are you staying only one night? Not even visiting your mother? You haven't been home in a while. I'm sure she wants to see you."

Though she was the unknowing cause of all his plans, Ahmed felt a little invaded. He hadn't intended to tell her until the deed was done because talk was cheap. If it turned out she wasn't involved with another man, one day soon he'd be able to say, *I saved a village, perhaps a whole region, from outside exploitation. I did it because I love you, Ajia, and Africa, too.*

All he said was, "I'll see my mother before I leave."

Her Stoney Tangawizi arrived and Ahmed worried the barman might overhear them.

"Let's go outside," he said.

He stood and led the way to the veranda. Nodding at hotel guests lingering over their shared al fresco meal, they stepped into the large walled garden. Its clipped lawn and surrounding flowers reminded him of photos he'd seen of the White House Rose Garden, except the blooms here were exotic. Off to the left, glittering candles in glass jars framed the hotel's lap pool. They walked along it toward a metal sculpture—a large African face reminiscent of the heads on Easter Island.

"What you said before?" Ajia asked him. "About fixing Africa for me?"

"Yes?"

"So you've decided to end up a wanted man, like your father?"

Ahmed felt a mix of shame and anger. He tried not to think about the father he'd probably never see again because he'd helped Osama bin Laden bomb U.S. embassies.

"If you're doing it for me, it wouldn't change things between us, anyway," she continued. "We're not meant for each other. You're Arab."

"I speak Swahili, like you."

"Yes, but you have no African blood."

"So you are suspicious of Arabs, like most of Tanzania?"

"A little."

"Ajia, we're both Muslim."

Upset, Ahmed led her to the side of the building where no one could see them. "Let me prove myself."

"You can't save Africa, Hanif. If the spirit healers couldn't when the wazungu came, if the Maasai couldn't, the Zulu, and so many others, how can you?"

"Just wait and see."

She sighed and looked at the white hotel, resentment marring her beautiful face. "This shouldn't be here. My people owned this coast. We built coral palaces and traded all over the Indian Ocean

… excuse me, the African Ocean." She stepped into shadows were he could only see the graceful curve of her neck and the anger shining in her eyes. "You know the ruins out on Kilwa Island?"

"Yes, I do," Ahmed said. "I used to play there as a boy."

"Before the wazungu came, every ship had to pay tribute to pass Kilwa Kiswani."

"I know."

Ajia covered her face and muffled a sob. "Sometimes, Hanif, sometimes …"

What was this emotion? He reached for her, but she moved away.

"Sometimes I wish I were a man."

"Why?"

"Long ago, queens often ruled we Swahili. I know their names—Sabana binti Ngumi, Mwana Aziza, Queen Maryamu of Yumba are just a few. They governed. They waged war. All along the Swahili coast, women ruled. Today, no woman has that power, thanks to Islam and the Omani Court set up in Zanzibar in 1830, followed by the last wave of Hadrami immigrants from Yemen in the 1870's. You Arabs subjugate women!"

"I will not do that!"

"Today I'd have to be a man to fight them."

"Fight who?"

She balled her fists. "The whites, the wazungu."

"Oh." He resisted patting her shoulder.

"When Vasco da Gama came here," she stabbed a finger toward the ocean; "do you know what he did? The royal women of Mombasa wouldn't hand over their gold bracelets when he demanded them, so he cut off their arms! Cut off their arms! I wish I'd been there so I could cut his throat the minute he stepped foot on our land."

"I do too," Ahmed said.

"Oh, Hanif! Sometimes I wish I could grow ten feet tall and carry a big, big gun. I'd walk all over Africa and shoot every one of them I saw."

His heart beat fast at the image. "I would help you." He reached out to stroke her hair and she allowed it.

"I would do it, Hanif, if I could. Look what they've done to us. Africa isn't ours. They strut all over it, steal what's beneath the ground, and treat us like dirt."

"I'll help you."

She pulled away. "You're Arab. You were slavers."

Ahmed didn't point out that the Sultan of Kilwa was, too. Kilwa and other Swahili kingdoms had a history of raiding Bantu villages in the interior and taking slaves. In fact, in the 18th century, the Kilwa Sultan made a deal with a Frenchman for an exclusive on slaves. Since meeting Ajia, he'd read about the Swahili. Their genes were solidly Bantu with a mix of Arab, Persian and Portuguese thrown in, but their history wasn't as innocent as she imagined it to be and, true, neither was that of the Arabs.

She moved closer to him. "If you do decide to do something foolish, something desperate …"

He couldn't risk revealing his plans at this late stage. "I was just talking …"

She looked up at him. "No, Hanif, you were not. Your friends here have girlfriends and wives and children."

He stepped away from her, pacing, holding his head. "What do they say?"

"That you are about to do some kind of jihad?"

He went back to her and, though it was haraam, forbidden, took her by the arms. "What if you are right? What if a company is about to destroy another village, this time in Mbeya where you were born, ruin its ground water, cut down its trees, pollute its earth? What if the robbery and murder they call mining is about to happen again with government consent?"

"It always happens with government consent, or ignorance."

He let go of her. "What if I could stop it, Ajia? I would if you—Ajia, is there another man in your life or not?"

Now she was the one pacing under the moon, waves of the ocean she called African dashing on the beach below, palm leaves swaying in silhouette against the sky.

He went to her and tried to wrap her in his arms but she resisted.

"You and I are not meant for each other, but I don't want you to be hurt. There is a Swahili saying: *A person who plays with a razor cuts himself.* I have a kanga with that as its jina. Even if you aren't up to something, my Swahili friend would hurt you badly if he knew I was here with you."

He laughed. "I am not helpless. I know another saying, though. *You will be troubled with what you have no knowledge of?*"

She laughed and he tried to hug her, but still she resisted.

She said, "What about: *I thought of you as gold, but you are such a pain.*"

He wanted to touch his lips to her smooth forehead. "What about: *Blame your character, not your fellows.*"

"Okay, that's a good one. It means take responsibility, but remember this one: *To aim is not to hit.*"

She was so beautiful. Ahmed lost control. "*Ninakupenda*, Ajia!" I love you.

In modesty, she lowered her eyes.

"Hanif, the truth is, if someone were to save a whole village of African people, especially from my homeland, I would not be sad. I would rejoice." She sobbed. "Oh, Hanif, how I would rejoice. Nothing could mean more to me. Look at us! Mere servants and employees in our own land, once unequalled. Now there is drought and tribal warfare, both sides armed by the wazungu to keep us weak. There is disease. Where did AIDS come from? I will tell you. The wazungu. They did something to kill us so they could take all of Africa, but the plan backfired and they caught the disease, too. Now they are starting to buy up whole tracts of our land for nothing and turn it into farms for their countries, making us work in unhealthy conditions for starvation wages. Oh, Hanif how I would rejoice if even one village, one family, is saved from them."

He barely dared to move. It was the first solid encouragement she'd ever given him. There was a Swahili saying for this moment, like for all moments. "*A little is enough for those who love.*" Wanting more, Ahmed reached to hold her and this time she didn't pull away. He stood there, so grateful for this closeness, her chest rising and falling against his with each breath. He felt like a knight who'd been given his lady's favor. No, not a knight. Whites were the ones she hated. In his heart, he wished she knew wazungu like his friend, Zach Dunlop. He wished she didn't hate anyone. Then he wouldn't have to, either. He'd be content to hold her in the moonlight for the rest of his life. Some Jihadist he was.

"Can we go down to the beach?" she asked.

It felt like she'd read his mind. Knowing he had zero chance of persuading her to come to his room, Ahmed had checked earlier and found a busy but navigable road between the beach and the hotel. They would be safe since this was the diplomatic quarter. Also, the beach was full of lounge chairs.

"Yes, I know the way."

They left the hotel grounds and reached the beach, not speaking, Ahmed full of anticipation and Ajia full of doubt, he was sure. Being alone with a man, much less alone on a beach at night, was as haraam as haraam got. Sure enough, she lingered under the palm trees and looked up to the hotel.

"We can go back if you want, Ajia."

The whirl of emotions on her face was all the reply he needed. She was afraid, she was determined, she desired him, yet she hesitated.

They heard a distant rumble and far-off lightning split the sky.

"A sign from God," she said.

"A good sign?" he asked.

"To the Swahili, there is no better sign. Lightning means God is pleased."

He took her hand and they walked to the nearest lounge chairs. She sat on one, looked out to the Indian Ocean, and softly sang. Like the jina on her kanga, most Taarab songs gave guidance and comfort about life. This was one of the cheeky new Taarab songs about someone who wanted an apple and couldn't have it. The song wasn't about apples.

Ahmed let her finish then came and sat beside her, knowing her music was an invitation. She was still carrying her Stoney Tangawizi and drank the last of it. He took the empty bottle and she lowered her head.

"I spoke wrongly, Hanif. We Swahili are peaceful. I'm sure you know our most important saying?"

Ahmed knew it. *"Mungu ndie muamuzi wa kila jambo."*

"God is the judge for everything."

"Yes."

It spoke volumes about the spiritual, accepting ways of the Swahili, yet it hadn't prevented Ajia from sobbing about the robbery and the murder foreigners engaged in while supposedly just doing business in Africa.

"Mungu ndie muamuzi wa kila jambo," she repeated and looked up to the sky, breathing deeply, almost panting, and saying something over and over under her breath. He watched, mesmerized, and made out her words, *Subhâna-Llâh, Subhâna-Llâh,* Holy is Allah, Glory to God. Suddenly she sought and held his gaze. To Ahmed's joy and amazement, Ajia began to unwind her kanga. She lowered the band around her chest until moonlight shone on breasts so ripe it seemed life-giving milk could spring from them at a caress.

Ahmed groaned, but didn't touch her, aware of the great sin it would be. He thought of Zenia Dunlop and what she'd done on the plane. Ajia couldn't be like such a woman. "Ajia, you are virgin, yes?"

"At this moment."

"You should not do this."

She scanned the deserted beach and started unwinding the bottom kanga.

Ahmed tried to focus on their Islamic duty, as heaven in the form of woman fully revealed herself to him. It was obvious from her pubic hair that she had never been instructed in the *unyago* rituals of Islamic Swahili women. Only at her wedding, in the feminine realm of the bedroom, surrounded by women sex instructors called *somos*, would she learn what she must do and never do. As a henna artist applied elaborate designs to her body, signaling her coming loss of virginity, the somos would teach Ajia to remove her pubic hair and, weekly, her husband's after they wed. At some point her father, the witnesses, and the sheikh would arrive. The women would veil themselves and leave so Ajia could give her consent three times, testify to having received the bridal gift, could say prayers and sign the wedding contract. Legally, she'd be married, though she would not yet have seen her groom. While she waited for him, the somos would tell Ajia never to refuse her husband vaginal intercourse except when menstruating. Other means should be employed then, except the sin of anal sex. She'd be instructed to keep other women away when he was at home; to keep her body, her bedroom, and their sexual relations private, making each act sacred in advance by saying *kupiga bismillah*, In the name of Allah.

Having been raised in Tanzania, Ahmed knew Swahili ways.

Instead, they were on a public beach to which he'd sought out a path, hoping for the unthinkable. Before him was all he'd longed for. Yet, how could he harm her so grievously?

"Ajia, does this mean … does this mean you will marry me?"

Her voice was thick with passion. "Save the village and I will marry you."

His hands needed no more information, nor did his lips, or his eyes, which embraced her, tasted her, drunk in the sight of her. Ajia naked. Ajia all his.

Their first kiss stormed through them as lightning lit the sky and when it was over, Ahmed urgently discarded his clothes.

They didn't say *kupiga bismillah* before he kissed what hadn't been kissed, touched where she'd never been touched and entered where no one had been, she whimpering at first then panting softly, he soon breathing like the white oxen on the Oyster Bay Hotel wall.

Chapter 14

Ariel Fubini understood the word *sullen* like she never had before. Seated in back of her dad's new Range Rover, her parents in front, she stared out at the Connecticut landscape, and sullen was the only word that she could think of to describe her mood. Today was supposed to be triumphant. At last she was being let out of her father's sight. Allowed to board at Choate for her final year, she could discover what it was like not to be guarded every second she was alive.

Knowing why her dad had watched over her was no help. In fact, it made things worse. She learned he'd used his money and his freedom to pull the most outlandish stunt Ariel had ever heard of in her life: clone Jesus. In the process, she'd been kidnapped. Then, because her dad couldn't govern himself even a tiny bit, he'd taken all her freedom away.

Today was supposed to be the best day ever. She'd begin a new life of independence and new opportunities. Instead, last year's school clothes were packed in suitcases in the trunk because she'd cut short her and her mom's shopping trip to go home and learn from her dad why she was kidnapped when she was eight.

Her dad said the clone he thought long dead might be alive. Did he book a flight to this Porlezza place to find out? No, he'd taken her credit card to make sure she couldn't go. Independence over.

"Are you all right, darling?" her mom asked from the front.

"No!" Ariel fumed.

"Try not to worry about all this, Ariel. I'm sorry we told you."

Ariel sat up, angry. "Not sorry you *did* it, just sorry I know."

Her mom looked at her dad and said, "I didn't do it."

They all resumed saying nothing as the dense forest rolled by. Choate was only an hour away, but the drive seemed to be taking forever, probably because Ariel couldn't scream out loud like she wanted to. They passed a lopsided barn. It had been straight before the earthquake.

She sat up. "Dad, wait. We just had an earthquake. Connecticut never has earthquakes. What if it's the end of the world, Dad, and that's why Jesus is here?"

He sighed. "It's not the end of the world and he's not Jesus—just some lunatic."

"Dad, you do realize that's what they said about him the first time?"

"Ariel, we're not discussing this," he said. "You're starting your last year at Choate and that's what you should focus on."

She dropped hard against the back seat, furious. "Are you really a Christian or is all that a lie, too?"

Her mother turned around, frowning. "Young lady, don't speak to your father like that."

Ariel folded her arms. "For your information, I've decided to switch to Judaism. Jesus was a Jew so it's good enough for me. Besides, I'm half-Jewish, right Dad?"

They'd told her the truth of the family name. Rossi was the surname her persecuted Italian grandparents adopted when they came to America to escape the Nazis. Their real name had been Fubini. When the last Jesus clone episode broke, Dad had changed their surname back to escape the press.

After a few moments, her dad said, "You can practice Judaism if you like."

"You mean I have religious freedom like the Constitution says? Gee, thanks, Dad."

Ariel fumed as the trees whizzed by. How could they only have reached Southbury? She thought of asking to stop at Denmo's for a hot lobster roll, but the thought of it made her stomach queasy.

She'd thrown up again this morning. Strange because she wasn't a thrower upper. Her classmate Lucy was. Lucy threw up before and after every exam. Ariel concluded the argument with her dad must have unnerved her.

Suddenly she felt dread. "Oh no!" she said aloud.

Her dad looked in the rearview mirror and her mom, Adeline, turned around, but this wasn't a suspicion she could share with them.

"I meant, 'Oh, no I forgot something.'"

"What?" Adeline asked.

Good question. "I think I forgot my, um ... soccer shoes."

Adeline smiled. "No, I packed them." She faced front and her dad resumed looking through the windshield.

Ariel waited a moment, took out her cell phone and checked the calendar. She was late. Impossible. She closed her eyes in despair, remembering the one time that escaping her dad's surveillance had turned into a nightmare. Her thoughts exploded into a continuous stream of *Ohmigods!* She couldn't be pregnant, she just couldn't be. She had to think.

Her stomach in her mouth, she asked, "Dad, can we stop at a drugstore? I need some ... things." *Hundred percent guarantee he wouldn't ask what.*

They were almost at I-84 E. He said, "What about a K-mart?"

"Good enough."

He slowed, took the next U-turn and they were there. Ariel hopped out and ran inside. Too ashamed to ask where the pregnancy tests were, she scanned the pharmacy aisles and found one that claimed 99% accuracy even before a missed period. Managing not to die from humiliation, she bought it from a female cashier then asked where the bathrooms were. The woman looked at her sympathetically and pointed her to the ladies room.

Ariel rushed there, trying not to panic. If she was pregnant, she couldn't finish her last year at Choate. The school had more rules than congress. The whole first third of the student handbook was about honor codes, integrity, discipline and dismissals. Not until page seventeen did it even tell you the dress code. Almost everything was forbidden, especially sex. Choate's aim was to graduate smart students who weren't liars or drug addicts and certainly not ones who were pregnant.

She went to the very last stall, read the instructions then commenced urinating on the stick. Two pink lines and she was pregnant. One and she was not. She had to wait three minutes. An eternity.

Ariel stared at the little window, quietly praying, "Please, God, just one line. Just one."

One minute, two minutes. It was taking forever.

There it was.

Two lines.

She couldn't help it. Ariel let out a loud stream of *OhmiGods*!

"Ariel?"

Her mother? How could it be her mother? Why didn't she stay in the car? Too late, Ariel fell silent. Then she saw her mother's feet outside the stall.

"Ariel, what's the matter? Open up, sweetheart."

Frantically, Ariel stuffed the telltale stick and its box into the tampon receptacle.

"I'm all right, Mom!"

"You most certainly are not! Open this door!"

"Mom!"

"Open this door young lady!"

Ariel opened the door and her mom rushed in. Unfortunately, there was room. Ariel had picked the handicapped stall to make sure she could maneuver.

"Darling, what happened?"

Her mom's eyes searched her body head to toe with that laser scan mothers have.

"Nothing happened. Nothing's wrong," Ariel said feebly.

Now her mother was laser-scanning the stall. Her eyes stopped at the partly open tampon receptacle. Stupid receptacle! Why hadn't it closed? Instantly her mom opened it, saw the pregnancy kit and the stick with two lines. Her life was over.

"Oh, darling!" her mother said in a voice so tragic it could have been Shakespearean. "Oh darling!"

Almost instantly they were back in the Range Rover, the car still parked, both her parents turned around and gazing at her as if she were a space alien.

"Ariel, it's all right," her father said, not looking the least like anything was all right. "We'll help you. First, who is the father?"

Ariel burst out crying so hard that her mom got out of the front seat and came into the back to hold her.

"It's all right, dear. Your dad and I will make it all right."

Ariel kept sobbing. Each time she tried to stop, the thought of what she'd have to say made her cry again.

Her dad asked, "Is it a boy from school?"

She nodded.

"Well, thank goodness for that. At least they're all good families."

"Just tell us who, sweetheart," her mom added. "Tell us who. We'll take care of it. We won't embarrass you."

"What's his name, Ariel?" her dad insisted.

Ariel flung herself out of her mother's arms and cried. "I don't know! All right? I don't know!"

"You mean … you mean you've had sex with more than one Choate boy?" Her dad would use this same voice if he were asking, *You mean you've clubbed more than one white baby seal to death?*

"No, Dad! I didn't have sex with anybody. I didn't! It's just …" How would she ever explain? "You know my friends, right?"

"Yes."

"Jessica and Nicole and Emily, Chris and Brandon and John and Kyle?"

"Yes?"

"Well, the eight of us hang out, you know, and sometimes … sometimes we drink too much and sometimes we…OhmiGod!"

"Don't tell me my daughter is in some kind of *friends with benefits* circle!"

"No, Dad, for heaven's sake, but…well, we drank and…smoked something—"

"Drugs, Ariel? Drugs!" her dad's eyes couldn't get any wider.

"We thought it was just pot, but apparently we were wrong. It was the last time we hung out—"

"Wait!" he said. "I drove you there. That was supposed to be a girls' slumber party!"

"I know, Dad. It wasn't. Anyway, we all fell asleep and then when I woke up, something had happened, I could tell. But I don't know who did it. Nobody remembers anything, Dad. He probably didn't even know what he was doing. I sure didn't. Now I'm pregnant and I don't even remember it?" She wailed, "How is that fair?"

Now her dad sounded like he'd been shot and was dying. "We'll need to ask all four of the parents to get DNA tests from the boys then."

In terror, Ariel shrieked, "Oh, Dad, please don't do that to me! Please don't!"

"What else can we do?" her mother cried.

"I don't know. I don't know. We can … I can just have the baby by myself. We're Catholic so there's no other option, right?"

There was silence.

Her mom said, "Choate will expel you when they find out. You'll have to withdraw."

"But it's my last year! Can't I just go for a while? Just a little while?" Ariel started crying again.

Her parents whispered to each other.

"Yes, darling," Adeline finally said. "Yes, you can go for a little while. And there's always a chance …"

"That I'll miscarry?" Ariel said.

Her mom glared at her dad and hissed, "Some guarding, Felix. Well done!"

Shaking his head, her dad pulled out of the K-mart parking lot as she sobbed.

Chapter 15

"*Qui è, signore,*" here it is, sir. "*Non c'è radio.*"

Instead, the waiter deposited a small portable TV on the breakfast table where Jess and I sat, looking down on the sloping grounds of the Hotel Parco San Marco. All morning I'd been trying to follow Jess's advice—stop worrying, stop unnecessary thinking, focus on the energy of my body and what's right in front of me. This last happened to be very pleasant because it was Jess. We'd almost finished breakfast.

"Jess, did you know there's this U.S. preacher who's always saying *nothing is impossible for the most high God*. They say he's got the fastest growing church in the world."

"Preachers often teach fear, not the Gospel's true good news."

Jess was adjusting the portable TV. "Fortunately, anyone may choose at any moment to believe the power known as God is also within and that they may call on that power—that they are loved, safe, invincible as promised in the Twenty-third Psalm."

I finished my ham, wondering what it would feel like to be invincible.

Jess continued, "The result is to have no fear of other people or of tomorrow because you know you can't be harmed. You are happy."

I certainly was. I was full of energy, vibrating with joy, *being still and knowing God* with my Jess.

Finally he stopped fiddling with the TV and picked up his coffee. "Watch, Mother."

I put my glasses on and looked at the TV. It was some kind of business report. People arriving in Africa—a man and woman; no, a minister and his parishioner. Officials met them. They were on their way to a village called Udugu. It was in trouble and they planned to save it.

I gasped when a photo of the village came on the screen. Hadn't I looked at that same image the whole time I was pregnant with Jess? The whole while Sam, my first husband, was courting me? I'd seen it in an old issue of National Geographic and it made me cry. How I'd pined over it, imagining my lost African home. There the village beauties would look like me, not Marilyn Monroe. When I thought I'd lose Sam to Coral, a woman so pretty Marilyn could only have wished to look like her, that photo had soothed my heart. For months I imagined living in Udugu—elephants, red earth, huts beneath a green, green hill. There I'd have a chance to be what Coral was. In Udugu, extra full lips, big backsides and wide noses were surely beauty marks. That was long ago and I didn't feel insecure about my looks anymore, but I sure had then.

I watched until the segment was over then I sighed. "Jess, you have no idea how I once longed to be in Udugu. It was my heaven on earth."

"Would you like to go there?"

Why hadn't I tried? "I'd love to, Jess. I really would."

"Take my hand, Mamma." He reached out "We can be there in an instant. You've read it a thousand times in your Bible: *If you have faith … nothing will be impossible for you.* Take my hand and we'll be there."

My vibrating joy vanished. "But—"

"Matthew was actually there with me. He was a disciple. He knew me … I mean me when I was Jesus. He recorded what I said fairly accurately. He and Thomas did. Matthew wrote the first Gospel. Trust the Gospel of Matthew, Mother. Trust my words. Luke said it, too in 1:37: *For nothing will be impossible with God.*"

A tear slid down my cheek. "I'm a disappointment, aren't I?"

Tenderly he wiped the tear away. "You are just human. Fortunately, what that means is about to change. Will you help?"

"I'll try. I will."

"Can you have faith in yourself? Can you believe in your own ability to work miracles through faith?"

"I'm ashamed to admit it, Jess, but I can't. That's the trouble."

"Do you have faith in me, then? Do you believe I can work miracles?"

'You're here and that's impossible, so yes. I believe you can work miracles, Jess Johnson. That I do believe."

"I can take us to Africa instantly. You must only believe I can."

My heart sped up. I didn't believe he could. I covered my eyes and shook my head.

He patted my hand. "Don't worry, Madre. One more question."

I looked up.

"Do you believe in airplanes?"

We burst out laughing, like always. I smiled at him. "I do believe in airplanes."

"Good."

He looked conspiratorially around. "Do you believe in cell phones and that flights can be looked up on them?"

Lightly I smacked his hand and took out my cell.

He told me, "I think the nearest airport to Udugu is Dar es Salaam."

I didn't have any practice at all in looking up flights like this, but I pulled up a search engine and typed *flights from Milan to…* "How do you spell that city, Jess?" and when he answered, typed *Dar es Salaam*. I clicked on the first link and a blizzard of flights appeared.

"We're not making any of these morning flights, honey. And— wow, the two-stop flights are quicker than the one-stops." I looked at him. "I think our best bet is this 5:50 pm Royal Dutch Flight out of Malpensa Airport in Milan. Flight 1628. We'll land in Dar es Salaam tomorrow at 9:20 am local time."

Jess stood. "Let's go."

"But sweetheart, we haven't paid the bill."

I motioned to the waiter who hovered expectantly near. Instantly he came.

"Si, signora?"

"Per piacere," I said. "Quanto costa?"

Looking disturbed, the waiter stepped back, and raised both hands in the Italian gesture that in this case meant: *I will not touch your money.*

Jess beamed at him and shook his hand.

We checked out of the Hotel Parco San Marco with no trouble, and took a taxi to Lugano, Switzerland to catch a train, unearthly beauty of water and sky passing on our left, slopes of green on the right. It was only seven miles away. Around Italy's northwestern lakes, two countries came together. We pulled up to a blush pink stucco train station, scrubbed clean like the Swiss do. Inside I bought tickets to Milan's biggest airport, two hours away. We'd change in Milano Centrale to the Malpensa Express.

Jess was strangely quiet during the trip.

Was he mad at me for not believing? What reasonable person would? The idea of being transported to Africa in the blink of an eye was like rubbing a lamp in an Arab fairytale and getting a genie. Why had Jesus said, *ask and it will be given to you* when some things plainly couldn't be given? Or did the Bible, genies and magic lamps have something in common? *Truth is written everywhere*, Jess had said.

I tried to stop thinking, like he advised. After all, my son was next to me. I didn't care if it was by a miracle or by a magic lamp. I just wished he'd talk to me instead of gazing calmly out of the window as if talking and not talking, being with me and not being with me, were the same.

During the whole trip whenever I tried to start a conversation all he said was, "Yes, Madre," or "Is that right?" or "Really?" Then he'd go quiet again.

In Milan, I thought we'd missed the 2:55 pm Malpensa Express, but we hadn't. It was late, like Italian trains sometimes are. At last we arrived at Malpensa Airport and got off the train. Other people on the platform had luggage, of course. With nothing to roll or carry, we zipped past the train's red engine into the underground level of Terminal 1. From there we'd fly to Amsterdam. Though Africa was to the south, we had to fly north to reach it, switching to another KLM flight to Nairobi, then to a Precision Air Flight to Dar es Salaam. I'd never heard of Precision Air before today and hoped it really was precise.

We took a lift to the departure level. By now it was almost 4:00 pm. Terminal 1, though spacious, was full of people. They stood in ticket lines, sat on the rows of orange chairs, or on their luggage. Light shone on them from paned windows reaching to the ceiling. Off to the side, at a green and black station labeled *Secure Bag*, a man in black and yellow operated a machine that wrapped luggage in green plastic for a fee. Overhead, signs pointed to Gates A and B. On the walls, massive video screens flashed ads.

We stopped beneath smaller screens that said, *PARTENZE*, Departures. When a flight was boarding, it blinked. Ours wasn't listed. It was too early.

As I started for the ticket lines, Jess said, "I'll wait here."

"Okay, but come when I wave to you?"

He nodded.

The line was long and so was the wait, but no one seemed in a rush. I got in a conversation with the woman in front of me who wore gold hoops, a shawl and colorful clothes like a gypsy.

"The line is long, but it's moving," she said, reaching in her purse to take out her passport.

Passports! Why hadn't I thought of them? Given the bizarre events I'd experienced in life, I always kept mine in my purse. Jess had no passport, though. I brought him to Italy as a baby and before dying in my arms on Lake Maggiore, he'd never left the country. Could he mesmerize the ticket agent like he'd done the waiter?

I looked behind for him. He stood in the wide floor space behind the roped-off lines. A little girl holding a pink rollaway suitcase stood there looking up at him. She had a long ponytail, wore a white blouse, a ruffled skirt, and hugged a teddy bear in her free hand. Were they talking? I couldn't tell.

Jess wasn't glowing, thank goodness. Still he was different somehow. An invisible aura seemed to surround him, as if sun shone where he was and everywhere else was cloudy. That's why the girl with the pink suitcase smiled at him. Jess was giving off an aura that let you lay your burdens down.

Asking the woman to hold my place, I left the line, intending to make my way toward the floor space where Jess was, vaguely telling myself I'd warn him about his aura, not admitting I wanted to be in it myself.

I noticed the rows of seats in the main area were less full. Where had the people gone? Suddenly I realized that, like me, they were coming toward Jess and the girl. Something was happening. Why did I leave him?

The little girl raised her arms. Jess picked her up and sat her on his shoulder. Out of the corner of my eye I saw a longhaired woman run toward them. She wore a ruffled skirt that matched the girl's. It was probably her mother. At first the mother looked upset but as she got closer she smiled. I could see worry leave her. She, too, was going where the happiness was. In the next moment, four more children were there with Jess, none unruly. Now it was five of them, then ten. The space was large. I'd taken perhaps eight steps, yet the number of children grew before my eyes, adults joining them, looking delighted, as if a carnival had appeared in the middle of Terminal 1.

What was going on?

As I tried to make headway, the group became a crowd and the crowd a throng all going to him.

A different reality existed where Jess was.

"Scusimi, scusimi per favore," I said and inched my way forward.

Pressing toward him, they ignored me. Those near reached out to touch him. As for me, soon enough I couldn't move. I couldn't catch my breath. Surrounded, no one meaning to hurt me, I was being crushed.

I heard background music. *Pie Jesu. Merciful Jesus. You who take away the sins of the world.* Sung by that little blonde girl who'd won a contest in America.

Pie Jesu, Pie Jesu.

I couldn't breathe. I had to take at least one breath. If not, I'd black out. It seemed ridiculous. A moment ago I was fine. Now I was penned in and couldn't move, couldn't call out to my Jess and let him know I was in trouble. I would pass out if I couldn't breathe soon.

"Take my hand."

Who said that? Oh, yes, it must be Jess. He'd been saying that all along. *Take my hand. Take my hand.* What he really meant was to believe in the impossible, that mountains could really move, that I could fly through the air, that I could do anything, if I asked, believing.

"If you have the faith of a mustard seed."

Who said that? It must be Jess. Did he know I couldn't breathe? Did he know the crowd he'd called with his happiness was pressing the life out of me?

Pie Jesu.

One breath. Just one. If I could take it, I'd be fine. Instead I was seeing colors. I was blacking out. I wouldn't wake. I knew it. I would die. How silly. Yet it was happening and no one knew.

"Take my hand."

What good was belief when reality was my body's need for breath? Did belief produce air, fill lungs, prevent death? I was dying. Moments from now I'd be gone, surrounded by happy people who were crushing me.

Pie Jesu, Pie Jesu.

"Take my hand."

Since I had no other options, it couldn't hurt to try. I told myself I could fly and, why not, I believed it. I could move mountains. I took his hand.

An instant later, I lay under the gnarled spreading limbs of an ancient fig tree, as the sun touched the horizon. A dignified old man with short graying hair lifted my head and made me drink from a gourd. He had strong arms and wore cowrie beads over a cloth garment tied across his chest. He looked African.

He smiled straight into my heart. "*Karibu, mama.*" Welcome, mother.

How did I know that's what he'd said?

Jess walked toward the fig tree, looked down at me and grinned.

The old man picked up a stick and hit a big drum. Then he lowered himself to the dirt at Jess's feet, played a musical instrument with his thumbs and, his eyes shining, sang, *sauti ya Mungu*, voice of God.

Obviously, it was a dream.

Chapter 16

From 7:30-9:00 p.m. all dorms, including sixth form houses, must remain quiet, with an atmosphere conducive to studying.

Ariel, Jessica, Nicole, Emily, Chris, Brandon, John and Kyle who called themselves *Hasayeah*, which stands for *the eight* in the Harry Potter snake language of Parseltongue, were all sixth formers. Not required to be in their dorm rooms until 11 pm, they decided to meet in front of the SAC, the Student Activities Center, and go longboarding.

Longer than skateboards, thus the name, the longboard's larger, softer wheels made them feel they were surfing on the ground. Since their freshman year, during lunch breaks and at the end of the day, Hasayeah had been a regular sight at Choate Rosemary Hall, speeding on their longboards across campus in a line, down hallways, across lawns, doing stunts over benches and picnic tables, breaking formation in graceful patterns then reforming the line. They rode to and from class. They took turns leading. Kyle taught them to jump over things. He taught them timing. From speed demon Chris they'd learned precision and control. Emily taught them how to do rolling figure eights like snakes. They learned fearlessness from Ariel in games of chicken with each other and fast-approaching walls. Recently they'd taken up dancing on the moving boards. On weekends they tackled more daring locations in town. Often, if one of them tripped, each of them did.

Scions all, they were expected to graduate from Choate, attend Harvard or another of the eight Ivy League colleges and become, for instance, President of the United States like former Choatie JFK. Secretary of State would do, as would governor or senator though, obviously, not as thrillingly. They were meant to found the next Facebook or Apple, win the Nobel Prize. If an Oscar was won, Hollywood careers were tolerated.

Getting a girl pregnant, or becoming so, was not.

One by one they rode their boards to the SAC. Ariel arrived first then Emily of the long dark hair and Nicole of the fat blonde corn rows then solemn and serious Jessica then all the boys solidly together as if, too late, they'd girded their loins. They were the only mixed longboarding group on campus. Usually girls didn't longboard and, even if they did, guys didn't want to longboard with *chicks*. Ariel had been the first. She'd talked her girlfriends into it. When they didn't whine and cry at scrapes because Ariel ordered them not to, the guys let them come along. Ariel had wondered if their friendship would survive this new crisis, but they'd all shown up. Without talking, Hasayeah fell into line.

Ariel's default place was behind Kyle, as first of the girls. She noticed that today, by coincidence, both she and Kyle wore jeans and hooded Choate sweatshirts. John and Chris and Brandon were in khakis. Was God telling her Kyle was the father? She felt she had become more religious since learning she was pregnant, breaking into frequent silent prayer that often began with *Oh God!*

They rode quietly, not joking or shouting in glee. The last time they were together, they'd awakened into a nightmare, Ariel crying and asking who'd had sex with her. If nobody said anything, perhaps it would go away.

With Chris in the lead, they rode past the lanterns and lawns, the oaks and the firs, the athletic fields and ponds, the brick and white clapboard campus buildings, zipping across asphalt and brick, over bridges, down hills, the wind in their hair and flapping their clothes as an orange and blue sunset draped the horizon. No one fell. To Ariel they seemed determined to remain upright today. When Chris raised his arm and gestured to the Seymour St. John Chapel, they sped toward it and at the lantern on the lawn exited the path to sit beneath one of the great old trees that framed the white portico.

They looked up to the church steeple when the carillon chimed 8:00 pm. No one had spoken yet. Ariel knew they were waiting for her.

She cleared her throat. "Well, as we all know, my vagina has been compromised."

Brandon sniggered. No one else.

"The result is I am pregnant."

"Dude, sick!" Kyle exclaimed.

She grimaced at him. "That happens to be the point, Kyle. I'm not a dude. I'm female and one of you made me pregnant."

Hasayeah stared at her, ruined scions, presidential aspirations drifting off in puffs of bad dope.

"Why did we ever smoke that weed?" Emily asked. "We all knew better."

"It wasn't weed," Ariel said.

"Guess not," Brandon mumbled.

"Doesn't anybody remember anything?" Ariel implored. "Anything? Even dreaming about sex?"

The boys looked at each other. "We do that every night, Ariel," Kyle said. "It's like …" he faltered. "You know the good behavior society expects of guys?"

"Yes?"

"It's all a crock, Ariel. It's not how we are."

Having looked horrified all the while, Nicole of the blonde cornrows and the biggest trust fund among them said, "You mean it really could have been any of you? It really could?"

Kyle nodded and reluctantly so did Chris, then Brandon then John.

They started talking or rather whisper-yelling at each other.

Kyle, who was a member of the a capella Maiyeros, dissociated from the spat and started singing The Beatle's *Yesterday*. It was how he dealt with things, including stress. He was their portable soundtrack. A squabble would begin and Kyle would start singing *Come Together*. They'd longboard into an amazing sunset and he would sing *Here Comes the Sun* except he'd change it to *There Goes the Sun*. He loved the Beatles. Tonight he hadn't sung until now.

Ariel studied her friends objectively for perhaps the first time because she was suddenly different from them. In their faces as they spoke was consciousness of privilege, and, she now realized, an underlying fear. It had always been there. What were they afraid of? Outsiders who wouldn't understand them? Being thought a fool? Shaming their families? Choate and their parents had taught them how to comport themselves. They hadn't expected disaster to come from among them.

On Emily's face, on Nicole's, on Jessica's she also saw sympathy with Ariel's plight, the tips of their eyebrows rising in sadness for her, but also knotting and lifting now and then in sheer terror. They sat a bit apart, as if wanting distance from the unthinkable.

Not the boys. They just looked terrified, their eyes round, their pupils pinpricks. One of them was going to be a father.

"Kyle, stop singing about yesterday!" Ariel snapped. "What's done is done; we have to deal with it."

"We'll all get DNA tests, right guys?" Kyle said. "We don't have to tell our parents, unless … you know."

Brandon and John nodded. Chris looked around for an escape route, like the girls.

Ariel stood. "No! I'm not doing this to you. I love you all too much. If you want to forget you know me, get up and leave. I'll understand."

Chris stood, no one else. Eventually he sat down and glued his eyes to his smart phone.

Emily said, "They're going to expel you."

"I know," Ariel said.

"Hey, dudes!" Chris said, suddenly laughing.

He was answered with seven relieved *whats*.

"Something happened at the airport in Milan today."

"What happened?"

Chris kept laughing. "This is so whack. People are actually saying Jesus was there."

Ariel grabbed Chris's cell phone and started reading, "OMG, guys! I've got to go there!"

Everyone stared at her.

"But Jesus—I mean the guy—isn't there anymore," Chris reasoned. "I mean, it's an airport. Somebody said he was with a woman buying a ticket to Africa."

"Where in Africa, Chris?"

"How would I know?"

She gave Chris back his phone and used her own to dial her house. Her father answered.

"Dad, it's me."

"Hello, sweetheart. How are you feeling?"

"Dad, have you seen the news?"

"Uh, no not this evening. Your mother and I have been talking about you, of course."

"What do you know about the clone and Africa?"

"Africa?"

"Yes."

"Nothing, Ariel. Why do you ask?"

"Think, Dad. Is there any connection at all? Anything with Maggie?"

"Not that I know of. When I knew her she'd never been there. She just … well, used to carry this photo around of an African village. It seemed to mean a lot to her."

"A village? What village?"

"Well, I don't remember the name. I … it's been years. I … Udugu might have been it. What's going on?"

"Turn on the news, Dad. If I were you, I'd book a flight." Ariel hung up and said out loud. "I sure am." Then she searched for Udugu on her cell phone's browser and said. "They speak Swahili over there." No one replied as she kept reading. "They call the whites, wazungu. That's the plural. The singular is mzungu. I guess that's me."

"Where are you going?" asked Nicole.

"To Africa," Ariel said, not looking up. "Jesus is back."

"Oh?" Emily said.

It took two heartbeats before they all talked at once.

"I have to get back to the dorm…"

"I've got a lot of homework…"

"I've got a late practice…"

"I told my sister I'd call her…"

"I think I left my math book at the infirmary…"

"I've got a study session…"

Sadly, Ariel stared at them.

Kyle said, "I'll go with you, Ariel."

He stayed as the others left, picking up their longboards, saying goodbye, hugging each other, mournful because they knew Hasayeah wouldn't skate across campus together ever again. When they were alone, Kyle took her hand. With all her heart, Ariel hoped he was the father of her child.

"Kyle, you can't come. You'd get in trouble."

That was an understatement. On the long list of things Choaties were forbidden to do—smoke, gamble, have sex, do drugs, drink, curse, spit, be rude, wear jeans, hack the school's computer, wear sweatpants to class, violate curfew, cheat on exams, lack integrity, respect or compassion—leaving campus without permission was probably number one. Choate could protect you from yourself only if you were here. If she wanted, she could study abroad for a term in China, France, Italy or Spain. She could do a summer exchange in Japan.

Africa? No.

Going there a day after the Matriculation Ceremony in which she'd recommitted herself to the principles and values of Choate Rosemary Hall, would be the biggest infraction of the Honor Code, ever—way beyond the punishments of the many lower disciplinary levels: Restriction, Warning, Censure, Probation and Suspension. Even if Ariel managed not to be pregnant, the consequences of missing check-in for more than one night without her murdered body being found were severe. When they knew she was alive and well, she'd be expelled. No need for Kyle to be.

"Just drive me to the airport?" she asked. JFK was two and half hours away. "I've got to find out where this village called Udugu is, get money from my ChoateCard and buy a ticket."

Her dad had forgotten that. He relied on fatherly authority—as if his words, once spoken, controlled her legs, which were now incapable of going where they'd been forbidden. Not only did her ChoateCard serve as school ID, she could use it to withdraw cash

from her school account. Her parents always kept a couple
thousand in it, just in case. But the Student Services Kiosk in the
SAC had already closed. It wouldn't open until 8 a.m.

"I'll drive you to the airport when you're ready," Kyle said.

They got on their longboards and, holding hands, skated into
fast-falling night.

————

Zach Dunlop had been bumped from his Newark flight, the
one that would have gotten him to Dar es Salaam four hours after
Zenia and Paul Joseph landed. Normally, all he had to do was offer
to buy a first class ticket and he could get on any plane. Not only
was the Newark flight delayed, it was overbooked, but no one
would give up their seat, though he offered to pay handsomely out
of his own pocket. Instead of solving the problem, this somehow
offended the flight attendants who refused to announce his offer
to the plane, which took off without him.

Not something he was used to. The delay also caused him to
miss the only other flight out of Newark last night, Lufthansa
through Zurich at 6:47 p.m. Desperate, Zach next tried to book a
private jet, only to discover last minute jet charters to Africa
weren't available at the drop of a hat, at least not for him today. His
quickest option to Africa would be the same flight Zenia took,
twenty-four hours later.

Now, last on the plane, Zach boarded Flight 204, frustrated and
befuddled. His life usually went so well, people called him lucky. It
hadn't been since yesterday. It was as if the entire airline industry
conspired to keep him from following his wife. He made his way
toward the center of the plane, trying to remember the last time
he'd been in coach. It had to be before he and Zenia moved out of
Manhattan to Hewlett Bay Park Village, that's for sure. The
multimillion-dollar home they'd bought was underwater by
almost a million now, but Zach didn't care. They had no need to
sell, even if they did move to Ohio. At least the delay had allowed
him to go home and pack properly this time, change into jeans, a
cotton jacket and shirt. He didn't want anyone to wonder why the
man in the four thousand dollar suit was sitting in coach.

Stowing his carry-on overhead, he sat down, wondering what possessed Zenia to run off to Africa like this. For years he'd tried to penetrate the layer of frost under which she hid—the perfect wife, the perfect society hostess, the perfect church member—always unkindly judging others who fell short of her mark. After a while he'd given up, accepting Zenia for who she was. There were enough good things about her that he told himself he wasn't God and shouldn't judge. Now Zach had the uneasy feeling that his tolerance had been a mistake.

Yesterday, for all intents, his wife of eleven years ran away from home for reasons he couldn't fathom. Even a warning of potential danger hadn't fazed her. Repeatedly he tried to reach her cell before her flight took off, but she'd either turned it off or set it to "do not disturb." Only now did Zach realize a gulf had opened between them in which neither his status as her husband, nor her respect for his judgment, made a difference to his wife.

Settling into his seat, Zach noticed a girl bent over in her seat in his aisle's middle row. Her black hair covered most of her pale face. At first Zach thought the girl must be searching for her purse, but when she stayed like that, he began to watch her. Soon he realized the girl was soaking tissues with her tears. Zach looked uncomfortably around. Few men were constituted to ignore a crying female and especially not Zach. He wanted to console her, but nothing in the girl's appearance invited that. She made eye contact with no one, made not a sound, did not shudder or give off weakness of any kind. She just cried non-stop from a fresh, private grief.

Someone must have died.

As the plane taxied, Zach glimpsed a man across the cabin who obviously was similarly conflicted—feeling the urge to help, but seeing no way to approach a young woman he didn't know. They lifted their eyebrows in silent agreement there was nothing they could do and looked forward as the plane entered the runway and took off.

After a while, Zach glanced over to see if the girl had stopped crying. She hadn't. Now and then she sat up, only to grab more tissues so she could bend over and soak them in tears. She was well-dressed and looked patrician, not that it mattered, but Zach imagined it was his own daughter crying all alone in the darkened plane.

He decided the girl was going to make herself sick if she kept this up. Again he caught the eye of the man across the aisle, who shrugged. Zach put his hands on the armrests and made an *I'm going in* face and the man opened his palm as if to say, *good luck, friend.* Swallowing, Zach rose, went over and sat in the empty aisle seat beside her. "Pardon me, young woman, but did you know that tears make airplanes fly slower?"

The girl gave an upset, guarded stare. "I'm fine, thank you."

Zach lifted doubting eyebrows and said nothing.

"Okay, I'm not."

"I'll leave if you like, but I'm happy to stay."

The girl lifted the armrest and scooted over so there was a seat separating her and Zach. "You can stay."

"Why, thank you. My name's Zach Dunlop. If I had a daughter like you I'd hate to think of her all by herself crying."

The girl looked him up and down.

"Unless, of course, she really wanted to slow the plane down."

She laughed. "I'm Ariel."

"Nice to meet you. Were you going to cry the whole flight?"

Ariel sniffed. "Maybe."

"I shouldn't joke. Did you lose someone?"

"Yeah, me." Ariel blew her nose.

"Oh. Well, we'd better find her right away. She's probably looking for you, too."

She made a gloomy face.

Zach tried to look sympathetic. "Since we don't know each other and we'll never see each other again, feel free to tell me anything you like."

Ariel gave a fierce stare. "I'm pregnant. I don't know by whom. I've just run away from my school. No *Last Hurrah* for me in a great dress."

For a minute Zach's head spun. That's what he got for asking.

All he could think to say was, "Last Hurrah?"

"It's a bit like prom, just more formal because it's boarding school. The boys wear tuxedos."

"Oh."

Ariel rested her forehead in her hand. "By 7:30 tonight my prefect will see I haven't signed in on the house log and tell the faculty member on duty, who will tell Patricia—she's my form dean—who will immediately search all over campus for me or for someone who's seen me. Then she'll call the dean who'll call my parents. They'll think I've been abducted and call the police."

Zach was glad he'd never been to boarding school.

Ariel choked and wiped her eyes. "My parents are already so heartbroken they can hardly talk."

"So you decided to go to Africa?"

Ariel sat back and stared at the ceiling. "Yeah, why not?"

Zach smiled. "I understand completely." Actually, he was hoping Zenia's sudden departure wasn't for reasons as drastic.

Ariel started humming as she frowned at the ceiling.

"What's that?""

She looked at him. "What?"

"That song."

"Oh." She studied his face. "It's my favorite. *Can't Be Tamed.* Nobody knows, though."

"Why?"

"Girls like me aren't supposed to be rebellious."

"What does it say?"

"I can't be tamed, I can't be changed."

"Can you?"

She sighed. "I wish. How about you?" Ariel asked.

"Me?"

"Yes. Why are you going to Africa?"

Zach reached in his wallet and pulled out a photograph of Zenia. "My wife has run away with our minister. I'm following her."

Ariel laughed. "Where did they run away to?

"A village called Udugu."

Ariel gasped and sat up. "You're kidding. I'm going there. You think that's where Jesus is, too, don't you?"

Zach frowned. "Jesus?"

"Didn't you hear the news?"

"What news?"

"People are saying Jesus showed up in a market in Italy day before yesterday. He was with a woman who fainted, a black woman. My dad thinks it's the woman who carried that Jesus clone years ago. Did you hear about that?"

Zach was stunned. "I more than heard about that. I met her."

Ariel's mouth dropped open. "You did?"

"Yes. I helped her and her child escape, along with the scientist who created the clone and his sister."

"Ohmigod!" Ariel said, her eyes wide.

"What's the matter?" Zach asked.

"That was my dad and my aunt!"

"Your father is Felix Rossi?"

"Yes, that was his name then. He's changed it."

"Well, I guess I was wrong," Zach said.

"Wrong about what?"

"The not knowing each other part."

"Ohmigod, this is so weird. Tell me all about it. What happened?"

They hardly slept on Flight 204 to Johannesburg. On their connection, Flight 186 to Dar Es Salaam, they found seats together and by the time they approached their destination, Ariel had heard the whole story from Zach—all about the organization he started called OLIVE, Our Lord in Vitro Emerging. How a dangerous man had hunted her father and the clone—a New Yorker named Theomund Brown, now dead. How Zach's father, Congressman Dunlop, had done the bidding of Brown, but Zach had eavesdropped on his dad's meetings and with the help of OLIVE foiled the planned murder of the clone and its mother.

"What a story!" Ariel exclaimed. "Well, personally, I think it's the second coming and I don't intend to miss it. My life is falling apart. It makes sense that the world is, too."

Zach had given her the window seat so she could have the better view as they watched Africa come into sight.

Zach said, "Did you know we had an earthquake in Connecticut?"

"Yeah, it quaked our house."

They grew silent as Tanzania appeared below the clouds.

Quietly, Ariel said. "Zach, you're a cool dude. I can tell. I think it's no accident that we've met."

"What do you mean?"

"God must have put us on the plane together."

Zach thought of his overbooked Newark flight, the absence of available jet charters and wondered if the girl was right.

The plane dropped, filling his stomach with butterflies. He gazed down on brown earth through the clouds.

"Well, Miss Ariel, you're landing on a continent you've never visited and me just once. We're going to the same village. Shall we join forces?"

"Definitely," Ariel said, looking down.

"Shall we go straight to Udugu?"

The plane banked sharply, throwing them back from the window.

"Definitely," Ariel replied. "I have five hundred dollars."

He smiled. "Then we're rich."

They laughed and watched Dar es Salaam approach, ocean and scattered white clouds filling the window and through the clouds a city of trees and low buildings hugging the shoreline, trimmed in white sand. They gripped the armrests as the wheels set down.

"Zach," Ariel said. "We've come halfway around the world to find a guy who thinks he's Jesus, at least I have. Do you believe in him?"

"The clone?"

"I mean the original Jesus."

Zach smiled. "I do, but I admit I'll be satisfied if I simply find my wife. If Jesus appears in the process? All to the good." He didn't want to tell her he thought it was the second coming, too.

Felix Fubini, formerly Rossi, closed the door to his daughter's dorm room at Choate Rosemary Hall, his wife Adeline asleep on Ariel's empty bed. They'd had to give her sedatives, his wife was so distraught. Ariel hadn't signed into the dorm's house log last night or been seen or heard from since. The Wallingford police and scores of volunteers had scoured the campus, the town, and the surrounding woods looking for her. If Ariel was still in Wallingford, she wasn't above ground, a rookie policeman had said, causing Adeline's collapse. Felix looked up and saw Ariel's form dean, Patricia, hurrying toward him down the hall—gray carpet, cream walls, nothing to distract from serious educational pursuit. Patricia's short, straight hair bounced away from her head with her quick steps, but her face was composed. She had a paper in her hand.

"Mr. Fubini, this may be important," she said in an analytical tone. From the first, she'd exuded calm, belied only by swift movements.

He rushed toward her. "Yes, what?"

Patricia handed him what looked like a banking receipt. "She's withdrawn a great deal of money from her ChoateCard."

Felix frowned and didn't say the obvious. Had Ariel done it voluntarily or did an abductor somehow force her to withdraw the funds? Then, remembering the credit card he'd taken back from her and why, he felt new alarm.

"May I talk to her friends myself?"

"Hasayeah? Yes, we've assembled them."

He followed her controlled, rapid progress down the hall to a common room with casual tables and chairs, a small kitchen and a bulletin board. Three girls and four boys huddled together, whispering

"This is Ariel's father," Patricia said, and they all sat up straight.

"I know most of you," Felix said. "And you know me. As you can imagine, Ariel's disappearance is ..."

"Quite unprecedented," Patricia said, helping.

"If any of you even suspect where she might be ..."

He noticed one of the boys didn't meet his gaze. He had his feet on a longboard and was moving it back and forth.

"You're Kyle?" Felix asked him.

He looked up. "Yes, sir."

Felix saw guilt on his face. He was too young to hide it.

"Kyle, all of you—" He looked at each one. "I know you'd hate to betray Ariel's trust, so I won't ask questions. Will you just nod if I'm right?"

They stared at him.

Felix pushed once black hair out of his eyes. "This may sound odd, but is there any chance … I mean could Ariel have somehow gotten it in her head to go off to Africa?"

Patricia emitted her first gasp. All of Hasayeah held his gaze except Kyle, who looked down at his feet, pushing the longboard.

"Kyle," Felix asked. "Did she go to Africa?"

Kyle closed his eyes and put his head in his hand. After a moment, he nodded.

Chapter 17

Ahmed could not bear to be parted from Ajia. After her deflowering—in which he took inexpressible joy—he persuaded her to come to his suite at the Oyster Bay Hotel. She would not give herself to him again, but went to the bathroom and locked the door. He could hear her bathe, reciting yet another traditional Swahili phrase. *Mungu atanilinda ubaya wenu hautanifika.* God will protect me, your evil deeds will not reach me.

But his evil deeds had already reached her and Ahmed was very glad. He pictured her on the other side of the bathroom door, stepping out of the water and sitting on the sculpted block of ironwood in front of the elegant white tub. In his mind he thrilled again at the long, coppery limbs, the high breasts, the previously secret place where she'd felt pain, but him such pleasure. When she finally came out, she didn't meet his gaze, but stood, looking down at the white carpet.

She whispered, "I am too ashamed to go home. The Qur'ān says. *'And come not near until adultery. Lo! It is an abomination and an evil way.'* Ahmed, I cannot believe what I … what we have done. My parents will be infuriated. I don't know what came over me." Softly she cried.

Ahmed felt proud of her tears and her shame. He wanted to hold her, but knew this wasn't the moment. He had wronged her, but he would make it right. "I will marry you."

Anger blazed through her tears. "Unfortunately, Ahmed, in Tanzania there is no Las Vegas to run off to and get married!"

"Can you just go home to get your birth certificate and passport? If we have that, we can file a notarized *Certificate of No Impediment* and take it to the nearest Registrar of Marriages. Twenty-one days later, I can marry you."

"Assuming no one produces an impediment, Ahmed. The man who has been visiting me will. What am I to do?"

He stood. "Or, Ajia, we could apply for a Special Marriage License to eliminate the twenty-one days."

She looked mournful. "Yes, I suppose so. But don't forget I am a Swahili bride. You must also provide a dowry, remember; I must be asked for my consent on the wedding day; and vows must be taken in the presence of my father. My family will not accept you otherwise!"

Fresh tears slid down her face and Ahmed knew why. Even this would still deprive Ajia of the greatest moments of a Swahili bride's life. The weeks of beauty treatments, her body perfumed with sandalwood and dressed in rich clothing her groom had provided. After days of celebration the vows would be taken—he in the mosque, she elsewhere. Then, to the sound of the women's joyful ululating and shouts of *Bibi Harusi, the bride has come,* she would show herself to the wedding guests and enter womanhood.

"Come on safari with me," he said.

She looked up, wiping her face.

"We have already done a haraam thing," he added. How can that be worse? Anyway, if I am going to Udugu, we can't delay."

She said nothing.

"Ajia, do you still want me to save Udugu from the wazungu?"

She walked to the sofa and sat near him, looking at the ocean through the green shutters. "That is why I gave myself to you. To persuade you. Has a jinn possessed me, Ahmed?"

He took her hand. "No, Ajia. You are my love. I have wanted you since we met when I came to hear your group sing Taarab. Your lovely voice transfixed me. Do you remember that you sang *Binti,* the version by Safari Sound? Perhaps it was an omen. Come with me on safari. We will get married somehow."

She sighed. "I have no clothes."

Thanking Allah for the benefits of working at Silverman Alden, Ahmed reached into his pocket, took out the roll of cash he always carried, opened it, rose and showered Ajia with cash. It was an impulse. He had no idea how she'd react.

Ajia gazed, open-mouthed at the falling money and then looked at him in horror.

Swiftly he said, "This is part of your dowry!"

"Oh." She lowered her eyes. "I have to call home or they will worry."

During the call, he could tell from her expression that her father was very irate. "No, Baba, I cannot come back. Don't worry. I will make you proud of me." She hung up and, taking a deep breath said, "If I went back, he might feel he ought to beat me for leaving the house and staying away all night and he's never beat me. I will go with you, but no more of what is haraam. Where will you sleep tonight, Ahmed?"

She spoke bravely. They both knew there were local men who, in Ahmed's shoes, would feel justified in forcing sex on her now. Ahmed wasn't that kind of man. His heart sinking, he pointed to the tan sofa. "There. You take the bed."

It was draped in white curtains tied at each of the four posts. Without a word, Ajia rose and untied them. She sat on the white bed and closed the curtains around her. After a while, Ahmed turned out the lights and slipped off his shoes. He could see her shadow as she undressed. He could hear her African Ocean through the green-shuttered doors. In his mind, he made love to her over and over half the night.

He awoke to the words of the *Adhan*, the Islamic call to prayer, "*Hayya 'ala-s-Salah. Hayya 'ala-s-Salah,*" Rise up for prayer. It consisted of three parts, cleansing before prayer, the successive positions assumed on the prayer rug, and the actual prayers themselves. He went to the bathroom to perform *wudu'*, ritual ablutions before *salat*. First he used the toilet and applied water to cleanse himself since toilet tissue didn't do a good enough job for prayer. Ajia was still asleep, had told him not to wake her because she would not perform salat today. He hadn't argued. Women were not expected to perform salat during menstruation, labor and childbirth.

Forming the intention for purification, he whispered his, "Bismillah" In the name of Allah, then three times washed his hands to the wrists, filled his right hand with water and washed his mouth, quietly gurgling the water each time. Usually, these ablutions alone put him in a prayerful state, but Ahmed was still distracted by the events of last night.

He collected more water and inhaled it into his nose three times then blew it out, then washed his face thrice, moved to the right arm then the left, washing them up to the elbow three times. He put water in his hands and washed just once from his forehead over his head to his neck and back, placing his fingers as prescribed, cleaning his ears. He washed his right foot to the ankle three times then his left, cleaning between the toes each time—the right hand for the right foot, the left hand for the left. Four more times today he would repeat wudu' as preparation for salat, just after midday, in the afternoon, just after sunset, and when night had fallen. At Silverman Alden, his office had a private bath, given him for this purpose. The firm wanted to keep their second best trader happy. Had Ahmed not bathed last night after Ajia slept, he'd have to perform a full ablution because he'd had intercourse.

Ahmed was particularly meticulous this morning because he'd defiled himself. He'd definitely touched Ajia with lust and she wasn't his wife. The Prophet said no man could always keep to the straight path and Ahmed had proved it last night. According to the Qur'ān, what he'd done was a lot worse than drinking beer and listening to music. Yet Ahmed didn't truly believe he'd sinned since he loved Ajia and would marry her the instant he could.

To make up for his faulty thoughts, he recited the *Shahada* slowly and deeply, "There is no god but God, and Mohammed is the messenger of Allah." Only then did he open the bathroom door and unroll his prized possession, a 3' x 5' Ottoman prayer rug from the great Cairo weavers to do the two *rak'as* required at dawn. He placed it at an angle he knew to be one degree of north going clockwise, where Mecca was. Barefoot he stood on it, his feet slightly apart the width of his shoulders, his gaze down, and assumed the first position, hands to his ears, palms out, thumbs behind his earlobes. He whispered, "Allaho Akbar," God is Great," forcing away awareness of Ajia's breathing and the memory of their time on the beach.

He brought his arms to his chest, right hand over his left wrist and said, "In the Name of Allah, the Beneficent, the Merciful. All praise be to Allah, Lord of the Worlds."

For the first time during salat, Ahmed felt tears come to his eyes. He was impure. He was in love.

"The Beneficent, the Merciful
Master of the Day of Judgment.
Thee only do we worship.
Thee alone we ask for help.
Show us the straight path.
The path of those whom You love and favor
Not the path of those who have earned Thine anger, nor are leading astray.
Be it so."

Always before in the mosque, praying this prayer with the men, he'd felt joined to both God and them. Now, he had sinned. He had led Ajia astray. How could he be so happy?

He bent over at the waist, saying *Allaho Akbar*. Only during *Fajr*, the morning salat, were all prayers said aloud. He put his palms on his knees, his fingers spread, repeating three times in Arabic, "Holy is my Creator, the Magnanimous."

The several positions of salat and their accompanying prayers would make his sins fall away like leaves. He should have insisted Ajia rise and perform salat for the same reason, though if her monthly cycle had come she wasn't required to.

"Allah hears the one who praises Him; Our Lord, Yours is the praise," he said while straightening. Arms at his sides, he said, "Allaho Akbar" again then, both hands to his knees, he lowered himself to perform the first *sadjah* in which only his forehead, hands, knees and toes touched the ground. Three times he repeated, "Glory be to my Creator, The Most Supreme."

Now Ahmed sat, curling his right foot beneath his buttocks so that part of his weight rested on it. He said, "*Allaho Akbar*," rose to his feet, hands at his sides and performed the second sadjah, forehead, hands, knees and toes to the ground. Rising a final time he said, "Allah hears the one who praises Him; Our Lord, Yours is the praise," and sat back on his curled foot again, reciting the final prayer.

At last he felt the intense joy of salat, felt divine love. At such moments, he wished he didn't handle investments for those bent on Jihad, wished that his father weren't a wanted man, that he himself wasn't contemplating violence. He'd tried to explain this feeling to Zach, had demonstrated salat to him and Zach had observed that some of the positions were similar to yoga and the repeated prayers were like chants used by mystics and gurus everywhere. Make a habit of them and they induced a quiet state of mind. It wasn't anything peculiar to Islam, Zach had said, but our universal connection to God. That's when Ahmed knew converting Zach would be hard.

When he finished the final prayer, Ahmed lowered his head then slowly turned it to the right to address the angel who records good actions. "*As-salaam alaikum wa rahmatullah*," he said then repeated it, turning his head to the left for the angel who records bad deeds.

He'd abjured his evil deed.

Quietly he sat on the sofa and watched Ajia through the bed curtains as she slept, averting his eyes when she rose to go to the bathroom.

She came out and asked, "We are going through with this? You are determined?"

Ahmed was determined, though what he really wanted was to sin again. He'd do anything for her. He controlled himself and they went downstairs.

In a white room full of chic African art, under two elegant chandeliers made of strings of white coral, they joined the communal dining table, Ahmed confident now that Zenia wouldn't recognize him. She hadn't last night when they checked in. He realized she probably had little contact with people of Arab descent and couldn't differentiate between them well.

Paul Joseph's group was already at the table. To Ahmed's pride and irritation, the men stared at Ajia as they entered.

"Habari gani," he said to them.

Only the African among them replied in Swahili. The rest said, "Good morning."

Ahmed had forgotten about Zenia Dunlop, who sat next to Paul Joseph, looking as innocent as the dawn when, according to the Qur'ān, she should be flogged with a hundred stripes. He didn't want to believe this was really his best friend's wife and that she'd done what he thought she had. Yes, he and Ajia had sinned, but they intended to get married. Zenia already was and to someone else. He wanted to confront her, yet he couldn't reveal his identify or raise suspicion. Nor could he resist.

"Did you sleep well, Mrs. Joseph," he asked, goading her as he seated Ajia.

She looked up, startled. "I'm Mrs. Dunlop."

"Oh, I apologize," Ahmed said. "Zenia, I think I heard?"

Paul Joseph visibly tensed. "Zenia Dunlop is my parishioner and very kind to come help with my mission ... Mr. Hassan was it?"

"Yes. Hanif Hassan," Ahmed said. "Very kind and thoughtful of you, I'm sure, Mrs. Dunlop," he continued as the hostess poured juice and coffee for them. "Is Mr. Dunlop joining you?"

He felt Ajia kick him under the table. He knew he was being impolite.

Zenia stared at him. Was she remembering him from the Christmas party? Apparently not. "No, Mr. Dunlop is not joining me."

Ahmed knew he shouldn't be questioning a woman he didn't know.

"How are you getting to Udugu?" Ahmed asked Paul Joseph.

Paul Joseph didn't reply. Was he pretending he hadn't heard the question?

Ahmed repeated it, making sure to sound pleasant, and the man with the Boer accent said, impatiently, "Cessna. The best bush transport. No Ixtra seats, though." He turned to Paul Joseph, "I'll leave the van here, rather than use long-term parking et the airport."

Paul Joseph nodded and everyone resumed eating the salty but savory marmite on unbelievably good multigrain toast, drinking the juice and coffee. Ahmed and Ajia ate the eggs, but not the ham.

Ahmed couldn't forget about Zach, his trust betrayed by an adulterous wife. It was none of his business, but Ahmed felt a desire to avenge his friend.

He cleared his throat and spoke up, faking a smile. "Had I a wife as lovely as you, I wouldn't allow her to travel without me."

He heard Ajia gasp as Zenia Dunlop's gaze fixed unsmiling on her.

"This lovely girl is not your wife?"

Everyone stopped eating to stare back and forth between them. How could he have made such a mistake?

He knew Ajia must be crushed, but she didn't flinch. She glared back. "What is your business in my country, Mrs. Dunlop?"

Zenia seemed surprised to be challenged, but she also didn't back down. "You are right in describing it as my business, young woman."

Hate blazed from Ajia's eyes. "The business of whites in Africa is of no concern to Africans?"

The important-looking African man cleared his throat. "Allow me to introduce myself. I am the Honorable Bahari, Mahfuru, an MP and member of the Parliamentary Committee for Land, Natural Resources and Environment. We welcome Mrs. Dunlop's interest in Tanzania."

Now it was Ahmed who kicked Ajia furtively. She lowered her eyes. "Of course. Enjoy your visit, Mrs. Dunlop," Ajia said, stood and left the table.

Ahmed flushed, as angry with himself as he was with Zenia Dunlop for upsetting Ajia.

"Pardon me," he said, and rose to go after her.

Ahmed passed the hotel's uniformed chauffeur, assumedly on the way to tell Paul Joseph and his party that their transport to the airport was ready. Where was Ajia? Not in the lounge behind them. He looked in the bar with the photo of noble-faced white oxen. He looked in the lobby and saw only two zebras carved in white driftwood and the hotel's limo parked outside the iron-studded wood door. He went upstairs to their room and found Ajia crouched at the door, her head on her drawn-up knees.

"Ajia, I apologize."

She looked up, her eyes full of tears. "What a thing to say to strangers! *'Had I a wife …'* What a thing to say to that hateful woman, with me sitting beside you."

———

uchawi - witchcraft
wachawi - witches
mchawi - a specific witch

Ahmed didn't know where Ajia was taking him. He'd planned that they laze away an hour or two on the Msasani Peninsula, either at Oyster Bay Hotel or on Coco Beach. Then, Ahmed would take Ajia to the Hyatt Regency's Kilimanjaro Hotel. While she shopped for clothes and was pampered in its spa, he would buy gold jewelry—the essential rest of her dowry. Ordinarily, he'd fly her to Johannesburg or Dubai, where the world's best was on offer, but they had no time. He'd already told his safari company to expect another guest.

Instead, she insisted he call a taxi. Now they crawled through Dar es Salaam's heavy traffic into neighborhoods less desirable than those of the Msasani Peninsula, where most of the ex-pats lived, or green and spacious ones like Chang'ombe to the south, where Ajia lived or Upanga, his mother's home. The taxi pulled into one of the streets around bustling Kariakoo market where the locals in Dar shopped, Ajia craning her neck to read signs. He couldn't believe it. Their chances of being mugged here had to be a hundred percent.

"Ajia, tell me where we're going!"

"Kuacha!" Stop, she told the driver before a shop with a hand-lettered sign. It said *Babu Enzi, Herbalist*, and listed what he could cure, which included regaining a lost lover or spouse. Ahmed didn't like the look of the place or the name Enzi, which meant power. Usually, healers didn't have such names. Their power spoke for itself by curing.

"Are you sick?" he asked her.

"No, stay here," she said and before he knew it she was out of the cab.

Ahmed started to go after her then realized that, being Swahili, she'd have an easier time around Kariakoo market than he, a well-dressed Arab. He sat in the cab, watching her disappear into the herbalist's ramshackle shop. Two western tourists in khaki shorts ambled by, unintentionally offending with their bare legs. Either they hadn't taken time to get tourist advice or didn't care. Innocently they gazed about, sitting ducks for Kariakoo's expert pickpockets who would certainly target them, if just for the shorts. Tanzania was a poor country. Only outside of the cities were tourists' belongings sure to be safe. Ahmed sat a long time, waiting, watching the market's hubbub, smelling delicious smells. Suddenly Ajia appeared, carrying a paper bag.

"What's that?" he said as she got in.

"It's from the mchawi—something to ensure the success of your plan."

Ahmed decided to say nothing. Officially, he didn't believe in witchcraft, but this was Africa, where western notions of logic didn't apply.

Chapter 18

It was the best dream I'd ever had. I was in Africa. I was home.

When I opened my eyes, women stared down at me, their sienna skin, wide noses, and full lips similar to mine. A strong smell filled my nose—parts smoke, fire, earth, grass and sweat. I lay in a hut on a woven palm mat, a center pole supporting a thatched roof above. Something cool was on my forehead. A leaf of some kind. Outside I could hear children sing some childhood song, their voices clear, sweet, and full of joy. Where was Jess? What had happened to the strange old man who made me drink from a gourd under a tree? Had I fainted and been brought in here? Impossible. It was just a dream.

As I sat up, hands reached to help me, lips smiling and speaking a lilting foreign tongue. I got to my feet and saw other women scowl at me. All barefoot, they wore colorful head wraps and skirts, some with traditional blouses, some western style. We were crowded into a round hut of packed mud walls, a few pots and low stools scattered about, a floor of leveled mud beneath our feet. They said, *Bibi,* over and over, as if it were my name.

Forgetting they wouldn't understand me, I said, "I'm Maggie Morelli."

A young woman took my hand and held it. "We must address you with respect. "*Habari, Bibi* Maggie." She was one of the smiling ones. I had the sense that her intricately printed green head wrap and matching dress were her best clothes.

"Thank you. What does Bibi mean?"

"Honored grandmother." Still holding my hand, she turned to the other women and said, sternly, "*Mwanamke mwenye heshima ni mgeni wetu.*"

Wondering what she'd said, I returned her happy smile. "I'm not a grandmother, at least not yet."

"For us, Bibi is like calling you madam. I have told them you are our guest."

From the whispering and suspicious glances, I didn't think all the women liked that idea. A frowning old woman said mchawi when she looked in my direction. It made me nervous, but I didn't show it.

"We welcome you," the young woman said with sincerity. "*Tunakukaribisha!*"

"Why, thank you, child. Thank you." I was beginning to think she'd never let go of my hand.

"*Tunakukaribisha!*" she repeated to the women.

Clearly, she was on my side. "What is your name?"

"I am Suma. You remember Babu?"

She must mean the old man. I nodded.

"He is my real grandfather. Where do you come from, Bibi?"

"America, originally, New York. Then Italy." It felt strange to talk to a figment of my imagination. "What does mchawi mean?"

Suma didn't answer, just glared at the old woman who'd said it. I started to feel uneasy and wished Jess was here.

Suma led me outside and the women followed, talking excitedly. Immediately I realized the intelligence of the hut's mud construction. There was easily a twenty to thirty degree difference between the fast-cooling night and the warmth inside. No doubt the hut would be cool when the sun rose.

We stood near a campfire in the middle of a compound defined by encircling stones that opened to make a path to the rest of the village. Two other huts were there as well as the huge tree under which I'd first awakened, a big drum hanging from its outstretched limb.

Night had fallen, though I hadn't seen one like this since I was a child in Macon, Georgia. From horizon to horizon, the sky was ablaze with stars. How could there possibly be so many? Among them hung the moon, a pale jewel in clusters of diamonds. A great cloudy formation strewed itself across the starlit sky. It looked like a nebula or galaxy. Then I recognized the Southern Cross and realized it must be the Milky Way itself, its dust more visible than

I'd ever seen. The enormous African sky dwarfed the village, the real creation up there. For a moment I felt vast, too.

"Very hot. Unusual for Mbeya lowlands," Suma said.

That's where I was? "I thought this was Udugu,"

"Yes. Udugu in Mbeya. Very hot because of unusual drought. Last month it rained too much. Now topsoil washed away."

I gazed at the bare red dirt on which the village sat, and only a few yards away jungle rising up a dark green hill. Strange drought. The village looked just like the picture from National Geographic I'd carried long ago. Sam, my first husband, had asked for it before he died. I hadn't imagined Udugu's night sounds, though—strange snorts, warbles, buzzes and tweets, owl-like bleatings that rose to a crescendo, a bird whose call was like a rusty hinge, an occasional bellow from something large—made a constant chorus beyond the firelight. Without ever seeing the photo, had Jess magically brought me here? My eyes and ears must be lying to me again.

"This compound belong to Babu," Suma said.

"Your grandfather?"

"Yes. Years ago, he was our mganga wa pepo. He told us you and your son would come, but they didn't believe him."

"Um-ganga?"

Suma smiled. "Mmmmganga. He was once our spirit healer."

Alarmed, I thought *voodoo*, but didn't say it. Just then Jess and the old man came out of the largest hut and I stopped feeling uneasy. Whatever was going on, Jess would take care of it. When Suma saw them, she gave a radiant smile.

Jess rushed to me, an eighteen-year-old happy to see his mother well. "Are you all right now, Mamma?"

"I'm fine. What could be wrong in a dream?"

He laughed. "You are not dreaming."

I was about to point out we'd just been in the Malpensa Airport in Milan, so we had to be imagining these people and their village, but Jess hugged me and his arms felt real, though I knew they couldn't be. I could hear the women murmur as we embraced. He put his cheek against mine in comfort. Behind him, I saw Babu. Compared to most of the villagers he was tall, as tall as Jess. For clothes he wore a long dark cloth tied across his chest and secured with straps of cowrie shells and beads. Babu's short hair and beard had begun to grey. His forehead was lined, but lean, long muscles made him look far from helpless. Most compelling were his eyes— fully present and unsurprised. When he looked at me, I felt seen. Only then did it strike me—where were the other men?

As if in answer, I heard male voices on the path to Babu's compound. There were the missing men—not dressed like Babu, but in western shirts and pants. What had happened to their traditions? All these years, this village had been my symbol of Africa in its original state. The man in front wore a brown suit. He was younger than Babu and carried a kind of club he seemed to use as a walking stick. Menacingly, he shook something else at us. Apparently, we were subjects of a conflict. A few of the women, picking sides, ran down the path to join the men. I felt Jess take my hand. My joy at being in Udugu vanished as the man marched toward us, shaking whatever was in his hand.

Suma came and stood beside me.

"Who is he?" I asked. "What's going on?"

"It is Baba Watende, our healer and chairman now. He says you are evil spirits Babu brought and unless you go immediately tragedy will befall us."

Something glinted and I saw that Watende held a cross. Weird that the religion Jess inspired was being used to threaten us.

"No one saw you come," Suma added.

Oh, that. I couldn't explain my presence here any more than Baba Watende could. "Why do their first names sound alike?"

She smiled. "Babu means grandfather. Baba, father. They are titles."

I hoped that meant Babu had seniority.

The men moved along Babu's stone-lined path, chanting something, their voices deep and threatening. I was afraid to ask Suma what they said. They stopped before entering the circular compound. Babu went to meet them.

"Habari, bwana," Babu said, sounding as if it were an ordinary night, the fire casting light and shadows on the men of Udugu, who wore shirts and slacks in the middle of the jungle—Babu in his cloth and cowrie shells. The atmosphere was so tense, I asked Suma what they said.

She smiled. "He said, 'How are you, sir?'"

"Nzuri," Watende replied, his posture stiff, his voice a challenge. With the cross in his hand, he reminded me of the young preacher who'd joined our church years ago when I lived in New York. Full of passion, fear and inexperience, nobody liked his sermons until he loosened up.

Suma translated his reply, "I'm fine."

Babu gazed past Watende to the group of men. "So long since you come to see me," Babu said, Suma translating.

The men responded with grunts and grumbles.

"You brought no rain! Then too much!" one shouted.

"Now you bring *pepo mbaya!*" another said.

Looking apologetic, Suma translated that to *evil spirits.* Fully alarmed, now, I looked around to see how Jess was reacting. He seemed focused on Babu and no one else.

"Babu," Watende said, "we have come to give you a chance to rid Udugu of these spirits before they do us harm."

I didn't see weapons, but I could sense the men's fear—as if they wanted to sweep into the compound and destroy us all. How could I blame them? If strangers appeared out of thin air in my house, I'd be frightened, too.

The wind rose and on it Babu's voice. "My uganga family, Mungu, the one god, sent this mother to us and her son."

Hesitant murmurs followed.

Watende replied, "Mungu has deserted you. So have the *mzimu.* So have the spirits of the fig tree and the wind."

Babu began walking, gazing at the people with those eyes that deeply saw. "They did not desert me. I did not lose my powers. Five years ago our ancestors, the mzimu, told me to stop healing and making rain. In a vision they showed me the white father, Paul Joseph, would come. They warned me not to resist."

The tension dropped dramatically when Babu said the ancestors had instructed him. I saw awe on many faces, as if he said he'd heard the voice of God.

Watende, unconvinced, angrily raised the arm holding the combination club and walking stick. "Too many bad things have happened...strange weather, disease, hunger. What have we done that the mzimu would punish us with these things?"

"I asked this question as well," Babu said. "Do you remember the story of Chief Kalulu, what he did when the Germans came?"

Many nodded.

"Kalulu promised that, to make the Germans leave, he would dry up the stream that fed the village."

Voices rose in agreement.

"Kalulu visited the mganga wa pepo, a spirit healer like me. Soon there was an earthquake. It dried up the stream. The Germans left. After a while another earthquake restored the stream. In their history books, the Europeans say this happened."

"Why do you tell this story?" Watende asked. "A few years later the British came and imprisoned Kalulu. Tanzania did not need spirit healers, but warriors." He accented the point with his club.

"What is that?" I asked Suma.

"A Samburu war club, called *Rungu*. Thrown well, it kills. Don't be afraid. He always carries it."

Babu replied to Watende, "Constant warfare is what made us weak to foreign invasion. As for the rain, we know the long rainfall season failed us again. We know the short rains begin soon, but may not come. Something has changed the weather. I have prayed for an end to the drought of Mbeya and these weather changes that dry up our springs and streams, that bring cold and heat in the wrong seasons and make our crops fail."

"Then it was you who brought the flood!" Watende said.

Babu gestured to Jess. "He and his mother are the answer to our prayers."

"But how did they come," Watende insisted, "if not by witchcraft?"

"How did Kalulu stop the spring?"

Jess surprised me by stepping forward. "Watende, I have heard that some in Udugu once flew through the air."

Loud murmurs followed, people speaking to each other as if

resuming old arguments between believers and nonbelievers, young and old, men and women. A few of the women ululated like Arabs, as if to say, *Amen, we used to fly through the air.* Others grumbled and I heard the old woman say mchawi again.

Jess continued, "The oldest human knowledge survives in Africa, yet you turn from it."

Someone shouted. "We turn from pepo mbaya who do us harm."

My skin crawled. What was Jess doing? He shouldn't be encouraging them to believe in what sounded to me like voodoo.

"What is your name?" Watende asked Jess.

"You may call me *Mfaraja.*"

The women stopped talking. Everyone grew still.

"I have only heard that name in the Bible," Watende said. "The Comforter."

Jess nodded. "I am he."

Silence fell under the great sky. Jess motioned to the men. "Enter your sacred circle once more. Play the sacred *ngoma* drum. Sing the sacred songs. Be as you were when you flew through the air. If you do this, believing, the rains will come at the right time once more."

Watende said, "Mfaraja would not say this. It is against the Bible."

I knew Jess's answer before he spoke. He'd been preaching it to me since he showed up in Porlezza's market. He'd used it to explain why I could go halfway around the world with a thought. Jess didn't think these Africans had practiced witchcraft or voodoo. He didn't believe that at all.

"Does the Bible not say the kingdom of God is within you? Does it not say that all things Jesus did, you can do, too, and more if you have faith? Does it not say nothing will be impossible for you? In Africa, you knew this, you did this. You have never stopped believing. Like Kalulu who banked the stream, Africans did the impossible through their waganga—spirit healers like Babu."

Was Africa the repository of lost knowledge about the human race? I wasn't afraid anymore. Jess had brought us to Udugu because somehow it was in his plan. It was part of why he'd shown up in Porlezza in the first place. I just wished his plan would take friendlier-looking forms than Watende's scowl. However, nobody else was frowning now—only Watende and the old woman. They all smiled welcomes to Jess. The men on the path entered the circle, moving toward him, craning to see him. Having learned my lesson in Milan's airport, I stepped aside to avoid being crushed.

"We will have ngoma," Babu called, "to welcome Mfaraja and his mother, Bibi Maggie."

"No! *Kufanya mwavi sumu*," Watende said.

On my left, Suma looked dumbstruck and didn't translate. I peered up at Jess and whispered, "Sweetheart, do you know what he's talking about?"

"He wants to do a poison ordeal to find out if we are witches." Jess spoke as if it were a reasonable request. I'd had enough. Where I found the courage to walk over to Watende I don't know, but walk I did. I put my hands on my hips when I reached him and said, "We are doing no such thing, Mr. Watende!"

Suma must have rushed behind me because she started translating for Watende, who stood his ground, looking impassively at me. I stood my ground, too, wondering if I'd lost my mind. The old woman who'd called me mchawi ran over, took Watende by the arm and backed him away. Suma said, 'He is our local chief, our chairman, and that is his mother."

I thought, *For goodness sakes, Maggie, you've tried to intimidate the chief!* I heard tittering and did my best to ignore it in case this was really happening. I hadn't asked to come here and I didn't want to be poisoned—in or out of a dream. Jess might be divine, but I wasn't. I couldn't pop in and out of death like him.

"How can you claim to be a Christian?" I insisted, "and talk about poison ordeals?"

Suma translated. Watende replied, "Christianity and *mila ya desturi* are different." I just had to find out what mila ya desturi was. Sensing I'd said enough, I didn't ask.

As Watende and the old woman glared at me, Babu raised his arms. "*Sisi kuuliza tu mababu.*" We will simply ask the ancestors,

Suma translated. "*Kisha sisi kufanya ngoma.* Then we do ngoma."

Suma whispered that ngoma meant drum as well as drumming and the ceremonies and feasts at which drumming occurred. Babu had brought ngoma to the village after traveling to the Swahili coast, she said. As she spoke, the compound turned into a beehive of activity. Two people were building a bigger fire. Another scattered water on the dusty red earth. Women appeared with bowls of food and a beverage Suma said was *pombe* beer. Some of the men left and returned, dressed like Babu and carrying small drums.

Watende just glowered at everyone. He and his mother took seats on two stools and he leaned on his walking stick/club as Babu went to the big drum—he, it, and the tree silhouetted against the bright African sky.

He struck the drum repeatedly and in two seconds I had a headache, probably from not having eaten since breakfast this morning at the hotel. At least I thought it was this morning, not yesterday or last month, though I couldn't be sure. I squeezed my forehead and Suma said, "Music is medicine." She led me to a log, patted my shoulder and passed me a bowl of food—a corn gruel with bits of meat and vegetable. When I hesitated, she smiled and said, "It's not poison," then she handed me a folded palm leaf for a spoon. Babu drummed as we ate. The gruel was delicious.

When he finished, Suma stood and began to sing in an astonishing voice, *Mungu yu mwema, yu mwema, yu mwema.*

All the women around the fire replied, *Yu mwema, Yu mwema, daima*

I didn't understand the words but I knew the way they sang. It was *call and response*, heard in small churches everywhere, I suspected, but certainly in the churches in which I was raised— first in Macon, Georgia then in Harlem, New York. Suma sang the call then the rest lifted their voices in response, even the few who still didn't look happy I was there. They could have been singing a spiritual, except I'd never heard one so vibrant.

"Do you know what it means?" I asked Jess. He sat beside me on the ground with his back against the log, lounging as if he were on our sofa at the Hotel Parco San Marco.

He looked up in thought and replied, "It is an old Gospel song the missionaries taught them, *Mungu yu mwema*, God is good."

I smiled with my whole being at the singing women and the beautiful night. How clear and self-assured their voices were, full-throated confidence at being themselves in their own land.

Then the men joined the singing and the sound of all their voices seemed to reach me through the earth. What had Suma said? Music is medicine? I could believe it, there in Udugu's night, because if my body ached I was no longer aware of it.

Babu joined us and sang, too, and soon the music had rinsed my mind of trouble and fear. This might be a gospel, but it was pure Africa in its power. The villagers seemed to know how to sing together to create stupendous sound. All their voices were beautiful, as if no one had ever told them people needed training to sing. They all could and did, not missing a note. With no one consulting anyone, the song changed and with it the air became charged with energy. I felt waves of thrilling vibration throughout my whole body and suddenly I knew without doubt they were consulting their ancestors about Jess and me.

I surrendered to the music and opened my heart. In moments, or was it hours, I felt a ball of energy in my stomach move up to my throat and then explode between my eyes where I saw people with dark faces smile at me as if it were the most natural thing.

Did the others see them, too?

I heard clapping. Curious, I opened my eyes. Women were rising to make a circle around the fire. Two of the younger ones carried babies in slings, one on the hip, the other the back. Some had leafy branches in their hands that they waved as they danced. I saw Watende nod to Babu, who rose and took his place under the fig tree by the great drum. The men who had smaller drums stood and placed them between their thighs. They made a circle around the women. Drumming is too small a word to describe the sound.

I felt I could fly through the air if I tried.

Now I believed Africans had done that. Now I believed they could conjure rain and dry up streams.

Babu's deeper drum became infectious and the dancing

changed. Some made a line and rhythmically jumped from side to side, their bent arms swinging back then forward to clap their hands high. It crossed my mind that this could easily become the next dance craze in America—Europe, too. They could call it the Hop and Clap. Then I remembered clap had two meanings. Maybe they would just call it the Udugu Hop. Others swayed from foot to foot or stomped in place, swinging their arms to the old man's drum. I realized why water had been sprinkled on the ground. It kept down dust from the dancing feet. Soon I knew where the singer, Beyoncé, had learned to bounce her backside. She'd been to Africa and seen young women do what I was seeing now. At home this dance would bring catcalls. In this village, it was dignified.

"In some places it's called Mapouka," Suma said as she did the dance.

Jess looked no more amazed by these incredible events than he was when the towels magically arrived at our hotel. I hoped we were here for more than a whim of mine because when I'd dreamed of Africa, this was it: nature, song, dance, drums, community, magic, hearts beating into the earth.

Suma came and took my hand. "Ngoma, Bibi Maggie. We are welcoming you. Join us." Jess stood and immediately started jumping up and down like a Maasai warrior. The women laughed, covering their mouths shyly. As for me, I was totally uncoordinated, but I knew I had to dance. Assumedly, I was too old to bounce my backside, so I didn't try. The drums lifted my feet and I was no longer a spectator.

For hours beneath the starry night the celebration went on. Only slowly did I conclude it wasn't a party, but a ritual of deep significance—the drums, the dance and song sending the villagers one by one into trance. Once there, some ran about as if possessed, others fell to the ground, writhing, others sat down, their eyes closed, their faces wreathed in smiles.

Even more slowly I realized they intended to continue all night.

However, I was exhausted and by now urgently needed to find the facilities.

I looked around for Suma and whispered my situation in her

ear. Nodding, she lit a torch in the fire and had me follow her into the dark to a smaller hut in back of the compound. It had a thatched roof like the rest. Inside I found a round column about the size of a toilet seat, made of the mud building material they used. A hole in the center of the column extended below the ground. Large leaves on branches stacked in a corner must be their toilet paper. Luckily I had antiseptic wipes in my purse.

Suma beamed proudly, "No long drop," she said.

Desperately I wanted to hold my nose, but resisted for fear of offending her. "Long drop?"

"Usually, only hole in ground. Babu make this when he say you come."

When she left, I lined the rim with leaves before I sat. All in all, I don't think I've ever used a bathroom so fast.

Afterward I told Suma I needed to rest and she led me to our hut. On the way, we passed two men still in western clothes and curiosity got the better of me.

"Udugu must have been prosperous before the drought," I said. "To have … fine clothes."

Suma gave me an odd look. Inside our hut she put the torch in a depression in the mud wall, pointed me to a palm mat and when I got down on it, put out the torch and lay on the cot beside me.

Perhaps I shouldn't have asked about the men's clothes. "I hope I didn't offend you, Suma."

After a pause, she said, "They are second-hand clothes, Bibi."

Startled, I asked, "All of them?"

"All."

"But how did they get to Udugu?"

"You don't know?" Suma sat up. I could see her by the moonlight filtering in.

"I'm sorry. No, I don't."

She seemed to listen to the ngoma still going on. "They are doing the rain making ritual. By now, Babu has brought out special stones that only fall during special rains. He is drinking milk. He is saying sacred prayers and calling the spirits of the rain. For five years he has not done this. I feared my clansmen would kill him for it."

"Kill him?"

"So many of our waganga wa pepo have died in witch killings. When the Germans came in the 1800's, not understanding us they called our healers witches. Then the British Witchcraft Ordinance of 1922 made it illegal for waganga wa pepo to heal. All they could do by law was make rain. Even today, for Babu not to make rain was very serious to us. I was so afraid for him. Naturally, the missionaries are against all uganga, because they don't understand the African way—that there are European diseases and African diseases that can only be cured by the waganga."

Before, it had seemed inappropriate to ask Suma personal questions, but now I couldn't resist.

"Where did you learn English, Suma?"

"In London. My parents took me there when I was a baby. There was a fire and they died. Babu sent for me and raised me here."

"I'm so sorry."

"They are not really dead," she said.

I thought *zombies*, but didn't say it. I knew she meant their spirits were with her. My very presence here, to say nothing of what I'd felt during the dancing and singing, was inexplicable. "Do you miss London?"

Suma looked out at the sky. "No."

She lay down and was so quiet I thought she must have gone to sleep, but when I turned on my side she spoke again. "It is not only Udugu that wears second-hand western clothes, Bibi Maggie. All of Africa does. Rich countries collect their used clothing and sell it to poor countries in bales. Up to a thousand pieces each."

Surely she was mistaken. "The governments do this?"

"International recycling agencies. Wholesalers import the bales. They're mostly Indians and Pakistanis because we Africans don't have that kind of capital. African middlemen purchase the bales on credit without opening them then they sell individual pieces to retailers who sell them to us at city stalls and rural markets. Udugu's clothes come from Mbeya city. Watende's suit could have belonged to a neighbor of yours."

"But doesn't your outfit come from Africa?"

"Yes, but most of the men don't want to wear our own clothes anymore. They don't want to look backward and weak. They want to dress like our … like our conquerors."

She'd used the right word.

"Long ago," she continued, "Watende's great grandfather was a chief, like Kalulu, who dried up the stream. The grandfather's village was not like this. It was a palisaded fort. When attacked, the farmers took refuge in it. He had many ruga-ruga."

"What are they?"

"You would call them pages—boys without family raised in royal courts to be loyal to a chief, except they were warriors."

"Is that where Kony over in Uganda got the idea?"

She didn't answer right away and again I wondered if I'd offended her. "In those days, all chiefs had ruga-ruga."

I changed the subject. "What happened to Watende's ancestor?"

"First the missionaries came then the Germans in 1893 then the British. Like Kalulu, Watende's great grandfather and grandfather were overthrown and killed."

I shook my head. "I don't understand why he wants to dress like westerners then."

"I've thought about this. Perhaps it is a kind of traumatic bonding, like your so-called Stockholm Syndrome. Only his war club reminds Watende his forbears were warrior chiefs."

If that was true, I felt sorry for Watende. "I've seen pictures of the Maasai. They don't wear western clothes."

"They fought for their way of life and won, but their land is being taken and they are forbidden to hunt the lion, except if one kills their cattle. Soon, all they'll be is tourist attractions." Suma's voice was resigned.

The Africa I'd dreamed of didn't exist anymore, not in its original state. I heard the women sing the song the missionaries had taught them: God is good. *Mungu yu mwema, yu mwema, yu mwema.*

Full of grief and useless denial, I fell asleep to the sound of far off thunder in the sky.

Chapter 19

It wasn't a puddle hopper. The FSX Cessna Grand 208 taxied on the runway cut into the African plain, scrub trees before them, the airport's tall pines that looked like upside down cypress behind them. Kevin van der Linden had arranged an executive-style eight-seater.

"I prefer not to fly on single props," Zenia had grumbled to Paul Joseph as they ascended the small flight of steps mounted on the inside of the passenger door. Open the door and a stairway appeared.

"It's a turboprop, a jet," Paul reassured.

She turned up her nose. "Even for jet engines, one is a small number."

When they'd sat in the plane's two rows of plush seats and looked around, he saw her eyes fix on the cockpit and then widen. "Where may I ask is the co-pilot?" she said loudly, pointing at the cockpit's empty right seat. A very young-looking man dressed in white shirt and black pants sat in the left seat. Busily he consulted two charts, one on a clipboard in his lap, the other smaller and draped over the yoke's steering wheel.

No one answered her but Paul Joseph, the others having swiftly learned to leave Zenia to him. "It's not as precarious as it looks."

She stared open-mouthed as the pilot put on earphones, wrote something, fiddled with knobs, rechecked the charts, wrote something, re-rechecked the charts and set the plane in motion, not even looking where he was going when he turned the Cessna from one runway to another. He knew the airport by heart, Paul was sure.

"Don't worry, he's fine," he said to Zenia.

She gasped and gripped the seat as the propeller increased in speed until it no longer resembled a propeller, but waves that left the engine and dissolved into the air.

Trying to divert her attention as the plane took off, he called to Hon. Mahfuru who sat in the first row to her left. "What are the names of those trees at the airport?"

Today Mahfuru wore a khaki tracker shirt and shorts. Paul Joseph was dressed the same, except his pants were long. Zenia, always suitably attired for the occasion, wore khaki, too—long brown skirt with a front pleat, tan short-sleeved shirt with a cowrie necklace she presently gripped tight. He wondered where she'd gotten it and how, even in Africa, her black hair managed to look like she'd stepped from a salon.

"What trees?" Mahfuru asked.

Zenia, who was in front of Joseph, suddenly composed herself and leaned into the aisle. "He means the ones outside the terminal. I noticed them, too. Quite lovely." Feigning extreme politeness was how Zenia hid being terrified. She'd done the same after they were almost caught in his private bathroom at the church. Relieved, Paul Joseph concluded she wouldn't expire before they landed.

"Oh! Ah ..." Mahfuru said.

"They're cypress, I think," said Givn, otherwise known as Kevin, who sat across from Paul. Steve Harris from the consulate sat unassumingly behind them in the third row, though to Paul Joseph he was the most important person there, given his connection to the White House. The Honorable Mahfuru and Kevin had permitted only one member of the press to join them—someone reliable, they said—a Mr. Nzuri, and he sat quietly in the seat beside Steve Harris, bothering no one, a camera in his lap, its lens cap on.

"Not the usual cypress. Their needles grow up and these grow down," Paul said.

Mahfuru looked embarrassed not to know the names of trees at his own airport. "I can tell you about the Mpingo, or African Blackwood. It is our national tree and very hardy. We in the government have a project underway to replenish the population. The Mpingo improves the fertility of the soil; livestock feed on it; it can survive fire."

"If it's hardy, why does it need replenishment?" Zenia asked, her eyes glued on the pilot as his gaze shifted from the sky back to his charts.

"It has been harvested for woodwind instruments, for furniture and carving."

"ConservItion is important," Givn agreed.

Paul Joseph didn't believe Givn meant that.

"Udugu is roughly two hours away as the vulture flies," Mahfuru said, pausing, "You say as the crow flies, do you not?"

"Yes, we do," Steve Harris replied from the back.

"Because this is your first trip," Mahfuru said, "I've asked him to fly over the Selous Game Reserve. It is a protected wildlife area. We'll be there shortly."

"Isn't the Serengeti the most famous?" Zenia asked, tearing her eyes away from the pilot to look at Mahfuru.

"The Selous is the biggest in Africa."

Soon they were flying over a stretch of green, but as the Cessna dipped lower, Paul Joseph realized it was, like much of Africa, earth and parched grass with scattered trees and bushes. It was in the spring that the grass would become a thick long carpet of green, even up close. As they flew lower, animals came into view.

"Oh, my goodness, look!" Zenia said and pointed as two lions took down a water buffalo. "One lion's got his own mouth over the buffalo's mouth. He's suffocating the poor thing."

"They're females," Mahfuru said. "The males have manes. They don't hunt."

"Did I know that?" Zenia said. "Sexist lions." She seemed to be breathing normally, now, and Paul was glad. He didn't want her to be terrified.

Steve leaned forward from the back. "The male fights when another male challenges him. In doing so, he saves the cubs' lives because if a new male wins he kills the cubs since they aren't his."

"Humph!" she said and sat back. "There are human males who'd like to do that, too, take my word."

"Seat belts!" the pilot shouted, causing Zenia's calm to vanish in a scream.

"What's the problem, man?" Mahfuru called.

"Vultures! Hang on!" the pilot replied.

"Vultures?" Zenia shrieked.

The pilot talked frantically as he banked the plane. "In the U.S. it's geese and gulls. In Africa, it's vultures. When they're frightened they dive. And they're big birds. The last thing you want to do in life is fly under a vulture you've just scared. It will go right through the fuselage. Hang on!"

Way too much information, Paul Joseph thought, as earth and sky spun outside the windows, the pilot maneuvering to avoid the birds. Suddenly, the Cessna leveled.

The pilot sighed into the mike. "We missed them."

Zenia said nothing else during the entire flight over the Selous Game Reserve. She displayed no interest in elephants stampeding, spooked by the plane, a herd of wildebeest that seemed to stretch to the horizon, a group of hippo floating in a river over which the plane swooped so low they could see the teeth of one who opened his wide jaws to the sky. She paid no attention to the graceful giraffe emerging from tall trees in which they'd been feeding. All the while, the pilot kept up a stream of less frantic commentary, punctuated by occasional gems from Honorable Mahfuru. Usually, Zenia would have taken notice of such rare bits of information, fanatic for detail that she was. Instead, she remained withdrawn and lost in thought as Africa's wild glories sprawled beneath the plane.   Conversation stopped across the aisle as everyone looked down. In a low voice, Givn exchanged intermittent words now and then with Mahfuru in front of him and Steve Harris behind. After a while it made Paul Joseph feel a bit left out, until he remembered Givn probably had a long acquaintance with both men because of AmerCan. He tried talking with Zenia on their side of the plane, but she didn't respond. Either she was scared to death or trying to hear what was being said on the other side. She didn't speak until the Cessna rose once more into the cloud-ribboned aqua sky.

"Where to now?" she asked, gripping the armrests.

"Next stop Udugu," Mahfuru said.

———

Swiftly the taxi took Ahmed and Ajia from the herbalist's shop near Kariakoo market. Like the airport, its stylized roof was also reminiscent of a canopy of trees no longer there, but still cooling the stalls and mats beneath it where every kind of goods or foodstuff was on sale. Soon they'd reached the Kivukoni area, full of embassies, museums and monuments. Clipped lawns and flowers reappeared. Having never made this trip before, Ahmed hadn't noticed the stark contrast. It gave credence to Ajia's anger at the whites, the wazungu.

The Kilimanjaro embraced them in sleek luxury. They went shopping in its marble arcade, Ajia ravishing in each African outfit she modeled for Ahmed. Overcome with love, he bought heavy gold bracelets for her wrists at the jewelry shop, covered her fingers in gold rings, and lavished precious necklaces, headpieces, and earrings upon her. At a souvenir shop, he bought her a traditional two-knot elephant-hair bracelet, a rarity actually made of elephant hair, yet it was cheap compared to the gold. According to legend, these animals were a bridge between heaven and earth, body and spirit. He put it on her wrist with the gold ones and slid the knots to adjust it, saying "Hereby I seal in the elements of fire, wind, sun and water to give you strength and good luck." Ajia smiled and said, "You know this? You are superstitious after all." One of its restaurants overlooking the Indian Ocean that Ajia called African. They had an early lunch under its potted palms, Ajia wearing one of the silk scarves he'd bought for her. They ordered another cab and filled it with a trunkful of her new possessions.

Instead of heading for Toure drive, Ahmed told the cab to turn left from Ali Hassan Mwinyi Road onto Malik drive.

Ajia looked surprised, but Ahmed smiled. "You said I should visit my mother, so we will." He hadn't anticipated the distress on her face.

"I can't. I am disgraced. She will hate me."

"She won't hate you." Ahmed said, determined not to entertain doubt. At some point, they would need his mother's help.

Ajia pleaded, but Ahmed ignored her, giving the Upanga district address to the taxi, which soon enough pulled up to the high white wall surrounding his mother's home. Columns topped by white globes separated the wall into long sections and each had four rows of glass cubes embedded in the upper half. Ahmed was proud of having bought this spacious former colonial home for his mother. He'd paid for this one-story gem with a single bonus from Silverman Alden, after making a trade worth a hundred million.

The taxi entered past the old guard house, pulled into the spacious driveway, and stopped before the home's three columned arches. Its red tile roof extended beyond the walls on all sides, creating a covered walkway. Potted ferns accented the large latticed windows. A garden surrounded the house. On one side was a detached garage.

Ahmed went to help Ajia out of the taxi, and he heard, "Ahmed, *mwanangu!*"

His mother appeared, draping an embroidered chiffon scarf over her head in the traditional Muslim way, to cover her hair when out of the house. Yes, he was her dear son.

"Shikamoo, Mama!"

Ajia lagged behind as he ran to her. They embraced, kissed each other's cheeks then his mother held his face in her hands.

"Karibu, Ahmed. Will you stay?"

"No. Ninasafiri." I am traveling.

A pretty Swahili servant girl came from the house and, looking for luggage, took possession of Ajia's trunk and bags. Only then did his mother notice he wasn't alone.

"Ahmed, who is this girl?"

Taking a deep breath, he turned and held his hand out to Ajia, saying, "Mama, this is the woman I love, the one who will bear your grandchildren one day. This is Ajia."

Ahmed's mother gave him a sharp look. It was wrong to meet his fiancée in this way, brought by her son, unaccompanied by a member of her own family. It was not done to announce he would marry a total stranger, whose family was unknown to his. Nevertheless, his mother's face broke into smiles, as he'd known it would.

"Karibu, nzuri binti." Welcome beautiful daughter. "Assalamu 'alaykum" Peace be upon you. His mother held out her arms and Ajia, plainly relieved, went into them saying, "Wa alaykum us salaam. Asante, pleased to meet you." Hand in hand they went into the house, Ahmed following in happiness.

Like Arabs who'd immigrated to Tanzania for centuries, his family had undergone Swahilization, abandoning their own culture and language in favor of that of their new home—just as immigrants to America did, but his mother had a little of Egypt here. The living room's white glass chandelier still hung above the round wood table, carved camels serving as legs bearing its weight. Plush chairs and embroidered sofas ranged around it. Imitations of Egyptian funerary jars sat on side tables, one topped with the head of a dog, another the head of a cat. Calla lilies spilled from a large dark vase. A long papyrus painted with hieroglyphs and an image of the goddess, Isis, hung on the wall. Crowned with the throne symbol, she wore the vulture headdress, an ankh in one hand, a scepter in the other. She had his mother's face. It was one of his father's wedding presents.

"Bibi Hassan, where shall I place these?" the servant girl asked his mother, one arm full of Ajia's bags, the other dragging her trunk.

Ahmed said, "It is her dowry."

His mother clapped. "Her dowry? Naomba kuona, Ajia?" May I see?

When Ajia nodded, his mother said, "Lay them all out in my room."

His mother led Ajia to the sofa and sat beside her. Ahmed sat near in a chair. The houseman entered the living room, carrying a tea tray, which he set on the camel table. He made an elaborate ritual of filling three cups. Ahmed could smell its masala spice.

"Such a pretty girl, Ahmed," his mother said, making Ajia blush.

He knew his mother brimmed with questions she wouldn't ask until they'd had at least one sip of tea.

When all were served, she raised her cup and said, "Afya!" Good health.

Before Ahmed and Ajia could reply, before anyone could take a single sip, someone screamed and they all rose, his mother spilling her tea onto the carpet.

"Msaada!" Help!

It was the servant girl. Her screams came from his mother's room.

"Stay!" Ahmed ordered. Grabbing one of the vases, he dumped out its flowers and water and headed for the master bedroom. Ajia and his mother didn't stay. They were behind Ahmed when he reached the door.

No one was there but the Swahili servant girl, pressed against the wall in his mother's gold-trimmed room, staring. On the white bed and the white chaise, Ajia's finery was beautifully laid. The servant stared at something on the floor—something curved and ceramic. It was an animal's horn, the open end plugged with cloth.

"Dawa za uchawi!" the girl cried, *bad medicine*. She thought the horn was witchcraft.

"No, no," Ajia assured, easing by him into the room. "Ni si uchawi," it is not witchcraft. She grabbed the horn, and finding her purse, put it in. She sounded amused, almost laughing. "Ni tu souvenir."

Ahmed realized what a good actress Ajia was. He knew it wasn't a souvenir. He should have taken the package from her that she got from Babu Enzo, the herbalist—insisted she discard it as soon as she got in the cab. Ajia herself had called Enzo an mchawi, a witchdoctor. Though she smiled, Ajia's eyes were round with worry. Would his mother believe her?

"It's just a souvenir," Ahmed assured his mother, still at the door, unmasked horror on her face. He went and put his arm around Ajia. "But, Mama, we should go. We don't really have time for tea. We are traveling."

His mother entered the bedroom, looked down on Ajia's beautiful clothes then up at Ahmed. "Yes, mwanangu, you should go. Allah go with you." Now, he didn't dare ask if he could leave Ajia's dowry there while they were on safari.

Ajia repacked her clothes because the servant girl refused. When a new taxi came, they got in. Ahmed kissed his mother goodbye, her face now blank, not full of joy like at first. As soon as they pulled away, he said, "Ajia, give me that thing!" but she wouldn't.

"You won't need it!" he insisted. "I've made plans."

"When I see you have good plans, I'll throw it away. I promise, Ahmed."

Ahmed sighed and gave in, wondering if his mother would now refuse to approve their marriage. If so, he'd take Ajia to America and all this nonsense of Certificates of No Impediment to marry, and witchcraft, would be over. Ajia couldn't refuse to go. They'd made love. She could no longer command the respect of a Swahili groom's family or the dowry of a virgin bride from anyone but him and Ahmed was thrilled. Taking up with anyone else would mean risking being called a *jamvi la wageni*, visitor's mat, or a *dala dala*, a public bus.

The cab pulled up to the Oyster Bay Hotel and moments later their guide arrived. They had set no meeting time other than *this afternoon* because unlike westerners, Africans weren't obsessed by clocks. Ahmed simply called before he left The Kilimanjaro and the guide said he was coming right now, *sasa hivi*, though that was unlikely. The safari would begin whenever they met. As often happened in Africa though, both parties, sensing each other, arrived at about the same time.

Very few tourists went to the Mbeya region in southwest Tanzania to go on safari. That's where Udugu was. Normally, tourists flew into Kilimanjaro's airport, about 300 miles to the north, and stayed at a luxury campsite in Arusha before embarking. Ahmed had arranged to leave from Dar es Salaam. He'd been forced to book with a firm that offered private safaris and itineraries designed to taste, however odd the destination, like Mbeya. Not that it didn't have a few attractions.

But why climb the Mbeya peak when one could go north and climb Mount Kilimanjaro, the highest in Africa? Why visit Mbeya's Ngozi Crater instead of the spectacular Ngorongoro Crater, a UNESCO World Heritage Site with its abundance of wildlife and culture? With the spectacular Selous Game Reserve to the southeast of here, why go to Mbeya?

The standard tour was about seven thousand US, the luxury version eleven thousand. People like him who wanted to go tramping off alone into the wild paid much more. With Ajia coming, Ahmed was doubly glad they would travel in customized Landcruisers, retire to sumptuous beds—he tried not to think about the beds—reside in tents with drapes, toilets and vanities, and be served fine wine from crystal glasses in the middle of the African bush.

The guide got out of his Landcruiser and at Ahmed's request began loading Ajia's trunk into the vehicle. As Ahmed went inside to get his suitcase and pay the bill, Ajia sat in the front seat, her horn from the mchawi, the witchdoctor, rewrapped and placed in her new safari rucksack. Before leaving his mother's house, she'd changed into long brown pants, a matching T-shirt and lightweight hooded jacket.

They were flying into Ruaha National Park, where they'd camp for the night. From there they'd begin a walking safari tomorrow morning. By the time they reached Udugu, Paul Joseph's party should be well settled in.

Chapter 20

It took effort for Jess to focus on his body, since he was not used to being in physical form. Focus was necessary, though, because when his attention wandered, his being sought freedom. The slightest lapse and he slipped into the space between materiality and the other realms, blissfully at peace, omniscient, omnipotent, no desires but existence itself. It was this loss of burdens, the limitless joy, which made near-death experiencers reluctant to resume life's sorrows, unless compelled by a strong duty or powerful tie.

The body was a heavy thing and cumbersome, its function to limit mobility like the mind's true function was to limit perception. Most human beings had no idea of their true powers, in spite of what he'd told them two thousand years ago, *whoever believes in me will do the works I have been doing, and they will do even greater things than the*se. That almost no Christians believed the words of Christ was something he often joked about with the disciples. They themselves hadn't understood this fully until after they died. Only one of them was on earth right now, but he was too young to be of help in this, humanity's turning point.

Jess looked with love on his mother, Maggie, sitting against the side of a hut next to Suma, Babu's granddaughter. After breakfast and morning chores, the women gathered there with their babies and toddlers to chat in the shade. Maggie did not remember her life as Mary of Nazareth, or their reunion in the realm she called heaven. She didn't remember their decision that she incarnate as Maggie Johnson to be his physical mother once again. Of necessity her mind was strong, since on earth she needed the ability to reason, but her mind's earthly strength blocked her awareness of truth. Getting her to Udugu had almost killed her, as a result. Of course, Maggie Johnson wouldn't have actually died. Nothing does. However, her physical presence was needed on earth at this time.

The ngoma from the night before hadn't ended. This was merely a pause. When it resumed, Jess would reveal himself to the people. Their response would be crucial. Not only their progress, but that of millions depended on it.

Watende had called a meeting of village elders with Paul Joseph and his guests who were on their way here. It would take place tomorrow. Jess must reawaken the souls of the villagers before Paul Joseph arrived.

To prepare, he'd walked the stone-lined dirt path to Babu's compound, sat under his sprawling fig tree, closed his eyes and slipped into the space between heaven and earth. It took determination to bring intention into that realm where problems could not exist—there being no *self* or *not-self* to argue with one another. Swiftly, Jess's consciousness entered the gray aliveness from which all manifestations come. Unbounded, all knowing, all loving, he could contact anyone. He could calm the seas, command the wind, the land, the animals. What he couldn't do was command a human being. On earth, free will reigned. However, unless their minds were fully closed—unless physicality had totally blinded them—he could touch human hearts. In this state, if he formed the smallest intention, infinite power was at his command. It was the realm from which miracles came.

In his earthly self, Jess had a great sympathy with Africa—sprawled on the world's cross as it was—despised, abused, rejected, suffering, as he once was. Yet Africa was a repository of humanity's lost spiritual power, like he'd been as Christ. Bleeding, dying, much of this land had not lost touch with God, nor had most indigenous cultures and some lands in the East. There was one important difference. He'd come to Africa rather than to India, for instance, because many here still knew they could fly, dry up streams, move mountains to the sea. Africa had no worldly power. Its power was in the the unmanifest and the unbound. Meekly, its people and those like them—whether aborigines in Australia, Mayans in Mexico, or yoga practitioners in New York—would inherit the earth, if he succeeded.

He pictured the villagers in their huts, in their fields, at their well, at their work—pictured the beautiful naked babies, the women in colorful cloths, the men all dressed like westerners until last night. In his mind, he saw Babu in his hut, heard him softly playing his nsanza with his thumbs. Babu was using his own spirit to help Jess.

Soon it was as if a generator had descended on the village of Udugu. Instead of emitting electricity, it vibrated joy. The babes began laughing and looking in the air. Some crawled in Jess's direction. People who'd been worried paused to notice the children, a breeze, the beauty of the wide sky. Smiles broke on faces though no one but Jess and Babu knew why.

Joined as he and the village were, Jess asked the God they called Mungu to help them start humanity's transition—here in Tanzania, where Thomas Leakey's Mitochondrial Eve had lain for 200,000 years; here in Africa, where humans began.

He sensed Babu approach the tree, heard him beat the ngoma drum. Opening his eyes, Jess saw the villagers joyfully coming. All except Watende who looked unhappily at them. How could Jess explain to him a reality beyond words? The mind, small and fearful, seeking reason, couldn't grasp or even glimpse spirit's vastness. All earth's words in all its languages were inadequate. Truth could only be experienced, not analyzed or understood. Once experienced, no explanation was needed. That's why the Tao Te Ching said, "*You cannot know the Tao, but you can be it.*" That's why the Bible said, "*Be still and know that I am God.*" Human beings had forgotten the literal truth behind these words.

Grabbing leafy tree branches to wave, the women made their usual circle and began singing the song they'd sung before: God is good. *Mungu yu mwema, yu mwema, yu mwema.*

The men brought their drums and began drumming. Soon the music and the dance would send many to the place where Jess was. From there they could do anything, if they believed they could. They could fly through the air. They could bring rain.

Jess wanted far more of them. He wanted them to raise a collective energy strong enough to spread and linger on the earth, to be taken up by others and sent out wider and wider, countering the coming darkness with light. If he succeeded, it would lift earth's low-level energy of fear, destruction and hate, raise the vibration of all humanity. The kingdom would come.

He smiled to recognize his mother, Maggie, among the women. She had discarded her American clothes and her American hairdo. If he hadn't known better, Jess would have thought he was looking at a woman born and bred in Udugu. She left the women and joined him under the fig tree. Jess could tell her earthly mind was in full control.

"Why does this all seem so real," she asked, "when I know full well it can't be?" All morning he'd been trying to reach her spirit, but the way was blocked by her logical thoughts, her spirit imprisoned by her mind, like a giant who imagined itself constrained by cobwebs.

"You changed your clothes," he said, to avoid answering her question.

"I don't want to wear those things anymore."

"Darkest Africa isn't dark?"

She clapped her hands. "Oh, no, Jess! It's full of life. Just look at the people. They're beaming."

Jess smiled. "Yes, I see."

"I feel like a queen in these clothes."

"An African queen?"

"Yes! I hate to admit it, but in America that's what I secretly wanted to be—a Jackie Kennedy, a Grace Kelly. Fat chance! But here, Jess, that's what I am. Don't you see how they're treating me? I know it's probably because of you, but—"

"No, Mother, it's you."

Mary of Nazareth, presently known as Maggie Johnson, grinned in reply. In Jerusalem she'd been mistreated, too, forced to give birth in a stable.

Jess took her hand, knowing physical contact would increase his chance of reaching her soul. He pictured her as he'd last seen her when his mortal life ended two thousand years ago—on Golgotha, weeping with Mary Magdalene and the mother of Zebedee's sons.

How beautiful she was to him then, how beautiful now, all her power imprisoned in a twenty-first century mind. If he could release it, she might make the difference.

Nearby a woman shivered and rolled on the packed earth in the custom of this tribe when they felt spirit. Missionaries had weakened them by declaring them wrong. Jess must show them they were right. They must only abandon fear—of each other when things went wrong, of displeasing their ancestors who, now with God, loved them without reservation. They must trust the one to whom they sang. The drumming stopped and Babu came to the woman on the ground. He and the others surrounded her and intensified their song.

> Wee sogoraga wee
> Wee kumungelo wee
> Wee garagara wee

"Jess, do you know what they're singing?" his mother asked.

"Yes, they are saying, 'Go off running with pepo; follow the angel leading you; roll over the ground after pepo is free.'"

"What's pepo again?" Maggie said.

Jess smiled. "It's their word for spirit. Close your eyes, Madre. Concentrate on the song. Then tell me what you feel."

She closed her eyes. After a while she opened them, smiling. "It's amazing. Their voices are so … strong; it's like you can feel every note in your whole body. You just stop thinking and kind of vibrate to the music."

Jess nodded. The sacred work had begun.

Chapter 21

Ariel Fubini had always hoped something extraordinary would happen in her life and her dream was coming true, though not in a way she could have anticipated. Thrilled, overwhelmed, and slightly nauseous in the packed, hot and humid terminal, she stood next to her new friend, Zach, fanning herself with her ticket as she tried to get Wi-Fi so she could text Kyle she'd arrived. No Wi-Fi, no bars. Did international roaming have to be arranged in advance? Dejected, she kept trying, while taking in the sights and sounds of Dar es Salaam's airport: women in imposing traditional long dresses, men in chocolate brown and olive suits, foreigners all dressed casually. Did Tanzania feel disrespected by its visitors? Ariel decided to change her short khakis for long pants as soon as she could.

Zach, oblivious to his surroundings, was focused on getting them to Udugu, where his wife must have arrived by now.

"Udugu airplane?" he kept repeating.

"Kesho asubuhi," the man behind the desk kept replying, until another agent with beautiful black skin came and translated that the next flight to Udugu took off tomorrow morning.

Zach, no longer her easy-going seat mate, visibly tensed. "A charter then?"

"Booked already," the translator said.

Zach blew out air. "What about later?"

The agent smiled agreeably, while shaking his head. "Charter pilots do not fly at night, sir. Never on nights like this."

"Whyever not?"

"They use VFR, visual flight rules, impossible in the jungle on most nights. They do not wish to crash into inky water or black ground instead of soaring into our African skies."

"Well, can we rent or hire a car to drive to Udugu?"

"Yes, of course," the man said, "but hiring a reliable driver may be difficult before tomorrow. As for a rental, the drive is more than 850 km or 500 miles over unfamiliar, unlit roads with wild animals. It would take perhaps fifteen hours if all went well, but you have less than four hours of daylight left. At night, it is too dangerous. Even if you reach Udugu, the village will be asleep."

Zach looked more distressed. "What about a bus?"

"Yes, in the morning. The Sumry line has two at 6:30 and 6:45 am from Ubungo Bus Terminal."

"You mean there's no way we can get from here to the Mbeya region today?"

The agent smiled gently. "No way."

Zach's lips pursed, not something Ariel suspected they often did. "Well, then, can you recommend a hotel that will arrange transport for us? A good hotel?"

"The best is Oyster Bay, but it has only eight rooms. If you don't have a reservation, I suggest you phone. There is also the Transit Motel Airport 3 miles away. No frills."

Zach said thank you, offered Ariel his arm, and led her through the airport maze to collect their luggage from the public hallway where it had been placed. Taxi drivers besieged them when they emerged from the terminal.

"Udugu? Udugu?" Zach said and the drivers raised their eyebrows and politely stared at him as if he was insane then left to surround the next arriving party.

"It doesn't look like we're getting to Udugu today, Zach," Ariel said, beginning to feel the effects of jet lag as well as nausea. A night's sleep in a bed sounded a lot better to her than bouncing along dirt roads all night.

Someone grabbed their bags and they looked up to see a slim, elegant man in a neat white shirt and dark pants, smiling. "Udugu early tomorrow morning. Hotel now?"

Ariel tugged Zach's sleeve like she tugged her father's sleeve. "Call the Oyster Bay, okay, Zach? If it's the best, your wife might have stayed there. Maybe we could get some information? And ..." She didn't want to sound like a wimp, though that's exactly how she felt … "I think I need to sleep. Guess it's being preggers and all."

"Oh! Yes, of course, Ariel. You need to sleep." He took out his own cell, for which he'd apparently arranged roaming, and located the hotel.

"Hello, Oyster Bay? I'm at the airport. I don't have a reservation, but do you have two rooms by any chance?"

Ariel could hear the man on the other line raise his voice in disbelief that someone would call from the airport and expect to find two rooms at a hotel such as theirs. Zach colored slightly as he listened. "Sorry, just thought I'd check."

She heard the other man mumble distressed apologies, then heard a loud, "Wait!"

Zach looked at her, his expression implying they might be in luck. "Two guests are checking out unexpectedly?" he asked. "Is there something wrong?" Then he said into the phone, "Whaaat? You're not kidding? Yes, we have a taxi. Hold both rooms in the names of Dunlop and Rossi—"

"Fubini," Ariel corrected.

"Dunlop and Fubini. We'll be there in—" he looked at the taxi driver who mouthed a reply "—less than an hour."

Zach hung up, looking troubled, his fingers flying on the cell. Ariel drew closer to see what he was searching for. He lowered the phone so she could watch. He surfed to an American newspaper website and paused at the screaming headline:

SHOOTINGS REPORTED AT COLLEGE ANTI-GUN RALLY.
DOZENS FEARED DEAD.

"Dozens?" Ariel whispered, reading.

Zach put his arm around her. "Don't be afraid. It's the end of the world, at least as we know it."

"Dozens?" Ariel cried again and started weeping.

Looking sympathetic, the taxi driver urged them to follow him to the cab. They passed outside beneath strange cypress trees with upside down needles at Dar es Salaam airport, its roof resembling the canopy of a forest long gone, Africans watching the mzungu named Ariel Fubini—at birth known as Ariel Rossi—cry.

Chapter 22

As the Cessna descended, Zenia Dunlop glimpsed a strip of dirt carved from the jungle green and frantically speculated about what it was—surely not their landing place. To her dismay, the Cessna banked, heading straight toward it and lined up. Miss this pencil-thin so-called runway a few feet in either direction and a wing would shear, a wheel crumple. Why in the world had she come on this primitive voyage? She closed her eyes. *Oh, yes, the White House.* After hearing gossip that a limo showed up at Joseph's bungalow, Zenia had someone call Lily Joseph, his wife. Her name wasn't really Lily, it was Delilah—the name of the temptress who cut off Samson's hair in the Bible. She'd changed it when she married a minister. Zenia knew because she'd had her investigated. Drunk as usual, Delilah cum Lily told the caller where Paul Joseph was and the news sent a bolt of jealousy through Zenia, making her concoct this plan. She gripped the seat and silently prayed, "God, I expect you to keep me safe," as the Cessna set down and jostled to a stop.

She opened her eyes and saw a small swarm of children stream from the nearby bush, shouting in glee. Since she couldn't have children, Zenia had made herself stop wanting them, had avoided contact with them. The exuberance of these barefoot, poverty-stricken little ones coming toward the plane surprised her—some of the youngest naked, most dressed in what looked like third-hand clothes. What did they have to be happy about?

"The local greeting party," Paul Joseph said, as the pilot opened the door, letting the steps down.

"Yes, I see," she said.

The pilot got out and offered a hand to his passengers as they descended. The children crowded around, saying *Hamjambo* and singing some joyful welcome song.

"Good flight, man," Kevin said to the pilot.

Paul Joseph peered toward the trees. "Not sure where the grownups are. I'll help you get the luggage out."

"We'll all help," said Honorable Mahfuru. Steve Harris from the consulate, Mr. Nzuri the reporter, and the children followed them to the back of the plane, but Kevin stayed where he was, luggage-handling apparently not something he was eager for.

Though it was only 11 am, Zenia felt she was melting under the sun's intense heat. Her clothes soaked in sweat, she headed for the shade of a tree.

"Be careful of snakes!" Paul Joseph called.

She stopped and returned to Kevin, pulling her safari hat down to shade her eyes. She'd use the chance to learn more about Kevin van der Linden of AmerCan and, as he spoke, listen for lies. Zenia did this with all people. Rather than tell Zach about the pelvic infection that left her fallopian tubes scarred beyond repair, she'd let him wait for children, which is how she knew people lied.

"So, you must be eager for this trip," she said to the man Paul Joseph called Givn.

He gazed at her. "Oy am. Ever since Bestor Joseph told me the si-tyoo-I-shun."

Instantly, her head hurt. "Excuse me," she said and went toward the men getting luggage, calling, "May I help?" Two of the children ran and took her hands.

Paul Joseph pointed to her aquamarine Henk carry-on, but immediately one of the children swooped it up and balanced it on her head. They did the same with the rest of the luggage, two boys carrying Zenia's large, made-to-order Henk.

Givn said goodbye to the pilot as Paul Joseph led their disordered safari toward Udugu, the children laughing, chattering and holding their new guests' hands. Zenia resisted the warm glow that tried to spread through her. She couldn't have a child. A whorl of dust blew up, enveloped them and went on, leaving the new arrivals grumbling and coughing. The children turned their backs to it and made no complaint.

When they reached the village, no one was in sight. She thought she heard the trace of a drum somewhere, but all she saw were empty houses, an occasional chicken, or sleeping dog. One enclave of brick and metal-roofed buildings seemed to hold the church, given the cross above the doorway. The rest of Udugu consisted of round or square mud huts with thatched roofing. Dirt paths separated them, bordered by patchy greenery.

"Where's the chief?" Zenia asked Paul Joseph as they walked.

"Tanzania doesn't allow that word since the cultural revolution. They call them chairmen now. I don't know where he is. Usually, the whole village greets me."

He led the way toward the enclave of small brick buildings and when Zenia entered the one she was told would be hers, it felt like she'd stepped into a blast furnace. How could it be hotter indoors than out? She thought of the metal roof and stepped outside, followed by the two children who seemed to have adopted her—a boy in a torn, too-large soccer shirt and black short pants and a toddler in a grimy green shift, probably his younger sister because when she cried he picked her up.

Where was everyone?

Alone she walked past the empty huts, each surrounded by parched vegetation. Zenia wondered if this was Africa's version of a drought, because she sensed a single good rain would make the parched greenery overgrow the village.

"My name Kilomo," the boy said. "My sister Koko. Who you?"

Apparently, Paul Joseph had been teaching them English. "I'm Zenia."

He held out his hand. "Hello, Mama Zenia."

Zenia flinched, then shook his hand. "Where is everyone, Kilomo?"

"*Nojoo*," he said, *Come*, and picked up his sister Koko.

Zenia followed him through the village. He stopped at a hut and retrieved a large green plastic bucket nearly as big as he was. "I fetch water soon," he said and led her to a stone-lined path where he put his bucket and his sister down. He raised his hands to his mouth, said, "Sssshhh," and motioned her to follow him through the trees. Soon she saw another enclave, this one of thatched-roof mud huts. All the adults of the village seemed to be gathered there, sitting silently on the ground in an unbroken circle, their legs extended, feet touching the next one's feet. Zenia had never seen anything like it. Under a tree behind the circle sat a boy who didn't look African to her, maybe Arabic. He had very curly black hair. His clothes seemed unnaturally colored. She felt peace when she gazed at him. Who was he? Next to him sat a woman. Nearby an old man softly played a thumb instrument of some kind.

In the circle, one of the women exclaimed and, as Zenia watched, rose into the air.

Zenia rubbed her eyes.

She looked again.

Sure enough, the woman rested comfortably in a sitting position a good two feet off the ground. Impossible. Next a boy in long pants left the circle and flew up to a hut's thatched roof.

Zenia saw it. At least she thought she had.

Certainly it couldn't have happened. She must be hallucinating. Before her eyes, the floating woman descended back to the ground and the boy vanished from the roof.

It must be the jet lag, the heat, or both.

In her hiding place, Zenia blinked and pinched herself.

Suddenly, the people began singing in their native tongue as the old man softly played his lilting music. The sound burst into Zenia and trembled in her veins.

From behind her, she heard, "What is this?"

She turned and saw Paul Joseph, Honorable Mahfuru, Kevin van der Linden and Steve Harris, march into the enclave and tower over the magical scene.

————

Paul Joseph's worst fears had come true. He'd known something was wrong when the people hadn't met his plane, only the children. That had never happened before. Thank God Mr. Nzuri, the reporter, wasn't with them. He'd wandered off to take pictures of the landscape. Paul Joseph didn't want photos taken of the whole village sitting in their heathen circle once again.

The old man rose and bowed. "Welcome, Pastor Joseph."

Betrayed, Paul Joseph glowered. Five years ago, when he first came to Udugu, Babu was the healer and the chief, revered by the entire village, which he regularly led astray in Godless rituals using his native drums, his potions and tribal songs. With God's help, Paul Joseph had converted the village to Christianity, all except Babu and his granddaughter. Grateful they hadn't interfered with the church, Paul Joseph calmed the village's early anger when Babu stopped his so-called pepo work. It was only because of Paul Joseph that the village hadn't run Babu off.

"What are you up to, Babu? I thought we'd agreed you would stop practicing your ... your healing sessions."

Serenely, Babu replied, "Perhaps you misunderstood. I did not promise this."

Paul Joseph saw that Kevin van der Linden looked far from pleased. "Yislikes! Troi-ing to turn this congregation beck to pagan ways, are ya?"

Paul was sure no one understood what he'd said. "Let me handle this," he whispered to Givn.

Babu smiled. "We join in fellowship." He held out his arms. "Be with us,"

The invitation left Paul Joseph speechless. He was dumbfounded that the entire village still sat there, as if their pastor hadn't arrived. Some weren't even looking in his direction, but at Babu and the boy beside him. Strange boy. Sausage curls. Western clothes. Something indecipherable about him. Not from Udugu, certainly. Whatever the reason for his presence here, it couldn't be good. Otherwise, why did Paul Joseph feel like shrinking from his gaze?

"I insist you end this!" Paul Joseph demanded.

No on replied.

A few of the women smiled kindly at him. Most gazed off into the trees, or at Babu, or the boy.

Finally, Babu stood, reached beneath his robe and withdrew a folded piece of paper. "Who is this gentleman?" he asked kindly, motioning toward Mahfuru.

Infuriated to be questioned instead of obeyed, Paul Joseph reddened and introduced Honorable Mahfuru, Givn and Steve Harris. "Steve's from the American consulate and Givn, I mean Kevin, is with a firm that wants to help the village and Mr. Mahfuru is from the government."

"Ah!" Babu said and, walking respectfully toward Mahfuru, handed him the paper. "Please, sir, if you will."

Honorable Mahfuru opened the paper and read it.

"What is it?" Paul Joseph asked.

"It is a *kihali*," Mahfuru said.

"And jest what is that?" asked Givn.

"It is a certificate from CHAWATIATA, the government organization that licenses traditional healers. Babu is licensed with the district cultural office and is authorized to heal."

"Legally, I may continue, is that correct?" he asked Mahfuru.

Mahfuru's face became an apology as he said to Paul Joseph, "That is correct."

Watende who'd arrived leaned on his war club. "What is the date of that kihali?"

Mahfuru glanced at it. "Last month."

"Well ... well, don't you 'ave one, Watende?" Givn asked. "Aren't you the boss here?"

Watende shook his head then shot a look at Babu. "Most healers do not bother with the kihali." Then he frowned at Mahfuru. "It costs too much."

Why, against all logic, did Tanzania keep licensing these charlatans? No amount of reasoning had persuaded the government to ban the practice of uganga.

Paul sensed the attention of the boy with sausage curls. Gathering courage, he met the boy's gaze. "Who's this?"

"A great one from afar," Babu said.

Joseph sneered, though the ridiculous thought to kneel and pray had actually crossed his mind. "Are you responsible for this ... this heathenry?"

The boy smiled like an angel. "Yes, I hope so in part."

It incensed Paul Joseph to be confronted with a disarming smile when his authority was being destroyed.

"Who are you?" Paul Joseph demanded.

A woman sitting beside the boy stood. "Who are you, is what I'd like to know, coming here and disturbing everybody?"

Paul Joseph frowned. "You're not from this village. You're American!"

"Yes, I am, and this is my son. I'll thank you to be respectful when you speak to him!"

Several of the people held their hands out to Jess and began talking all at once. "He is Mungu, Pastor Joseph! This is Mungu!"

"Bliksem en donder!" Givn swore.

Aghast, Paul Joseph cried, "God? You're telling me this boy is God?"

A lone woman who'd been smiling turned away from Joseph and lifted her voice in thrilling song, "*Mungu yu mwema, yu mwema, yu mwema.*" The others turned from Joseph, too, and in call and response fashion, answered: *Yu mwema, yu mwema, yu mwema.*

————

From behind her tree, Zenia wept, the song was so beautiful. Could whatever caused such singing be bad?

She watched Paul Joseph storm away, Kevin and Steve following. The Honorable Mahfuru lingered and joined in the song.

Zenia had no idea what had just happened. She was only sure that, for Paul Joseph, it was a defeat. Not a great start on her road to the White House or, she suspected, his AmerCan plans. She dried her eyes, crying not being her thing.

Kilomo picked up his water pail. "We go, Mama Zenia. The water is far away."

She frowned. "How far?"

"In your minutes, thirty, I think," he said.

"My goodness. Roundtrip?"

"One way." He started off, Koko behind him, waving.

Zenia wondered if Kilomo meant to fill his pail and, if so, how he could possibly carry it that far. She sighed and left to find Paul Joseph. It was too soon for him to give up.

————

Paul Joseph was so befuddled, felt so angry and confused, he sat alone in his church and put his head in his hands. Mahfuru, Givn and Steve had discreetly left him alone with his embarrassment. What had happened? How would he counter it? Why did his plans always go wrong? A few months' absence and the village had not only returned to its native religious worship, they were calling some strange kid God. Incredible! How could they so easily be led astray, unless ... he looked up at the wooden cross a villager had carved, savage but beautiful ... unless they'd never believed his message from the start, only pretended to adopt the Bible in exchange for the good things his mission had brought.

The conclusion was obvious. Once again he'd failed. Quite dramatically, this time—in front of an emissary from the White House, in front of Kevin who thought he had sway over this village. Rick Warren succeeded at everything. Paul Joseph flopped at everything, even converting a poor village like this.

When Zenia came to console him, he felt so humiliated she'd seen it, too, he wished he could disappear. How had his White House triumph ended in abject humiliation in this backward village?

"Don't be upset, Paul. I'm sure things will work out."

Bending to put her hand across his shoulder caused her breast to graze his face. Inflamed, Paul Joseph sat straight, looked around the church he'd built for the faithless village that had abandoned him, grabbed her hand and led her outside into the bush. He was sick and tired of doing everything right and having everything go wrong.

She gasped. "Where are we going?"

He didn't answer. He desired this woman and would have her.

Parting the foliage, watching where he stepped, he headed toward a place he'd visited many times before when he wished for solitude during his visits here—a particularly quiet, secluded spot where exotic flowers bloomed. It was far enough away from Udugu that they wouldn't be disturbed. When he reached it monkeys chattered, birds called at their sudden arrival. He stopped and pulled her to him.

She didn't resist. He knew she wanted him, too. It was clear from what happened on the plane. "Whatever will Lily think of us if she finds out?" Zenia said.

"Probably the same thing Zach will."

Breathing hard from the trek, Zenia looked deep into his eyes, stepped back, looked around, pulled open the snaps of her tan short-sleeved shirt, lifted her bra and bared her breasts to him and the jungle. Surprisingly large, they had small, pert brownish nipples that pointed slightly out. He found the contrast intoxicating.

"Well, come and get them," she said.

Instantly Paul Joseph did, putting his lips on one and his hand on the other then switching lips and hand. She held her cowrie necklace up and standing perfectly still stared down at his manipulations and kissings, then up at the trees, then down again and began saying, "Oh God, Oh God," sweat soon pouring off her breasts in the sultry heat.

Paul Joseph reached under her long tan skirt with the pleat in front. She hoisted it up out of his way.

Soon she said, "Let me see it, Paul. Let me see it."

She always said this and he'd concluded it was a kind of fetish for her. Paul Joseph unzipped his pants and revealed his glory. That's what she called it, anyway.

Again she became perfectly still and for a while just stared. Finally she said, "I'm ready."

He took off his jacket and spread it on the ground. She lay on it against the log he'd put there long ago, as if anticipating this. Bending her legs, she lifted them and bizarrely opened them wide.

Paul Joseph had never seen a woman behave like this. At first he'd found it strange, even off-putting, that she would dictate his sexual behavior in such detail—first her breasts then under her skirt, then he must show himself, after which she'd lie down and present herself in precisely this odd way. It was lewdly mechanical, but so potent that since Zenia first did it, he'd fantasized about her night and day.

She had instructions for the act, itself, too, which proved spectacularly effective for them both. Eagerly, Paul Joseph lay atop her and carried them out, the monkeys chattering when she closed her mouth and, to keep from being overheard, screamed deep and long in her throat.

Paul Joseph made a guttural groan, too. His church might be in hock, he might have a drunkard for a wife, his mission might have failed, but he was screwing Zenia Dunlop's brains out in the African jungle—the kind of woman who, if God didn't hate him, should be his.

They lay, holding each other, unmindful of the darkening sky in which clouds suddenly opened and drenched them before they could stand. Paul jumped to his feet, raised his zipper, and beat his fists at the sky, shouting, "This is supposed to be a drought, damnit! It's a drought! God, why are you sending this rain?! Givn was going to dig a well!"

Zenia stood next to him, lifting her face to the sky. "Perhaps Kilomo won't have to go so far for water, now."

Confused, Paul Joseph peered, as Zenia let the rain fall on her face. Then she opened her eyes in horror. "You don't suppose … you don't suppose…?"

"What?"

"You don't suppose Babu and that boy could have anything to do with …"

"With what?"

She clasped his lapels. "With the rain, Paul! With the rain!"

In utter disbelief, Paul Joseph listened to Zenia describe what she thought she'd seen—a village woman levitate, a village boy fly up to a roof through the air."

"It was the heat. You were hallucinating."

He didn't say villages in the African bush were once full of such ridiculous rumors. Her wild report brought Paul Joseph to his senses, though, and he remembered the meeting he and Watende had called for tomorrow morning. He took her arm and led her back to the village through the pouring rain. Perhaps all wasn't lost just yet.

Chapter 23

When the Reverend Paul Joseph and his party left, Babu decided to ask *the great one from afar*—now called The Comforter, *Mfaraja*, by the village and called *Jess* by his mother—whether their gathering should take a break. Babu had felt pepo flee them as soon as Paul Joseph arrived. It took focus, time, it took repeated practice for someone's pepo to descend and remain. Yet, now and then one chosen by the ancestors would be afflicted by a crisis that forced taking immediate refuge in Mungu, the one God. Such a thing was a blessing if the victim could respond.

Unfortunately, none of the villagers were in crisis at the moment, or able to sustain what it had been his honor to help Mfaraja create. For a moment, the kingdom of God of which Mfaraja spoke had existed in Udugu. Now it was gone. Only a few still gazed inward to their souls instead of outward to the world, and Babu sensed even this would not last.

"Mwalimu Mfaraja, may I speak to you?" Babu asked the wonderful boy beside him.

"Yes," Mfaraja answered.

"Shall we continue or shall we stop?"

The boy turned amazing eyes to Babu. All was well where this boy was. How could the Reverend not have felt it?

Mfaraja gave him a smile Babu would never forget.

"Yes, Babu. Let us stop. Today is not the day."

Next to the boy his mother sighed, "Thank goodness!"

Babu nodded. Such a strong one she was, bravely confronting the new arrivals on her son's behalf. Mfaraja patted her hand. How kind he was to his mother—this great spirit who still believed herself asleep and in a dream.

———

Zenia let Paul Joseph drag her through the jungle. As they struggled through the undergrowth and the mud, the downpour stopped and Africa's oppressive heat dried the ground and her clothes before they arrived at the village. What an uninhabitable place! How could it be the origin of humanity?

Just as they reached the village, Zenia saw Kilomo and his sister Koko, both of them dragging the green pail, filled with muddy water. Were they going to drink that? They must have no choice. The brief deluge didn't seem to have left so much as a puddle anywhere. Alarmed, she stopped.

"Paul!"

Frowning, he slowed to look back at her. "Yes, what?"

"Did we bring our own water?"

He gazed at the children lugging their muddy pail. "Don't worry, we have plenty and we'll boil more if necessary. You got vaccinated, didn't you?"

She nodded.

He gestured for her to precede him into the village. "So there's nothing to worry about."

Zenia sighed as Kilomo and Koko disappeared with their pail.

Back at the village, Paul led the way to her brick hut and said their party would meet at the church in half an hour. She freshened up in an incredibly primitive washbasin, which a girl took away and emptied. After using an equally incredibly smelly toilet, she left her hut to explore. She noticed more people moving about. The village's circle meeting—or whatever it was—must have ended. The ones her age said, "Habari," to which she learned she was expected to say, "Nzuri" for *I am fine*. The younger ones said, "Shikamoo!" which someone told her was a sign of respect, meaning *I touch your feet* and in response she was supposed to say, "*Marahaba.*"

She learned that "Mbwa" meant dog because twice people pointed down to a sleeping one, warning her not to step on it. If they were almost starving, how could they feed dogs? What struck her was how gentle they were, all of them gracious, all of them seeming happy, as if they knew something wonderful no one who lived in a city did.

At the village's far east, facing the rising sun, she located the compound of Babu, the old man she'd seen show a paper to Honorable Mahfuru when Paul Joseph interrupted their meeting. Babu wore native clothes.

At the far west she discovered the compound of Watende, who they called Baba. Why have such similar nicknames? *Babu, Baba.* Watende seemed to be their chief. He wore western clothes, perhaps only secondhand instead of third or fourth. When she encountered him on a path, he nodded politely to her, but did not speak. Neither did she. Zenia was only reconnoitering, trying to sense the atmosphere of this place, figure out how people in Udugu might look when they lied.

Nowhere did she see the curly-haired boy who'd angered Paul Joseph. She didn't see the black woman with the American accent who'd defended the boy.

Zenia returned to Paul Joseph's brick compound. A church, a schoolhouse and a rudimentary town store within its low walls, it commanded the village center. Zenia had seen no other walls in Udugu.

She stepped across the church's wood threshold into the greater heat inside, wondering why Paul hadn't figured out this wasn't the way to build in the jungle. In Nassau Country, sure, but not here.

She found Paul Joseph, Honorable Mahfuru, Steve Harris from the consulate, and from AmerCan Kevin-called-Givn sitting in chairs and huddled over, talking.

"Hello, gentlemen," she called.

Honorable Mahfuru was the first to rise, Steve Harris second, Kevin third. Interesting that Paul, who now thought he could have her when he wanted, wasn't quick on his feet anymore. Kevin, who seemed to her to be in control of things, only managed to beat Paul up by a tad. Steve, who like all diplomats had to be obliging to everyone, found his feet before Kevin. Honorable Mahfuru, whose government was penniless, broke the sound barrier rising for a woman who had cash.

Interesting.

"So what are we talking about?" she asked, joining them and

taking the seat Steve Harris pulled out for her. She'd been careful to give him blinding smiles. He was going to report to the President.

"That awd boy," Givn offered.

"Who do you suppose he is?" Steve asked Mahfuru. "You stayed behind when we left. What happened? What did the villagers say?"

Mahfuru spread his hands in amazement. "They say he is Mungu, God and—" Mahfuru wagged his head from side to side, "—they say other silly things, all unimportant."

Steve Harris, educated American diplomat, blew out breath and shook his head. "So God's a teenager?"

"Outright superstition!" Paul Joseph declared.

"Well, ewever e is, ow do we get rid of the Bliksem is my question." Givn leaned forward like a man who didn't intend to be opposed.

"Out of curiosity," Zenia asked, "why must we get rid of him? Perhaps the thing to do is indulge the village and make friends with him. I'll have Mr. Nzuri take photos of me here"—she looked around—"where is our photographer, anyway?"

"We dun't need im now."

"Oh, well, I mean as long as I get the photos, I'll be able to raise—"

"Yisss-likes, woman. There's a lawt more at steak ere than photos!"

Zenia zeroed in on Kevin/Givn. "You mean the well?"

Givn snorted. "Yeh, Yeh, and I plan to do a leettle mining."

She'd forgotten about the mining. Suddenly she wished she'd paid attention to what Zach said before she left—something about AmerCan; something about danger.

Paul Joseph lost patience and gestured impatiently with his hand. "Zenia, isn't it obvious? Kevin's an outsider. So is Steve. In a way, so is Mahfuru because he represents the government. I'm … I'm the only one the village completely trusts. If I explain things to them, they'll believe me. Then Kevin can proceed. He can dig a well. The Honorable Mahfuru can confirm AmerCan's title for use of the land."

"And I can report a favorable outcome to the White House," Steve Harris said.

Zenia smiled at Steve then, as cool as she could, asked Mahfuru, "You have to get the village's approval to use the land?"

Honorable Mahfuru cleared his throat. "It's a formality, so yes and no."

To Zenia that meant yes. Something other than the village's toilets was beginning to give off an odor here.

Paul Joseph added, "but with this ... this boy-god here, who knows what will happen?"

Taking in what they'd said, Zenia turned to Kevin. "What sort of mining?"

"The normal koind of course."

"Gold?"

"No."

"Gems?"

"No."

"Minerals?"

"Yeh, berheps! What's it to you?"

"Will it have any negative effects on the village?"

Kevin stood. "Listen, now. ThI don't ave water. Ya can't git more nigative than that! We're giving them a well!"

She nodded and rose, leaving the men and walking to a window, afraid now that she might have gotten herself into a mess, just like Zach had warned. Why hadn't she listened to him? It was habit. She hadn't listened to Zach for years. To her, the husband she once tried to love had become a machine—an always-pleasant moneymaking machine who in fact settled for far less money than he could make if he'd simply try. Zach called himself lucky and he was. Things fell into his lap, but what good was luck if you didn't make the most of it? With a congressman for a father, with everyone liking and trusting him, Zach could have gone into politics, made a killing and had power to boot. He could have been President. She could have been his First Lady and a darned good one, too. But no, politics was too sordid for Zach. Having billions was too sordid for Zach. Zenia's father had been a poor teacher.

She'd never been lucky a day in her life. Unlike Zach, she made the most of everything in her path. When Zach appeared, she made the most of him. It irritated her how he stupidly, patiently waited for her to give him the children she couldn't have—didn't even inquire about it anymore. She no longer felt a thing with him in bed. For years she'd fed Zach, screwed Zach, been a credit to Zach in public and tolerated that he bored her to tears.

Quietly, Zenia sighed.

Casually, she looked out at the people of Udugu—women grinding dried corn, stored from the last harvest? Was maize their big crop? Two men on a roof, laying new palm leaves. Children bouncing the balloons into the air that Paul Joseph had brought them. A woman plucking a chicken. A woman with a baby on her back breaking into song. A group of men making mud bricks for a house. A girl arriving with a water pail. Zenia took out her cell phone, doubting she'd get bars in the middle of Africa. To her surprise, they weakly appeared. Her homepage was a US newspaper's website. Dozens shot at a college anti-gun rally? Another quake in New England? A mass grave found of some dictator's victims in the Middle East? In Colorado, two women drove off a cliff like Thelma and Louis. Was the world going crazier faster? She shook her head then searched the web for news of mining problems in Tanzania, found an item and read:

a litany of problems plague the sector
violence, pollution, sexual assault ... but that was at a gold mine
windfall profits at the expense of the government
child labor
hazardous mining waste poisons groundwater

She waved goodbye to the men, left the church and the compound in search of the woman who spoke with an American accent and had called the boy-god her son.

Zenia didn't need to remain, having uncovered the lies.

———

I sat outside a hut in Babu's compound, watching Suma's cooking fire. It consisted of a hole dug into the ground in which wood was burned to coals. With a big leaf I caught escaping sparks before they drifted up and set someone's thatched roof on fire. I sat in a squat like the local women did. For them it looked effortless and they worked like this for long periods. For me, I can tell you it was a challenge. My knees had stopped complaining, except when I got up, but keeping my balance and not rolling over onto the ground was a lot harder. It happened once and I was trying to prevent a repeat.

Good at squatting or not, I wouldn't be anywhere else on earth right now but here in Udugu. Neither at night or in the day was Africa quiet and the odd cries, far-off growls, wild chatters and chirps now lulled me. My nose celebrated the vibrant smells after the rain—so raw, so fresh, that mother Africa could have been shaping a new Adam out of clay. Sometimes I felt guilty because my husband, Adamo and my son, Peter, weren't here. Once more I'd asked Jess if I could phone them and, with great sympathy, he again said no. Jess explained that his visit would be over if I made contact with my normal life because his return had created a shift in time.

That confirmed this was a dream, but I didn't care.

My heart had taken root in the soil here. My soul had entwined itself in the night sky. If it weren't for Adamo and Peter, I could easily spend the rest of my life in Udugu, sitting against a hut's wall and helping mind the children, helping Suma grind maize or build a fire, dancing in Udugu's ngomas, sitting in sacred circle and feeling the village breathe as one. All my life I'd missed this bond, a sense of community I'd never known, even in the 121st Street Baptist Church.

Here in Africa there was nothing to overcome, nothing to prove to anybody. I felt so authentic in being the Udugu version of me, I could barely remember being inauthentically viewed as a maid, as black mother of a non-black child, as the black wife of white men—first Sam, now Adamo.

My love for them wasn't inauthentic, of course, nor theirs for me, but both America and Italy had always viewed me as "other." Looking at the self-confident men of Udugu made me wonder what being a wife here was like. Yes, there was a little sexism. I'd seen it, but it seemed more natural than at home. Women didn't perform the hard manual labor because they didn't have the muscles of the men, who didn't take care of the babies because they had no milk to feed them. Suma said that, because she was a woman, she might have a hard time keeping Babu's land when he died, but now that the laws had changed she had a fighting chance. So there *were* downsides to being a woman here.

On the other hand, I had never experienced what Suma did every day—a womanliness that shared something with the stars and moon. Like them, Suma's glory was reflected in the villagers' admiring eyes. Her charm seemed to seep from the earth. Everyone loved Suma—as daughter, granddaughter, sister, potential mate, future mother. All my life I'd longed to be female like that.

Tears of gratitude filled my eyes at the gift of being here, poor though the village was. No place had felt more like home. Whenever I woke up from this, I intended to buy airline tickets for Peter, Adamo and me and come right back to Udugu.

"Here are the herbs, Hetta," I heard. I hadn't told them my real name.

I wiped my eyes and looked up to see Suma come from her hut, a plastic bag of herbs in one hand. She squatted beside me, picked up a banana leaf, put some of the herbs inside then folded the leaf into a small packet. Next she placed it on a square piece of metal that went into the coals.

"They must be hot to help your headache," Suma said.

My head had been aching since I saw the villagers fly. It became a pounding when Reverend Joseph came. I'd had to keep reminding myself this was a dream.

"How did you learn this, Suma?"

"From Babu. He teaches me. He wants me to be the village's mganga wa pepo when he is with the ancestors."

"May I approach?" someone said.

We looked up at the same time to see a white woman standing on the path to Babu's compound. Suma and I glanced at each other, our expressions confirming we hadn't seen this woman before.

"Yes, come, Bibi, join us," Suma called then whispered to me, "She must be with Reverend Joseph's party."

If Suma was calling this younger woman Bibi, too, it must mean madam rather than grandmother after all.

The woman came and squatted next to Suma then rudely reached across her to me, extending her hand. "I'm Zenia Dunlop. I'm a member of Reverend Joseph's parish."

I returned the handshake. "I'm M ... I'm Hetta Price." I'd almost forgotten and used my real name. Then I realized it didn't matter either way because this wasn't actually happening.

Zenia Dunlop offered her hand to Suma. "And you are?"

Suma smiled without shaking the hand. "I am called Suma. I am Babu's granddaughter."

"You mean the elder who beats the drum?"

Suma and I exchanged another glance. Had Zenia met Babu on a path and talked with him or had she seen the pepo session?

Suma nodded in reply.

"He seems a remarkable man. What are you cooking, if I may ask?"

"Oh!" Suma picked up a stick and nudged the charred banana leaf out of the coals. "Medicine," she said and gingerly unwrapped the leaf, sucking at her singed fingers. "Hold out your hands," she said to me. When I did, Suma shook the heated leaves into my palms. "Now put them to your forehead, Bibi."

I did, closing my eyes.

"Is she ill?" I heard Zenia ask.

"She only has a headache. May I do anything for you, Bibi Zenia?"

"Oh. I'd hoped to talk with the two of you. I'll come again."

I opened my eyes as Zenia rose. I needed to talk with this woman, too, find out if the Reverend and his people intended to cause more trouble for Jess. "My head doesn't hurt that bad. I can talk."

Zenia squatted again. "First tell me. Who is your son?"

I looked up. "You don't beat around the bush much, do you?"

"I've found it helps to get to the point."

"Since you've gotten to yours, let me get to mine. Why do you want to know?"

I saw fast thinking behind Zenia Dunlop's eyes. "The Reverend Joseph didn't react well to him on first meeting. Perhaps I can help avoid that next time. I assume you're staying in the village a while, or do you live here?"

Something told me to be honest with Zenia. It wasn't trust. I didn't think I could trust Zenia one iota, but I had a strong urge to answer Zenia's questions and I never ignore instincts that strong. To me, they are taps on the shoulder from God. Anyway, this was a dream.

"We'll be here until my son says it's time to go."

"Who is he?"

I took a deep breath. "Did you ever hear that story about somebody making a clone from DNA they took from the Shroud of Turin?"

Zenia frowned, then looked at me. "Yes! It was about twenty years ago?"

"That's the one."

Zenia looked confused. "And?"

I took another breath and with my eyes dared Zenia to make a smart remark. "My son's the clone. His name is Jess."

Zenia fell straight out of her squat and had to catch herself with one hand. "Excuse me," she said as she got back into position, her eyebrows still raised in surprise. "I lost my balance. So, in other words, you're saying you carried the cloned embryo and that's why you're his mother?"

Suma stared at me, too, her eyes wide.

"Yes, that's how I'm his mother though we don't look alike."

I could see a lot more thinking going on behind Zenia's eyes, along with a few unsaid exclamations that made her eyes go slightly wide now and then as she pondered.

Suma touched my arm. "Is your headache better, now, Bibi?"

I realized that it was and took my hands down from my

forehead, wiping away the herbs that stuck there. "That's better than aspirin, Suma, what do you call it?"

"Lantana."

Zenia interrupted, "Um, wasn't the clone supposed to have died or something?"

"Yes, at first that's what we told people just to protect him. Then, when he was ten years old he really died. A neighbor threw stones at him."

"Well, then how—"

I was getting fed up with this dream. "Mrs. Dunlop, is that your name?" I asked.

"Yes."

"I hate to tell you this, but you're just a figment of my imagination. You too, Suma. Yesterday, or was it day before yesterday... or, I don't know... last week, I got up one Saturday and went to the market in Porlezza like I've done a thousand times."

"Porlezza?" Zenia asked.

"That's in Italy. Anyway, I'm there at the market and the next thing I know my dead son is in front of me."

"That's impossible."

"Of course it is! I'm not crazy. That's why I know you're a figment of my imagination. You're just part of my dream. True, it's a long dream, a complicated dream, but somewhere in Porlezza I must have fallen asleep, or maybe I just dreamed I went to Porlezza and I'm still at home in my bed."

Suma and Zenia looked at each other. "You're not in a dream, Mrs. Price. We're real and so are you. So is this village."

Agitated, I got to my feet. "No, it's not. This isn't real. I'm telling you. This is a dream!"

Zenia stood, her eyes wide in confusion. "I'm not a figment of anyone's imagination!"

I found myself shouting, "Yes you are!"

Suma stood. "Ladies, ladies!"

"You're insane. I said I'm not!"

Words came out before I could stop them. "Yes, you are, and

you're a pretty darned nasty, nosey figment if I do say so myself."

"Then I'll show you!" Zenia shouted, reached across Suma and shoved me. "Do you feel that?"

My mouth flew open. My eyebrows draw tight. "Yes, and do you feel this?" I shoved Zenia back, Suma retreating, screaming something about the fire. One of Zenia's earrings had come off and was now being incinerated in the flames.

Zenia stepped back, huffing. "Normally I don't approve of this kind of behavior."

I stepped back, too. "Me neither, but if you shove me again, I'm shoving you."

"Damn it!" Zenia said, looking into the fire. "That's 24 carats melting!"

How could she be so shallow? "You poor thing."

Zenia looked up. "Let me ask you something. When someone gets ready to push or hit you in a dream, don't you usually wake up first?"

Surprised, I froze, thinking. I wrapped my arms around myself and took in what Zenia said. Yes, I always woke up. I was pretty sure everybody did. I focused on the fire, its charcoal, Zenia's burning earring. Why would she wear 24 carats in a jungle? I focused on the big fig tree, Babu's drum hanging from it.

"Suma, are you real?"

Suma nodded. "Yes, Bibi Hattie, I am." She came to me and took my hands. "Feel my hand in your hand. I am real."

I gazed at the African sky. "That means Jess has really come back from the dead. He really has."

"Impossible!" Zenia said. "Impossible! He'd have to be a god of some kind."

Finally accepting, I fell to my knees. "He is."

Zenia, breathing hard, turned on Suma. "I suppose next you're going to tell me you people actually flew through the air for a bit there yesterday?"

Suma helped me up, took my hand and stood beside me. Together we faced Zenia, Suma saying, "We did."

Chapter 24

Ariel sat at the Oyster Bay Hotel's breakfast table, sipping tea and chewing on toast. Their hostess had extolled the virtues of the marmite she served—a salty British yeast product, loaded with B vitamins. Even spread thinly on toast as recommended, marmite had almost made Ariel throw up. Also the eggs. Fruit. Everything but toast. Ariel wondered if she'd starve to death before getting anywhere close to childbirth.

Giving birth, what a strange concept.

Logically, it was how everyone got here, but Ariel had never imagined she'd be involved. Not at sixteen, anyway, not in a million years. As a child, she'd preferred stuffed animals to baby dolls. And what did the sex she'd missed feel like?

To keep from crying again she sniffed, drank more tea, and looked at her watch. Unable to grasp Swahili Time, she'd simply advanced the hands to the local time zone. If it was seven am here, that meant it was, what, eleven pm at home? By now, Hasayeah had abandoned its long boards. Unless they'd requested a *late night* to finish an assignment, her friends were now all *quiet and in their rooms*, as required. 11 pm was *lights out* for fifth and sixth formers, who no longer actually had to turn out the lights. Still, most were in their beds or on their way, their stomachs full of non-regurgitated food. She missed them terribly already, but at least they were safe, not shot to death at an anti-gun rally.

When had America become so violent?

Ariel imagined how the parents of the dead students must feel, then with a shock realized her own parents might feel the same. After all, she'd vanished. As far as they knew, she could be dead.

Feeling guilt, she looked up at the chandeliers—strips of white coral surrounding two hanging lights. She put down the tea and toast and said, "Thank you, ma'am," to the hostess. Bidding the other guests farewell, she rose from the hotel's communal breakfast table and went to find Zach. She'd ask to use his phone to call her dad. The hotel's first floor was mostly open, gorgeous spaces separated by billowing white curtains and super terrific African art. She found Zach putting his wallet away, having just paid their bill. He had on pale grey khaki everything and if she hadn't known better, she'd think Zach was a movie star. When he smiled, you wanted to get his autograph.

"What's my part of the tab?" she asked.

He turned cheery brown eyes on her. "What say I take care of the hotel? It's my pleasure to have such a fine traveling companion."

Ariel frowned. "No need. I have five hundred dollars."

"Don't worry about it."

"Did it cost more than that?"

Comically he lifted his eyebrows and pursed his lips.

"Ohmigod, you can afford it?"

He tried to make an even funnier face and succeeded. "Ah…yes!"

Ariel chose not to laugh. "I guess you're rich, then, like my dad."

"Yes, and I agree it should be a crime," he joked, looking wistful. "Actually, I've always wanted a daughter to spoil."

Understanding Zach, now, she grinned. "Well, in that case, maybe we can detour up to Oldupai Gorge at some point? Who knows if we'll ever have another chance to see it?"

"Oldupai Gorge?"

"You know, the Cradle of Mankind? Where the Leakey's first found prehumans?"

"Oh, African Eve."

"No, silly, she was found in Ethiopia. But humanity's Mitochondrial Eve probably lived in Oldupai Gorge right here in Tanzania."

Zach fixed her with a kind gaze. Had he figured out she was stalling about something?

"I guess I need to call my dad. I don't have bars. He's worried. My mom, too. "

Zach handed her his cell phone and showed her how to dial the USA. She took it out to the veranda and walked on the grass beside the pristine white lap pool. Instead of her dad's cell ringing as usual, the call went immediately to voicemail as if his phone was turned off. She left a message. "Dad, I'm in Dar es Salaam. I'm leaving for Udugu now. Don't worry. I'm fine." Ariel thought of calling her mother's cell, but decided against it, knowing she'd cry and beg and plead for Ariel to return.

Back inside, she found Zach poring over the hotel guest book, his sunny smile not in evidence.

She came up beside him and looked at the ledger. "Is something wrong?"

Zach said nothing, just stared stonily down at what Ariel saw was his wife's signature and, below it, that of someone named The Reverend Paul Joseph, who'd signed his name so close that the flourishes of his John Hancock ran into hers.

I don't remember exactly what happened after Zenia left Suma and me. I know I asked Suma if I could be alone for a while and she let me lie down in her hut. I know every now and then Suma brought me something to eat and drink. I know night came. I guess the truth is I was so lost, I couldn't have put one foot in front of the other. There's no roadmap for learning everything you thought you knew is wrong.

When I left Suma's hut, life would never be the same for me, Maggie Morelli. What I'd thought was unreal wasn't. What I'd assumed was impossible wasn't.

I just let thoughts bang into each other in my mind, and tried to slow my breath, tried to calm my pulse, not ready to see Jess and talk about it. Believe me, realizing that up is down takes some getting used to, much less that miracles happen. This wasn't a dream. My dead son had come back to life. Without setting foot in an airplane, a boat, a train, a car, I was in Africa.

I must have slept because morning came.

Suma brought breakfast and sat beside me. Maize again, some

kind of herbal tea. "*Umeamkaje*, Bibi. It means how did you wake?"
She'd been teaching me a few Swahili words.

"Well," I said.

"In Swahili that is *vyema*."

I ate a little, using a palm leaf. Then I put the food down.
"Actually, I didn't sleep all that vyema, Suma."

She touched my hand. "I know. You speak to your son now? I
told him about you. He said not to disturb you, so I did not."

"Yes, I'll speak to my son. Where is he?"

She rose. "I will take you."

Suma led me out of Babu's compound to a field with two long
strips of dirt that looked like a primitive runway. It must have been
where Paul Joseph's party landed. Jess stood in the center, a baby
monkey on his hip. I'd never seen one like it. It had a cute baby
face, lots of gray and white fuzz, but the hair on its arms and legs
was actually dark blue. It ate leaves from Jess's hand. When Jess saw
me, he tried to put the monkey down but it climbed up on his
shoulder and held onto his hair. Jess lifted it off him, put his face
to its face, smiling. Again he put it down. This time the little
monkey made a few squeaks and scampered into the jungle and up
a tree.

Jess came to me. "Madre, how are you? I mean, Umeamkaje?"

"Vyema, Jess. I slept well."

He smiled. He always smiled. Everybody in Africa smiled most
of the time. Perhaps smiling was a kind of magic. "You believe me,
now, don't you, Mother?"

I nodded.

"You believe what I said in the Bible is true."

I nodded, embarrassed, still feeling lost.

"I mean in the Gospels. Not *Revelation*. I never said I'd throw
anyone in a lake of fire."

"I know."

Jess hugged me. Then you're the first modern Christian,
Mother—the first to realize the Gospels are true. It's how God
made the world and us. Believe we can work miracles and we can
because—" He held me at arm's length and looked at me
expectantly. "Because?"

My eyes filled with tears of joy. "Because the kingdom of God is within us."

Jess started dancing like the villagers had at the ngoma and Suma, who'd been watching, broke into a ululation, grabbed a leafy branch from a tree and started dancing, too. I did my best, all three of us whooping it up on the village's dirt landing strip, blue monkeys screeching from the trees.

Chapter 25

Paul Joseph was impatient for the meeting to begin. Apparently, Watende had invited the chairman from a neighboring village that also needed a well. He hadn't arrived. Paul Joseph milled around Watende's compound, anxiously looking at his Swahili watch in which 12:00 and 6:00 were reversed on the face. This meant our 7 am was their 1 am. He granted this made more sense when you were on the equator where day and night were always virtually equal. Watende had said the neighbor chairman would arrive *asubuhi*, in the morning. It was almost noon, 6:00 in Swahili Time, and he hadn't appeared.

"It's the overcast sky," Honorable Mahfuru offered, mopping his brow. Living in air conditioning in the city as he did, he obviously wasn't accustomed to the heat.

Paul Joseph nodded. In the African countryside, people told time quite accurately by their own shadows on the ground, unless the sky was cloudy like today.

"The donder'll git ere when e gits here, like all of em do." Givn said.

Paul didn't like Givn's foul mouth. Routinely he referred to people as donders or bliksems, which technically meant thunder and lightning, but was also South Africa's way of calling people bastards.

Steve Harris posed next to Zenia for Mr. Nzuri, the reporter who'd reappeared—Steve in his diplomat-on-safari suit, she in safari couture, as she called it, though Paul was sure no jungle had ever seen a hot jumpsuit like that. Watende's mother ushered village children in and out of the photograph. She instructed them to lift beseeching faces to Zenia. In others, Zenia embraced the young ones.

Everyone sweated except the locals and Givn, who was a miner and always outdoors. The sun seemed to have burned his skin a permanent mottled brown.

Paul Joseph passed the time by admiring how Zenia's long black hair splayed down onto her thin, loose clay-colored jumpsuit and into the cleavage she'd exposed for the camera. He would have liked to take her out to his secret spot last night or this morning, but she had stayed to herself.

When she returned to her compound yesterday, her cheeks had been red as if someone had slapped her, or she'd cried. Only then did he realize he'd never seen Zenia Dunlop shed one tear. He'd seen her lust, fume, lose patience, but not cry. If it weren't for their assignations, he was certain God would find her an upstanding member of society, one of the purest of the People of the Book. He felt shame to have led her astray, but such was the weakness of mortal men. In truth, he couldn't wait for a repeat.

"Shikamoo!" Paul Joseph heard.

They all turned to see a man dressed in traditional garb approach Watende's compound, his walking stick in hand.

Babu called, "Marahaba!" to the younger man and went to greet him. They embraced then began the long formal Tanzanian greetings, each inquiring about the others' health, relatives and crops before getting down to business.

Watende greeted him next and, when the preliminaries were done, invited everyone to the back of his compound. He stopped before a series of large, different-colored pails, full of water. Paul Joseph recognized the green one from a dent in its side. Zenia had described it to him. It was Kilomo and Koko's pail. Watende was their father.

Watende nodded to Babu to do the talking. The old man had obviously figured out who was who because he addressed his remarks to Kevin/Givn with AmerCan.

"This is how we clean our water. From far away the children bring three pails." He picked up a cotton cloth from beside one of the pails. "The water is not clear. We must pour it through the cloth. It must sit for three days. Then we boil one pail." He pointed to an iron pot. "We use the water. The children then refill that pail."

"That leemits ya to a pail of water a day?"

Babu nodded.

"Unless you have more children and more pails?" Zenia interjected.

Before anyone could speak—no doubt because they were shocked—she turned from Babu to Watende, the village chairman. "It's appalling that these children have to drag a heavy pail of water long distances every single day." Her tone accused him. "Are Kilomo and Koko your children?"

Watende raised his war club, leaned both hands on it, and stared impassively at her, as if the empty air was demanding explanations of him.

His mother spoke, her tone indignant. "They are my grandchildren."

"Well, then, why don't you tell him, a strong man, to fetch the water instead of allowing those poor children—"

Paul Joseph was so aghast, it took him a minute to speak. "Zenia, please. This is my mission, if you remember!"

Her eyes blazed, but she closed her mouth and stormed away from the water pails.

Everyone followed her back to the center of Watende's compound—like eyes of a storm dragged by its sudden winds. In Paul Joseph's experience, no one had ever spoken to a village chief like that. He saw sweat seep from Zenia's belly below her slouchy belt onto the pale clay jumpsuit, the wind rippling its fabric. He knew unless and until he repented, which he didn't want to do, he was going straight to hell because of Zenia Dunlop. That she might ruin his earthly ambitions hadn't occurred to him before.

Everyone stared at her for a moment. Then Watende motioned to a circle of makeshift seats set before his largest hut. One by one they sat. Watende's mother passed out paper cups of what looked like water. Zenia suspiciously eyed it until Paul Joseph frowned at her, insisting with his glance that she drink. This meeting was why they'd come to Africa.

Zenia fixed him with her gaze then poured the cup's contents on the ground.

Paul Joseph couldn't pray about her. He couldn't seek God's help with unclean hands. He pictured Zenia informing him his hands were fine; the dirty parts were lower down. What was the matter with him, with her?

He focused on the meeting. The important people were here—the chairman Watende and his mother, the neighbor chief, Babu the mganga wa pepo with his certificate that gave him permission to heal, his granddaughter Suma. Having regained the confidence of the village—evidenced by the sacred circle they hadn't made for years—Babu's opinion could be important now. Also vital were Mahfuru from the government, Steve Harris from the consulate and Givn, of course. Paul Joseph, as the village's Christian pastor, spoke for God.

Honorable Mahfuru was saying, '...studied the situation in Udugu and we have a recommendation. The Reverend Joseph would like to explain."

"This is Mr. van der Linden with a company called AmerCan," Paul Joseph began.

Givn took off his hat and nodded agreeably.

"His company has wonderful news. They found possible reserves of gemstones on Udugu lands. They are willing to bear the full cost of mining, in exchange for a share of sales later and, for now..." Paul Joseph let his excitement show ... "digging you a well and installing irrigation so your crops no longer fail!" He slapped his knee in triumph.

Silence.

Watende spoke through his mother. "Last year the long rains were not long. The dry season was not dry. We can no longer predict the weather so we don't know when to plant."

Zenia interrupted. "Back home we call that global warming."

Watende ignored her. "A well and irrigation could do much for Udugu."

Apparently not liking being ignored, Zenia turned to Givn. "What about the risk of pollution? Surely you want this addressed so Steve Harris here can tell the White House what an environmentally friendly project this is. I'll make sure it's all over the society pages: AmerCan, Africa's green savior."

Mr. Nzuri, the photographer, snapped a photo.

Givn, eyes and mouth stretched in an unmasked urge to strangle Zenia, looked to Paul Joseph.

"I'm sure it will be fine, Zenia," Paul Joseph said.

Babu cleared his throat. "Let us hear about the environmental friendliness, Mr. van der Linden."

"Well, uh. We'll make stedies. Yes, stedies."

"Studies," Zenia translated. "They're going to perform studies to make sure they don't poison you and your groundwater."

Givn exploded to his feet. "Now, wait a minute ere, girlie!"

Babu rose and withdrew another paper from his robe. He walked up to Honorable Mahfuru and presented it.

"What's that now?" Givn asked.

Mahfuru sighed. "It's a CCRO, a Certificate of Customary Right of Occupancy."

"What's thet?"

Mahfuru re-sighed.

Babu spoke. "All Udugu land is covered by this. It passed from my father to his father, who was once the chief."

Mahfuru looked up at Babu. "As you know, the 1995 Land Policy vested all our lands in the President on behalf of Tanzanians."

Babu replied, "This is true and four years later, the Land Act said the President will, *recognize existing rights to land and longstanding occupation or use of land.*"

Givn said to Mahfuru, "I thought yew granted us a right of occupancy, a GCRO didn't you call it?"

Mahfuru winced.

Paul Joseph stared back and forth between them.

"That is not possible," Babu said. "Our customary right of occupancy is perpetual and can be inherited. My father transferred it to the village of Udugu so we may live on our land as we always have. Only we may give you permission to mine."

Givn turned to Mahfuru. "I thought yew said Udugu was part of yer Planned Lands or something."

Together, Babu and his granddaughter, Watende and his

mother, and the neighbor chief stood, frowning at Mahfuru. Whatever *Planned Lands* meant, the five of them apparently didn't like it. Without a word, the meeting's only local residents exited the circle in Watende's compound—leaving it to the foreigners and Mahfuru from the government.

"Look what ya did, ya beetch!" Givn shouted.

All furious femininity, Zenia Dunlop stormed off toward the jungle.

Paul Joseph excused himself to Steve Harris, Honorable Mahfuru, Mr. Nzuri still taking photos, and Kevin van der Linden of AmerCan, who'd quite rightly called the woman he yearned for a bitch.

Chapter 26

Zach and Ariel landed at a charter airfield 5 km south of Mbeya City, construction of Mbeya's international airport having been indefinitely postponed. On the flight, a British passenger had told them a joke. "How many people can you fit in a dala dala?" The punch line was, "One more!"

Soon enough they learned firsthand that a dala dala was Tanzania's version of a public minibus that ran on somewhat regular routes at somewhat regular times. The one presently jostling them down an Mbeya back road was so full of people, Zach almost expected a flat tire from their sheer weight. Somehow he'd found Ariel a seat. Zach himself stood crushed among the friendliest people he'd ever met, all of them interested in learning who he and Ariel were, why they were on a dala dala in Mbeya, and where they were going.

Zach informed them that the taxi he'd hired to take them to Udugu broke down a mile outside of Mbeya City then this minibus happened by.

Hearing this, several of the dala dala's passengers gave Zach detailed instructions on how to reach Udugu from where the minibus would stop. When all passengers were satisfied he'd been sufficiently directed, they started teaching him and Ariel Swahili greetings and phrases, laughing at their mispronunciations and patiently teaching and reteaching until he and Ariel could say, *habari gani* and its reply, *nzuri*, perfectly, as well and other key phrases like *Naelewa* I understand, *Sielewi* I don't understand, *Kila la Heri* good luck and *Kwaheri*, goodbye.

Zach found the generosity of the passengers so disarming, he wondered if the end of the world could really be near with such warmth still on earth. In spite of so little wealth, things constantly breaking down, and bus schedules often ignored, as he was told, the people of Tanzania seemed full of joy. When the minibus's radio broke and stopped playing Bob Marley, they sang—one woman starting a refrain that the others answered. Zach had never experienced music in this way. It vibrated not just in his ears, but in his whole being, and after a while he had to fight tears. The man in front of him, apparently noticing, raised his hand and said something in Swahili and to Zach said, "No more sing," and smiled.

For a while the dala dala bumped along in happy silence, now and then passing barefoot people on the side of the road who balanced pots, or firewood, or bundles on their heads as they walked. Occasionally they passed men or boys on bicycles, sometimes a woman. A rare motorbike would pass, never a private car. Eventually a woman passenger inquired whether they were hungry and, not believing their reply that they were not, opened a bag full of what she called *zabibu*, which turned out to be Concord grapes. She shared them with Zach and Ariel and everyone else on the dala dala.

Zach's life had contained memorable moments, but by the time the bus pulled to a stop near Udugu, he'd concluded his ride on the dala dala, standing up the whole while, was one of the greatest. He helped Ariel off. Waving kwaheri, they longingly watched the dala dala depart, kicking up dust, until it rounded a bend in the road.

Amazed, he and Ariel looked at each other.

"How can people be so great here and so awful back home?" she asked.

Zach shook his head. "I guess it's cities, industrialization. We take things for granted."

"Ohmigod, I've never had a better time in my whole life."

"Me too," Zach said.

Shaking his head, he took Ariel's backpack from her, slung it across one shoulder and his own carry-on across the other. Together they headed toward the large baobab tree the people on the dala dala had pointed out.

As promised, they found a footpath beneath it and, following instructions, he and Ariel kept looking down, careful of where they stepped and put their hands. Though February, the hottest month, was biggest for snakes here, a few might be about in September, or so the dala dala people had warned.

"Snakes will really try to escape if we come near them, right?" Ariel said.

"Right," Zach reassured her. "We're to stop if we see one and give it a chance to leave."

"They said most bites are to the ankles?"

"Yes, but since we're both wearing hiking boots we're safe."

"Good, because I'm totally not ready to die."

Zach laughed. "If death from snake bite was that easy, the dala dalas wouldn't be so packed."

Ariel laughed merrily and seemed to relax, happily swinging her arms. They came to a fallen log.

"Step onto logs, not over them they said, right?"

"Right," Zach said, and offered his hand.

She stepped up on the log and, seeing no snakes on the other side, agilely hopped on both feet to the ground.

"There's the rock they told us about." Ariel pointed to a large black stone. "I guess we're getting close to Jesus."

Zach reminded himself it was her motive for coming to Udugu. He was only here to find his wife.

He readjusted the backpack and bag on his shoulders. "Ariel, don't get your hopes up, okay? Just accept whatever comes. We had a wonderful adventure on the dala dala. I have a feeling there'll be more. Meeting Jesus may be one of them, but maybe not, so—"

She gave him a teenage-girl-insulted look. "You don't need to worry about me, Zach. I'm not a weirdo like my dad. I'm just—sort of hoping."

He chucked her chin, like she'd told him her dad did. "Well, I'm sort of hoping, too. I was there when the clone was born. I saw the child." He grinned. "I guess that kind of makes me a weirdo, too, so—"

The chattering of monkeys interrupted their conversation. Looking up into the trees, Zach saw flashes of dark blue.

"Wow, I think those are East Africa's blue monkeys! I read about them in my guide book."

They screeched and chattered, the noise increasing and Zach saw they were all looking in the same direction.

"Something's disturbed them. Ssshhh, let's listen."

They fell silent and strained for sounds that weren't monkey chatters. At first there was only what Zach took as the normal background of the African bush. Then he thought he heard a low growl. Worried, he took Ariel's hand.

"It could be wild boar. I think we'd best get out of here."

Carefully they continued along the path to Udugu, Zach gazing into the bush in case an animal lurked. He wished he had a weapon—not that he knew how to use one. Shortly he saw a movement, stopped, stood still, listened, then sure he was seeing things, went closer, Ariel behind him. Jungle thinned and gave way to a small clearing full of wild blooms. On the ground against a log a couple was having sex. Grinning, Zach started to back away then glimpsed long black hair.

Automatically, his eyes, his ears zeroed in on the woman against the log, who—both hands on the man's buttocks—eagerly pulled him into her, then shoved him back, then pulled him in. Years ago, Zenia used to do that.

That's who was doing it now. His wife. On the ground. Against a log. In the African jungle. His own wife was screwing another man.

He went numb, his first thought to keep Ariel from seeing this, shield Zenia from being observed in an undignified position. He must be imagining it. He looked again. His heart raced. His mind grasped the enormity of the traitorous act—another man penetrating his wife. He lost the ability to think.

Zach let go of Ariel and lunged into the clearing. He hurled himself against the man, toppling him off Zenia in mid-rut, the monkeys screaming now.

Vaguely he heard Ariel shout, "Zach, no!" heard Zenia's terrified scream, but all Zach saw was the man's startled expression organize itself into the stunned face of the Reverend Paul Joseph, sainted pastor of God who was fucking Zenia, his wife.

Zach lunged again, this time for Joseph's throat, kneeing him in the process.

Only for a second did Paul Joseph howl.

Zach's hands were around his throat.

Zach squeezed tight, trying to make Joseph's bulging eyes pop out of their sockets, but they weren't doing it. Instead, he glimpsed a heavy limb, picked it up, and brought it down on Joseph's head, then down again, saw blood but not enough. Zach lifted the limb again, but hands jerked it away from him. Hands on his shoulders pulled Zach off his enemy while voices, Ariel's and Zenia's, screamed that he mustn't hit Paul Joseph, minister of God, who'd been in Zenia's pussy, enjoying himself.

Zach fell to the ground and found two people on top of him, half naked Zenia, and Ariel, slight and pregnant. He mustn't hurt them. He just needed them to move so he could kill Paul Joseph.

Then someone else was there, an old man, a native villager, who was a lot stronger than he looked because he took over the duty of sitting on Zach. He said Swahili words that, against all logic, soon made Zach see the sky again, see the jungle, hear the blue monkeys chattering and, for the first time since he'd known her, hear Zenia, his wife, crying.

"I'm all right," he said to the old African man. "I'm okay, now."

The man nodded and let Zach up.

Zach rose and saw Paul Joseph backed against a tree bleeding, his pants half-zipped, his mouth open in astonishment. Zach turned to Zenia. Her jumpsuit on, but unsnapped, she was still crying and next to her Ariel was, too, like she had on the plane. They were crying as if the world had come to an end.

Zach felt disembodied. Time shifted into non-time and now stood still, a terrible forever.

"Why Zenia?" he heard himself say.

She put her hands to her head, wailing, then looked up to the trees. "Because he's got a cock the size of Kansas, okay?"

Ariel came to Zach and took his hand. He barely felt it, he was so numb.

"Come away, Zach."

"And who's this little whore, Zach? How many times have you fucked her? How many?" Zenia yelled. "Well, get your children off of her because I can't have any, you stupid idiot! Do you hear me? I'm barren!"

"Come away, Zach," Ariel said, pulling his hand.

The old man took Zach's other hand. Zach let them lead him away, Zenia shrieking from the clearing.

"He's got a cock the size of Kansas, Zach, okay?"

Chapter 27

Ruaha National Park was Tanzania's second largest. Serengeti National Park in the north drew the big safari crowds. Those few in the know came southwest to Ruaha to be off the beaten track. To Ahmed, Ruaha's prime advantage was that its most southerly part lay in the Mbeya region, less than half a day's walk from Udugu village.

He had arranged that the four of them pitch a temporary camp called a fly-camp near there. Ajia didn't know the two black Africans who would accompany them on the walking safari were his friends—actually, his dad's friends. Even if caught, they'd never turn Ahmed in so he could carry on the struggle for the cause of Allah.

Ahmed had also paid them well. They would stage an uprising in the middle of the night, using machetes to slaughter all the wazungu in Udugu in their sleep. As would-be jihadists, they were eager for such a chance. They had already spied on the village and learned where the wazungu slept—in the brick compound of the missionary. It would not be guarded. There'd been no attacks on missions in Tanzania since 2007 when a couple was robbed up north on the Kenyan border in Moshi and one had been killed.

How easy it would be for them to slip from the jungle over the compound's low wall and dispatch the whites in their sleep—the Reverend Paul Joseph, Zenia Dunlop, and the man from AmerCan. The others whose photos had been in the paper—the African-American named Steve Harris from the consulate, and Honorable Mahfuru from the government—would not be harmed, because anyone of African heritage was a victim, Ajia said. Only wazungu were responsible for Africa's downfall, and by supporting Israel, for the suffering of Palestinians, she pointed out.

Ahmed wouldn't participate in the attack. He'd never killed anyone.

His job was to find out exactly where each would be, if he could.

Yesterday, Ahmed's safari company had arranged a private charter from Dar es Salaam to a local airstrip then transported them by Landcruiser to this isolated permanent camp of eight luxury tents on stilts near a sand river called The Jongomero. To say the camp was spectacular was an understatement. Secure in their tree-height world, they'd watched elephants wander by in the night, seen a lion pass. Last night there must have been heavy rain upriver because this morning when Ahmed and Ajia placed their prayer rugs on the veranda and performed salat, their sand river was gone. When they finished praying, the sun rose on white surf on the Jongomero River, the trees and vegetation that grew to its shoreline glorious as they emerged from jungle mists. Reveling in the silence, they'd had breakfast alone here then, until time for their walking safari, played backgammon on one of the beds made from the polished limbs of jungle trees. Sleep and backgammon was all they'd done in those beds.

In the beauty and the peace, Ahmed forgot for a while that the wazungu were Ajia's enemies and Udugu needed saving. He thought Ajia forgot, too, on the banks of the Jongomero.

He did think of the famous paper hidden in his suitcase: *Rationalizing Jihadi Work in Egypt and the World*, the revisionist treatise by Imam al-Sharif, a leading thinker in Egypt's Al-Jihad. He wrote it from jail, effectively joining The Muslim Brotherhood in renouncing violence. Militant jihadism had started in Egypt. Would Egyptian jihadists spread a new, peaceful form? Ahmed longed to talk to his father about it, but there was no chance. Any contact between them could be fatal for his dad.

When their guide came to get them, they learned their fly-camp was already set up. Safari company staff had gone to do it yesterday. No guest had ever asked to camp near Udugu, before so extra time was needed to find the best spot.

Ahmed helped Ajia into the Landcruiser that would take them within a half hour's walk of their destination. She looked back at their stilted tent on the Jongomero and said, "This isn't meant for Africans, only for rich whites."

His dad's friends—the campsite's only two other guests—got in the vehicle, as did their cook, and when everyone had introduced themselves, the Landcruiser took off, an armed guide at the wheel. For an hour the guide pointed out the wild sights of Ruaha's landscapes—dozens and dozens of birds Ahmed had never seen, like grey bottomed swallows and the red-beaked Ruaha hornbill; almost extinct wild dogs with mottled coats and white foreheads in black faces; elephants taking a bath in the dust. Often Ajia stood up for a better view, the pop-up roof shading her from the sun. She pointed out two elusive cheetahs resting beneath a shade tree, and the guide informed them how rare such a sighting was. Lions abounded as did leopards, if also rarely seen, but the cheetah was an endangered species. When she sat down, Ajia whispered invectives about the wazungu whose activities destroyed cheetah habitats and reduced their prey.

They reached another dry riverbed on which four domed tents had been pitched, one for them, one for his dad's friends, one for the kitchen, and another for the staff.

Refreshments were laid at a table beneath an acacia tree—white tablecloth, red napkins, champagne, sweet fruit and sandwiches with aromatic cheese. An hour later the walking safari began, the two male guests begging off as previously decided, saying they'd drunk too much champagne. Their real duties would begin tonight.

Less than a half hour and they'd reached Udugu—not much of a walking safari, as Ahmed had requested. He expected the usual village red carpet: jubilant children, everyone gathering to greet him and Ajia to learn who they were, a welcome from the local chairman.

Instead, their progress was interrupted by an excited procession. Half the village seemed to be accompanying a man bleeding profusely from the head. From the photos he'd seen, Ahmed recognized Paul Joseph. He seemed barely conscious. Disheveled and in tears, Zenia Dunlop, Zach's wife, followed the men carrying Joseph.

Ahmed whispered to Ajia, "Wait here." Nodding to the guide to take care of her, he followed the procession to the mission's brick compound.

He asked successive villagers, "Samahani. Nini ni kosa?" Excuse me. What's wrong? Each shrugged and smiled a welcome.

An old woman who gave the impression of seniority directed Ahmed to a building with a cross above its door—Paul Joseph's mission church, surely.

Ahmed entered and saw two others, a white girl and man. They seemed to be praying. Was one of them Kevin van Der Linden? He heard an occasional sob. Instead of coming from the girl, it came from the man, who knelt before Paul Joseph's makeshift altar and its obviously hand-carved wooden cross.

Not wanting to disturb them, Ahmed sat by the door, wondering what had happened in Udugu.

He waited impatiently, debating whether to try to see Joseph or get back to Ajia. Suddenly the man rose to his feet, as did the girl beside him, seeming to have resolved something. They turned and approached the door.

Aghast, Ahmed recognized the man. It was Zach Dunlop his best friend, great guy and infidel who—according to plans Ahmed had set in motion for Ajia—would be murdered if he slept here tonight.

Zach took no notice of Ahmed as he passed, nor did the young girl who held his hand. Who was she? Was Zach also an adulterer? Ahmed was so stunned by these events he couldn't think. Should he warn Zach or leave him to the same fate as his wife? Then Ahmed realized his own danger. Zenia knew Ahmed as Hanif Hassan, Zach knew him as Ahmed Bourguiba. If they saw him and talked, it would ruin everything. Ahmed's only safe option was to leave, unseen.

He watched Zach and the girl head down a village path. Now was the time for Ahmed-the-jihadist to escape, but Ahmed-who-drank-beers-with-Zach found he couldn't go. Instead, he rushed toward them, put his hand on Zach's shoulder and called his name.

Zach turned, looking confused, then astonished.

"Ahmed!"

Ahmed said nothing, just stared at his best friend. The BuckyCube Zach gave him over beers when they last met was in his pocket, a pastime for long flights, long drives, waiting in line. Ahmed enjoyed disarranging the cube then restoring its order. He knew it also kept him from thinking overmuch.

"Ahmed, you're here!"

"Hi, Zach. I'm camped not far away."

"I had a hunch—" Zach looked toward the missionary compound. "Listen, I don't want to impose, but I'd sure like to get out of here for a bit. Is there a chance we could visit your camp?"

Praise Allah, Ahmed thought. *Praise Allah.*

"Come with me," he said and led the way back to Ajia and their armed guide.

Chapter 28

Ariel sat next to Zach at Ahmed's fly-camp dining table, listening. She was good at it. Instead of only pretending to pay attention when adults spoke, like most teenagers, Ariel actually listened and tried to make sense of what she heard.

The first thing she'd noticed when they followed Ahmed toward his camp was that the young woman named Ajia didn't like her and Zach's arrival one bit. Ajia raised questioning eyes to Ahmed when he introduced them to her. Ahmed's wording was quite odd, too, *Ajia meet Zach Dunlop. We work together. Would you ever guess a Tunisian like me named Ahmed Bourguiba would have an infidel for a best friend?* Ariel was introduced as an acquaintance of Zach's.

This caused Ajia to flash a brief look of resentment toward first Zach then Ariel before dutifully lowering her eyes.

Ahmed and Zach led the way and the women fell in step behind them, but not once did Ajia try to meet Ariel's gaze in greeting. Ariel concluded she and Zach were seriously unwelcome. Repeatedly, Ajia hinted that the two of them would surely find it more comfortable, more interesting, more logical to be back in Udugu where their luggage was before night fell.

At first when they reached the small camp, Ahmed went and spoke with the safari people, who then served food and a beer named Ninkasi I.P.A. For some reason Ahmed grinned widely at the beer and Zach groaned and grimaced, shaking his head. Nevertheless, Zach gulped down two bottles, avoiding Ahmed's inquiries about the procession in Udugu and the injuries to the man he called the Reverend Paul Joseph. From what she'd seen in the jungle clearing, Ariel wouldn't have guessed his title was *Reverend*.

Poor Zach. She felt more sorry for him than for herself, pregnant out of wedlock in her last year at Choate, the father unknown. Unable to face her tragic reality, she'd come to Africa in desperation. Zach had come because he loved his wife, only to catch her in the act of adultery. Ariel had always viewed desperate acts as positively Victorian—until she saw Zach's wife *in flagrante* and Zach's response; until she found herself on an amazing dala dala. She could now add *desperate* to *sullen* as moods she understood. No question that she and her gentlemanly traveling companion had both gone temporarily insane in coming to Africa. Who could think about luggage?

Ignoring Ahmed's veiled questions and Ajia's hints that they leave, Zach rose from the table and said, "Can I just lie down for a sec in one of those tents?"

Ahmed nodded. Ajia's lips mashed so tight together, Ariel thought they'd go permanently flat. Zach stumbled to the nearest tent, opened the flap and passed out on one of the cots. Ariel knew it wasn't just the beer.

Suddenly she was alone at the campsite's table, Ahmed and Ajia both staring at her, if with different expressions—perplexity for Ahmed, and the other ... well, murder.

Nervously, Ariel stood and pointed toward Udugu. "Tell Zach I ... went back for a bit, okay?"

Ahmed rose, too. "I'll go with you."

She raised her hands in a, *No, don't trouble yourself,* gesture and said, "Thanks, I remember the way," then rushed off before she could hear any objections.

As she entered the jungle, she thought. *Okay, Ariel, remember, don't put your feet or your hands anyplace you can't see.*

Careful to take her own advice, Ariel proceeded toward Udugu and had almost reached it when she heard, "Young woman!" from behind her.

Ahmed came up beside her. "You are Zach's good friend?"

Ariel paused and sighed. "No, I'm just a pregnant runaway from school who broke her parents' hearts. I met Zach on the flight and he was nice to me, that's all. I never laid eyes on him until day before yesterday."

Ahmed frowned disapproval. "You were sinful!"

"Nope, no I wasn't. I didn't even know it happened, I ..." Tears rose in her eyes and Ariel couldn't believe she was standing there confessing to a total stranger and about to cry. She turned and ran toward the village then swiftly screamed, feeling a sharp pain in her hand.

"Don't move!" Ahmed ordered and she complied, terrified, as the longest snake she'd ever seen, its body silvery gray, its eyes and mouth and tongue coal black, peered at her from the strike position then lowered itself and vanished into the bush at lightning speed.

She looked down and saw two pinpricks bleeding on the back of her hand. She was shaking when Ahmed reached her.

"What...what was it?"

"A black mamba!" Ahmed took off his belt and cinched it around her arm.

"Is it deadly?"

"Yes! One of the worst!" He tightened the belt until she knew all circulation to and from the hand had been cut off, yet still she saw her hand swell.

"Is there a medic at your camp?"

She watched him do a neck swivel back toward the camp, farther away, then toward Udugu, which was near.

"I think I feel dizzy!" Ariel said and the next thing she knew Ahmed had picked her up and then the jungle overhead and the sky above blurred.

———

When Ariel opened her eyes, she was inside a native hut, an old man bending over her. She heard someone yelling about there not being enough ampoules of anti-venom and the old man replied, "Be calm."

It occurred to her she was dying and she thought, *so this is what it feels like.* A moment later she was out of her body, looking down, blissfully happy, if vaguely sad for the girl lying there, sad for her dying baby. She watched the old man lift her head and pour something thick and dark down her throat. She knew it tasted awful, but it wasn't happening to Ariel herself, only to the body lying there. She recognized the old man as the one who'd sat on Zach and kept him from killing Paul Joseph. Behind him stood a boy about her age. Like her, he was in two places—in his body and up here with her, smiling. He was really cute and had curly hair.

Are you dying, too? she asked in a nonverbal way that ought to be impossible.

No, are you? he replied.

She hadn't realized it was up to her. *Not if I can help it.*

All right, then, back in you go, he said.

Wait, can I ask a question first? Who are you?

He smiled at her.

I knew it! Ariel said. *I just knew it!*

Then Ariel was back in her body, feeling the painful swelling and having a hard time getting her breath. A young African woman put some kind of wet palm goo on her snakebite and an older African woman loosened Ahmed's belt from around her arm. Then she felt an odd suction, like her veins were being vacuumed. She knew it came from the old man and the boy. Her vision began to clear and she looked at the young African woman putting the goo on her hand.

"The snake is dead," the woman said. "The men killed it."

Her head still clearing, Ariel nodded. "Thanks for taking care of me everyone."

"She will be well now," the boy said.

The older woman spoke to the old man in an American accent. "What did it? The anti-venom, you Babu, or my boy?"

Babu replied, "All worked together."

"She was pregnant," the boy said.

Was?

Ariel sat up and looked at the boy. "Was?"

"You will not have a baby, now," the boy said. He spoke into her mind, adding, *It is all right. Your baby only wanted to be physical a little while. She is happy and she thanks you.*

So it was going to be a *she*.

Ahmed stepped up. "If that is true, God has blessed you, young Ariel."

Babu gazed at her with compassion. "The herbs that saved you were not good for the baby."

"Oh," Ariel said, not sure how to feel. This meant she could go back to Choate, assuming they'd have her. It meant her parents might stop treating her like a new species that suddenly appeared in Roxbury, Connecticut. It was great to be alive and not a snake's dinner. It was strange to know something inside her would die.

"They call me Babu," the old man said. "I am the healer. This is my granddaughter, Suma." He pointed to the boy. "He is the *Great One from Afar* and that is his mother."

Ariel stared. "OMG! That's right! You just talked to me, didn't you? You're the clone and ..." she looked at the woman with the American accent, "are you Maggie Johnson?"

Maggie hung her head, as if embarrassed, then she seemed to make a decision. She nodded. "Yes, I am. And that's my son, Jess."

"You are not Hetta Price?" Suma asked.

"Yes," Maggie said, "I'm her, too. It's a long story."

"OhmiGod! I came here to meet you. I'm Ariel, Felix's daughter!"

Maggie leaned closer. "Yes, you are, aren't you? I didn't recognize you, sweetheart! I haven't seen you since you were eight years old! They kidnapped you to try to get to Jess."

Ariel nodded. "I know. Do I ever know! My dad hasn't left me alone since!"

Maggie reached out and hugged Ariel in a long embrace. "I'm so glad you're all right after that snake bite."

"Me, too," Ariel said, hugging back. Somehow Maggie's arms felt familiar.

Maggie let go. "How did you find us?"

Ariel searched their faces, confused. "You're all over the news!"

"Not again!" Maggie said and rose. "Not again."

Ahmed said, "What clone? What do you mean, *great one from afar.*"

Maggie sighed. "It's a long story."

Babu rose and faced Ahmed. "This is the Comforter, Mfaraja."

Ahmed frowned. "Who?"

The boy said, "When I was here before they called me the Jesus clone."

Babu added, "He is Mungu, the one God. As proof, when a black mamba bit a Maasai warrior I knew, he was ill for seven days. I saved him. She is well in an hour because of Mfaraja."

Ahmed gazed wildly about, smoothed his hair back with both hands, blew out breath, and said no more.

In the silence, Babu asked Ahmed. "Why do you come here?"

Ahmed's eyebrows rose. He stepped back. "I, uh…I'm on safari and I met the Reverend Paul Joseph and his party in Dar es Salaam and…uh, I said I'd pop in for a visit."

In response, Babu held Ahmed's gaze so long, Ariel wondered if Babu was trying to hypnotize Ahmed or read his mind. Finally, Babu said, "The Reverend is unwell, but you may join us."

"Uh, I've got to be leaving—"

Babu said more firmly, "You may join us!" and that seemed to decide things. He asked Ariel, "Do you feel you could stand?"

"Yes, I think so."

She rose from her bed of reeds on the hut's packed mud floor and followed the others outside. Night was falling. Far away she saw a mother and baby elephant silhouetted against the yellow and orange and purple sky, a symbol of what she hadn't asked for and now would not have, yet the baby elephant made her feel loss.

What must be the entire village had gathered in the center of Babu's compound—the elders, the adults, the older children—and arranged themselves in a circle, feet touching feet at the sides.

It was an odd and transfixing sight—all of these people in one place, touching each other, an unbroken circle of life.

Babu motioned for Ahmed to precede him to a great tree on the edge of the compound. Jess and his mother and Suma followed, Ariel bringing up the rear. It occurred to her she should be hungry by now, but she wasn't.

They sat together and Babu beat a great drum that hung from the tree. The sound literally sent chills down Ariel's spine. At length Babu stopped and his granddaughter, Suma, rose.

"Now I will tell the story of the Violet People."

Everyone smiled and murmured approval. Ariel couldn't wait to hear about the Violet People, but she didn't want to listen where she was. The night was too beautiful, the moment too magical. Not knowing who or how to ask, she stood and went to the circle, hands clasped under her chin. The people shifted and made room for her. Ariel took off her shoes and sat with them on the packed red earth, the sides of her feet touching theirs.

Chapter 29

Why am I here in this compound? Ahmed asked himself. Because an old man he didn't know had ordered him to be? Why did he feel cornered by these villagers sitting in the dust in their silly circle? And who was this plainly Arab boy, masquerading as a clone of Jesus?

It was getting dark and Ahmed knew Ajia would be furious with him. He pictured her pacing in front of their tent, pitched on the dry riverbed. In his mind he saw her silhouetted against the brilliant, darkening sky, more beautiful in her new womanhood than in his most captivating dreams—Ajia, sweet as honey dates, who wanted to kill all the wazungu.

Fate must have guided him to her.

For years Ahmed had felt alone, estranged, because he had no father in his life. No one there to take pride when Ahmed first fasted through the entire month of Ramadan, no one to teach him how to drape the white sheets of the *ihram* clothing when he first pilgrimaged to Mecca to fulfill his religious obligation in the sacrament of the *Hajj*. Sent away to study finance because he was good in math, Ahmed had done his father's bidding. He'd moved to New York and been hired into a major firm so he could oversee the secret American accounts of Al-Jihad. In the process, he'd come to like so much about America: the beer, the football, women in revealing clothes, the throbbing music with suggestive lyrics, freedom to be wrong as well as right. While straying from his Islamic duty in some respects, notably his night with Ajia, he had scrupulously observed the Five Pillars of Islam: to have faith, pray, be charitable, fast, and go to Mecca for the Hajj. Yet Ahmed lived in two worlds and knew he always would, unless and until he joined with his father.

Since meeting Ajia and deciding to help her, he no longer felt alone. Ajia gave Ahmed his jihad. Now, he would belong in his father's world.

He watched the young woman called Suma step into the circle of people. As she spoke, the old man, Babu, played his mbira, making soft, high notes fill the night. She spoke in English for the guests then in Swahili for the village.

"Long ago our ancestors lived in harmony and joy," Suma began.

The circle clapped in time to the mbira and said, *Amen.*

"Long ago when Africa was ours."

Clapping and more amens.

"These Africans were called the Violet People."

Someone began humming to the clappings and amens.

"Their skin was blueish/purple."

Clapping, hums.

"All ran with pepo. All spoke with the ancestors. All could heal."

Clapping, clapping.

"They played the Healing Drum and sat, as we sit, in sacred circle."

The old man played his mbira sweet and high.

"Then some of the Violet People went away to another place and lived in peace and harmony there for thousands of years."

Clapping, hums.

"The wanderers spread across the earth and lost awareness of their Violet Flame."

Amens.

"Today it calls us again. Spirit calls us. Pepo calls us. All over the world they sing the music from the Africans. Return now, sons and daughters, to the flame."

Ahmed wondered whether returning to the Violet Flame was anything like Islam's complete submission to the will of God and by *music from the Africans* if she meant Michael Jackson. The girl named Suma rejoined the circle and from within it a woman sang, "Mungu yu mwema, yu mwema."

The circle answered, in one deep voice, vibrating to the sky.

The old man went to his drum and beat a hypnotic rhythm.

Something was happening. Exactly what, Ahmed couldn't say. The girl named Ariel suddenly smiled in joy as if something wonderful had occurred.

Ahmed felt happy as he watched her smile. He felt himself relax like he hadn't in a long time, not since planning his jihad. A deep peace filled him, of a kind he'd only felt in rare moments on his prayer rug performing salat. He thought of Zach asleep at the campsite. It was just a joke to call him an infidel. The Qur'ān called disbelievers "kuffar," but that didn't include the "Ahl al-Kitab," Christians and Jews who were called People of The Book. Islam recognized them. Ahmed's father said Islam wouldn't have warred on them if they hadn't warred on us first. The Qur'ān said, *Let not believers make friends with infidels in preference to the faithful.* In the strictest terms, Zach wasn't an infidel, just non-Muslim.

The drumming continued and soon Ahmed felt his very heartbeat synchronize with it. The drum and the songs seemed to physically enter him and raise his body's vibration until he felt he almost throbbed with joy. Eyes closed, Ahmed felt himself smiling, smiling. Then, with no warning, tears rolled down his face. Something opened and he was one with them.

He heard the old man stop his drumming and take up his mbira again. The sound was sweetness itself. It was love. It made Ahmed stop thinking about killing anyone.

He opened his eyes. Why had he only discovered Imam al-Sharif's new thinking right before coming here? Why had he only studied the stock market, and not jihad? If such a one as Sharif, a founder of Al Qaeda, had concluded non-violence was the answer, could Ahmed ignore that and turn to violence? Sharif's first book, *The Essentials of Making Ready for Jihad* was a training manual used in Afghan camps. Shouldn't Sharif's new theory of moderation guide jihadists now?

Listening to the old man's mbira, Ahmed decided he was no longer sure. Therefore, he must stop his men from entering the village tonight. He actually doubted they'd even try, knowing Ahmed was still here. That alone would tell them something was amiss. The plan was for him and Ajia to be asleep in their campsite tents before the killing started.

Nevertheless, he had to make sure his dad's friends wouldn't come.

Taking out a flashlight, Ahmed tore himself away from the sacred circle that had captured his heart and slipped from the old man's compound. He had to find his way back to the campsite in the dark and the light would scare away prowling animals. Soon it was clear he didn't remember the way because he'd wandered down a path and returned to the same spot, but eventually he found the hut he'd seen when he carried Ariel to the village. It was distinctive for its small window with four glass panes.

Anxious to see Ajia and make sure his men stayed put, he didn't at first pay attention to the faint commotion that came from the village center. Even when the shouts grew somewhat louder, he didn't feel they had significance for him. Apparently, everything in Udugu was departing from the norm today. Only when Ahmed heard a woman's scream, followed by angry voices, did he stop his search for the path to the campsite and turn around.

To his surprise, he heard running footsteps then Ajia flew into his arms. Why in Allah's name was she here?

"What happened? What's the matter?" he asked.

"Ahmed! Save me!"

"What's wrong, Ajia? Tell me!"

Suddenly the angry voices arrived, their owners carrying torches, flashlights, lanterns, shaking their fists at Ajia and shouting. " *Mchawi! Dawa za uchawi!*"

Ahmed knew precisely what that was. They were accusing Ajia of witchcraft, black magic. Why?

"What did you do?" he demanded.

Terrified, Ajia cowered behind him as men from the village encircled them.

"Nothing, nothing!" she cried.

A villager stepped forward, a strange walking stick in one hand. The other hand held an animal's horn, a cloth stuffed in the open end. The man shook it, saying "*Imbombo itonga.*" Ahmed prayed it wasn't Ajia's. He assumed she'd destroyed it when she met his dad's friends.

The old woman who stood beside the man spoke. "I am the mother of Watende, the chairman of Udugu. He says, 'I saw her digging in the earth near our church. I watched. I heard her say evil words. I caught hold of her. I dug up this horn. It is filled with bad medicine, dawa za uchawi. Those who walked over it would fall sick and die. When I accused her, she ran." Watende lifted his clubbed stick. Ahmed had seen ancient ones in the Cape, called keerie, or hurling clubs. He looked ready to hurl it at Ajia.

Alarmed, Ahmed turned to Ajia, whispering. "That's the horn you bought near Kariakoo market!"

Her eyes wide, she nodded.

"Why, Ajia? Why did you come to the village?"

She wrung her hands in despair. "You did not return! I came to find you. When I saw you in that circle I knew you had betrayed me."

He grabbed her hands. "I didn't betray you, Ajia, I only—"

Two village men approached and tore Ajia from his arms.

"Mwavi!" Watende insisted. "Mwavi!"

Ajia screamed.

"What is mwavi?" Ahmed cried.

The old woman said, "Trial by poison ordeal. Tomorrow she will drink the bark of the mwavi tree. If she is not a witch, she will vomit the poison and live."

Ahmed couldn't believe his ears. "You can't do that! It's just ignorant superstition!"

"This is Africa," the woman replied. "We are Bantu. She tried to use uchawi. She will be tested with uchawi."

They turned to leave.

"Where are you taking her?" Ahmed demanded.

Ignoring him, the villagers yanked and hauled writhing Ajia toward a compound at the west end of the village. When they arrived, a cage of bamboo was brought to the center. They dragged Ajia to it as she cried out, "Ahmed! Ahmed!" Strong men kept him from her.

Others laid Ajia was down. Then women came. Ahmed watched in horror as the women hit and slapped her.

He shouted and tried to reach her, but the men held his arms.

"Ahmed, help me, *kunisaidia!*" she said, struggling to protect herself from the blows.

"Ajia! Ajia!" he called as the gold jewelry he'd bought his beloved was jerked from her arms, the earrings torn from her ears, the precious cloth that covered her body stripped away by the women. All that remained was the cheap bracelet of elephant hair.

There she stood—Ajia crying, Ajia naked—for everyone to see.

Chanting "Mwavi!" the women shoved her in the cage.

Watende motioned to two men. "Wewe! You! Wewe!"

"What is he saying?" Ahmed cried.

"He is calling them to guard her," the old woman said. "I will watch, too. You go now. It is over for tonight."

"Ajia, I will help you!"

Ahmed ran toward the east end of the village and the peaceful sacred circle he'd initially condemned. In the moonlight he ran, past mud-thatched huts, dogs asleep outside them, past grass and greenery no longer high because of the drought. Vaguely he wondered where Steve Harris and the man from AmerCan were. Had they heard or seen the attack on Ajia? Why hadn't anyone defended her? Had Paul Joseph? Or was he too ill to leave his bed?

Ahmed reached Babu's compound and hurried down his stone-lined path, completely confused. There was no drum, no mbira, no one sitting in sacred circle. All the people were gone.

Chapter 30

Paul Joseph wished that Kevin van Der Linden, called Givn, had joined the others setting bonfires along the jungle runway. It was hard enough not to moan out loud because of the throbbing in his bandaged head. Speaking with Givn was nearly impossible.

"Had ta twist tha bloke's arm. He didn't want to come, even when I pointed out, moonlight is light. Kept saying, 'If we can't see, we don't fly,' like it was some koind of slogan.' Had to bribe him. You owe me a million and a half, Joseph."

Paul Joseph choked. "What?"

Givn chuckled. "Tanzanian shillings. It's a thousand U.S."

Paul Joseph sighed, glad not to be facing destitution as well as injury and possible disgrace. Most of the village had streamed out to the airstrip—expressing apprehension about this unprecedented night landing, but excited and curious, too. Knowing how dangerous the landing could be, all wanted to help guide the plane. Givn, as usual, opted out of manual effort.

"Fine time ta 'ave a tree fall on yer ed," Givn said.

The girl named Ariel ran back to Paul Joseph. "Are you totally sure you won't let Babu look at you? He healed me of a black mamba snake bite."

"If a blek mumba beet ya, gul, yew wouldn't be 'ere anymore," Givn said.

Paul Joseph only shook his head. He didn't want to offend the girl by saying he'd never let that heathen, Babu, near him. Apparently, neither Zach nor Ariel intended to tell anyone how he was really injured and Zenia certainly wouldn't. From long contact with Babu, Paul Joseph knew he never carried tales, good, bad or indifferent. It was his only virtue, though. Otherwise, Babu was uncivilized and dangerous.

Ariel sighed. "I know Jess might have helped me with the snake bite, but I'm sure Babu is a gifted healer. You could have a concussion or be bleeding inside your head—"

"Ew is Jess?" Givn sneered.

Light from the bonfires flickered on the girl's face, showing her surprise. "You don't know?"

"Know what?" Paul Joseph asked.

"He's Jesus. He's the clone."

Paul Joseph and Givn looked at each other, rolling their eyes.

"Remember the clone? Nineteen years ago, a doctor Felix Rossi made a clone of DNA from the Shroud of Turin?"

"Oh thet," Givn said.

"Well, Felix is my dad," she said proudly, "which is how I know Jess is really the clone."

"That Arab boy who was at the sacred circle really thinks he's Jesus?" Paul Joseph asked, in spite of his head hurting. "And the village believes it?"

"Of course," Ariel said. "They've seen what he can do with their own eyes. He's Jesus and he's come back to try to keep the world from ending. Isn't that totally cool?"

Paul Joseph winced. "And Zach Dunlop believes this, too?"

"Of course!" Ariel insisted. "You would, too, if you'd stayed at the sacred circle."

Paul Joseph heard an engine in the night sky and looked up. He saw the headlights of a plane. The villagers cleared the runway and waved as the plane descended and lined up, guided by the fires. It set down hard on the packed earth then taxied to a stop. Almost instantly the village children surrounded it, the adults watching, but hanging back.

Steve Harris and Honorable Mahfuru hurried off the plane. Paul Joseph felt grateful to them. When no one could get bars on their cell phones, they'd trudged through the jungle to take a dala dala to town and fetch a plane to evacuate him. No way on earth he could have walked out.

Zenia hadn't spoken to him since the incident in the clearing and when informed her travel companions were leaving, at least temporarily, she refused to come. It was just as well. What would he and Zenia say to each other now?

Harris and Mahfuru came to help him, Givn hanging back as usual.

"Where's bliksem Nzuri, the photographer?" Givn asked.

"He said he'd had enough of Udugu," Harris replied. "Can we trust him?"

"If 'e knows what's good fer 'im, we can trust 'im," Givn said.

Somehow Paul Joseph reached the plane, got on, and fell painfully into the first seat. Shortly, everyone was on the plane and, the pilot grumbling under his breath, they took off into the moonlit African night.

"Listen, you oaks," Givn said, turning around to the others when the wheels were up. "We've got a problem. That *bakvissie* said the kid down there thinks e's Jesus end the villagers believe 'im."

"Bakvissie?" Paul Joseph asked.

"That silly girl."

"Jesus?" Steve Harris said.

Paul Joseph listened as Givn explained what Ariel had said. The girl seemed bright. Zach was certainly no dummy. So how could they believe such hogwash?

For the first time, Steve Harris lost his diplomatic cool. "What'll we do? If we don't stop him, it's all over for AmerCan. Isn't it, Mr. van der Linden?"

"Ebsolutely!" Givn said. "With 'im around, none of them are going to listen to yew, Bestor. You're not divine."

"No, I'm not."

"Can't one of yer governments do something? Izn't there a law? Some reason for errest? The UnIted States and Dunzeneea can't be 'elplus in the face of a mere boy!"

Paul Joseph sighed. "We can't crucify him."

"Woi not?" Givn said. "Donder that bliksem! It worked tha first time! People die all tha time in theez jungles."

Everyone sat back in their seats and gazed out at the starry night.

———

I didn't go out to the airstrip with the village. I wanted to, but Jess suggested I stay and take a walk with him.

"Is there danger, honey?" I asked as we fell in step.

"On earth, there is always danger," he said, "though most of it is easy to avoid."

"How?"

He gave me that *you already know* smile again and said, *"Judge not, do unto others as you would have them do unto you, love your enemies, love thy neighbor as thyself. Be still and know God."*

"Can it really be that easy?"

"Come, Madre," he said and took my hand, taking me on a path behind the village, not through it like we normally went. It gave me a chance to look up at the night sky again and be dazzled by its glory. Of all the wonders I'd experienced in Udugu, I suspected I'd miss this the most. Nowhere had I seen such a sky. In Africa, The Creation was easy to believe in.

He stopped at a point behind Watende's compound and put his finger to his lips as we went closer. At first I couldn't make out what was in the center, but then I saw a bamboo cage, two men and a woman nearby, talking. Something was inside the cage and at first I thought it was a large animal they'd trapped, but no, it was a person, a woman. The cage was too small for her to sit up, so she lay awkwardly on the ground, one arm covering her breasts, the other hand covering her private parts because she was naked. She drew her feet up close to her body trying to hide herself in back. Silent tears rolled down her face and the ear I could see was bleeding. How could they treat someone like that, especially a beautiful young girl?

Jess said, "Most who did this say they are Christian, but they are judging her, they aren't treating her as they'd wish to be, they aren't loving her."

"She must have done something."

"She tried to use witchcraft."

"See? So there's a reason."

"Yes, but instead of responding in fear, if Watende had asked her why, he would have learned she was born in Mbeya and that she wanted to harm the mission and its guests, not the villagers. He would have learned AmerCan's mine could destroy the village's groundwater. Even if she is their enemy, they are asked to love her."

The girl called, "*Mimi haja ya choo.*"

"What's she saying?"

"She needs a toilet."

The three who were on guard looked at her then turned away. As she sobbed, urine spread on the dirt beneath her. Her voice rose in supplication.

"Bismillâh ar-Ra.hmân ar-Ra.hîm

Al-.hamdu Lillâhi Rabbil 'âlamîn

Ar-Ra.hmân ar-Ra.hîm

Maliki Yaumid Dîn

Iyyâka Na'abudu Wa Iyyaka Nasta'în

Ihdinâs Sirât al-Mustaqîm

Sirât al-Ladhîna An'amta 'Alaihim Ghair al-Maghdûbi 'Alaihim, Wa Ladâllîn.

Amin."

"I've never seen anything like this!" I whispered to Jess.

"Yes, you have."

"Of course I haven't, Jess. I'd remember."

"You don't remember Golgotha, my mother?"

My heart literally skipped a beat, no several. I shivered and Jess must have sensed it because he held me in his arms. Had I seen his flesh torn, seen him die on the cross?

I listened to the girl. Now she was saying, Subhâna-Llâh, Subhâna-Llâh over and over and Jess told me it meant Glory to God—a way to express contrition for your own or another's mistake.

She sounded just as sincere as any Christian. "Jess, is she going to Hell because she doesn't believe in the Bible?"

"Of course not," he said, "She is saying the Fâtiha, the sacred prayer of the Muslims. Just like all roads lead to God, all prayers go to God and are answered, even when we don't at first understand the reply."

Ajia's answer appeared in the form of a man who approached on the compound's walkway. He was the one who brought Ariel to us after her snakebite—Ahmed, if I recalled. He rushed to the cage, the men rising to intercept him, but Ahmed reached it, sat, and snaked one arm through the bamboo, implying they've have to drag him away.

"Go!" the woman ordered Ahmed, but he refused.

The three consulted each other and the woman said, "Try to free her and you will be sorry." Ahmed glared at Ajia's jailers and they glared back. When the three sat down again, Ahmed began whispering to Ajia in her cage. I couldn't make out the words but his voice was soothing, comforting, encouraging. It was clear he loved her.

"We can't just watch someone be murdered like this!"

"You have witnessed murder before, Mother. Twice."

I closed my eyes, remembering the recital I took Jess to in Milan when he was ten, only weeks before a grief-stricken neighbor killed him. We went to La Scala for a performance of *The St. Matthew Passion* by Bach. In my mind I could hear it as I watched Ahmed and the girl, hear the monumental music swirl into Udugu's night, hear the flutes, the organ, the oboes and bassoons, the violoncellos and violins. I could hear the two choruses, hear sopranos in unison fling sorrow to the sky, basses sob, altos weep, "O guiltless Lamb of God, Slaughtered on the tree of the Cross."

Had I been on Golgotha? I'd certainly been with Jess the second time. Twice Jess had come to earth. Twice he'd been killed. Would it happen yet again? Once more, would I be there to see him die?

Outside the girl's cage, Ahmed dug up earth then reached into the cage, dug and reached into the cage, covering the soaked dirt. Taking off his shirt, he worked it through the bamboo and laid it atop Ajia. Once again he dug up clean dirt, but this time pressed his palms into it and then ran his palms down his forehead. He used his left hand to wipe the back of his right hand and vice versa.

"Do you know what's he doing?" I asked Jess.

"He's performing *Tayammum*, a cleansing without water."

"But why?"

"He is preparing to pray."

Sure enough, Ahmed performed the motions I'd seen praying Arabs make in their mosques on TV. "I hate to say it, but that's a really strange-looking way to pray."

Jess hugged me. "All prayer pleases God. Ahmed is abandoning violent jihad for the true jihad within."

Ahmed finished and reached into Ajia's cage. She took his hand. For a while they whispered to each other. Then her voice rose in the night, boldly singing a kind of song I'd never heard.

"What is she singing?" I asked.

"It is called Taarab music. She is saying, 'How I long for the sweet words we used to exchange; Other deeds I can't mention which we used to share; Great was the impact, never did I experience it before."

Ahmed whispered something to her. Her song changed, and Jess translated, "I don't care being blamed for loving you; whatever happens, you are the choice of my heart; I'm branded with evil accusations, but I don't care …." Her voice trailed off into quiet sobs.

"We can sleep," Jess said. "Nothing else will happen tonight."

He was wrong. Love was happening between the bars of the cage.

"Can you tell me the outcome of all this?" I asked as we started back to Babu's compound.

Again, Jess gave me his *you know the answer* smile. "Yes, I can. Each will reap what they have sown, like the girl."

Chapter 31

Arriving early at the communal breakfast table, Felix walked about the spacious white room filled with African art, trying again to reach Ariel's cell phone and let her know he was in Dar es Salaam at the Oyster Bay Hotel. He'd insisted that Adeline, exhausted by worry, not come.

He stopped in front of the hotel guest book and was shocked to see Ariel's signature. Since she didn't have a credit card or very much cash, he wondered how she paid for her room. The hotel looked like an art museum and cost a fortune. She'd signed the book just after a man named Zach Dunlop. The name had a familiar ring, though try as he might Felix couldn't place it. That she might be traveling with a man he didn't know made Felix extremely uneasy. He paused before a stunning photo of a young African girl, a massive gourd balanced gracefully on her head. It made him think of the burden Ariel bore. How terribly he'd failed her! His dear, sweet Ariel was pregnant, would be expelled from Choate, had traveled halfway around the world alone, her life in ruins. How had he failed her so completely?

Unable to sleep, he'd sat up late in the lounge last night under a magnificent portrait of beautiful white oxen. Wanting to be clear-headed if Ariel called again, he'd drunk the Stoney Tangawizi the bartender recommended. It was the most potent ginger ale he'd ever tasted and Felix was instantly addicted to the delightful burning it produced in his mouth and nose. As he wondered if it was available back in the States, three men entered the lounge and said hello.

Two black and one white, they made a somewhat odd trio. The larger and taller of the black men was clearly African, the other looked preppie, like he'd just stepped off an Ivy League campus. The white man's tan seemed permanent, as if he'd spent his life under the African sun. Felix guessed he was South African from his accent when he ordered a Carling Black Label. Felix was impressed when the luxury hotel produced a Sprecher Mbege, Tanzanian banana beer, for the African. He'd read about it on the flight and assumed it would be hard to come by, but there it was, signature parrots on its label. The American ordered a Guinness Draught as if he were at Gryphon's Pub at Yale and sure enough, the Oyster Bay delivered.

The men raised their glasses to each other and then to Felix, and moved to a more private corner of the lounge. Felix had been about to turn in when he heard one of them say *Udugu*. He started to call out that he was going there, but something in their faces made him stop. Instead, he ordered another Stoney Tangiwizi and did his best to eavesdrop while pretending to be engrossed in a book.

What he heard them say last night, or thought he heard, was unnerving. Order an evacuation of the village? If the boy gave trouble, arrest him or make him disappear? Ignore the American woman who said she's his mother? People would think her crazy, anyway. He listened for names, but made out only one: AmerCan. Later in his room, Felix had looked it up and discovered it was a Canadian mining firm doing business in Africa. A PAC belonging to its U.S. subsidiary had spent millions on campaign ads for the President.

Since Ariel was in the middle of this, Felix took pains to arrive at breakfast early next morning and give himself a chance of learning more. He tried not to speculate about what boy they meant and who his mother might be. Jess had died eight years ago. It couldn't be him.

As he sat down to the breakfast table, his chair shook. He rose, assuming a leg was uneven, but no, all were steady on the floor. He sat again and once more the chair shook as if a huge vehicle were rumbling by. Hearing rattling above his head, he looked up to the chandelier and saw its strings of white coral sway.

It was an earthquake!

Felix shot up and ran to the garden, looking up just in time. An upper window broke and glass fell, shattering on the concrete pool. Swiftly he heard screaming, saw other guests arrive in the garden, some still in nightclothes—including the three men.

"Be careful!" Felix warned, pointing to the glass. Just as he got the words out, the shaking stopped.

Everyone froze, looking and listening.

"End of earthquake?" Felix said.

The proprietor, a cheerful woman, said, "Best wait to see if there's an aftershock."

The guests talked excitedly as they waited in the garden and Felix ambled over to the three men he'd eavesdropped on. The two black men had managed to get into their clothes, but the short one with the South African accent might have stepped from the 18th century, given his silk dressing robe—dark green with a quilted collar and handsome piping.

"Lucky we're all in one piece," Felix said when he reached them. "Are earthquakes common here?"

"We had one two years ago just off the coast," the large black man said, "but not as strong as this."

"I just left one behind in Connecticut," Felix replied. "Feels like they're following me. Are you going on safari?"

The men looked at him, at each other, said "No," in one voice, then moved away.

———

Zach awoke in the fly-camp, not knowing at first where he was. Then the memories returned. Zenia having sex with Paul Joseph, the crude thing she'd said about his cock. When Zenia felt cornered, she resorted to obscenity. He'd guessed she couldn't have children, still it hurt to have the truth flung at him like that. It shouldn't have surprised him to find her screwing her own pastor. As far as Zach was concerned, hospitals and churches had a lot in common, the former full of sick people needing help to get well, the latter full of sinners who needed help to be good. Just like hospitals exposed you to germs, churches exposed you to sin. In the past, he'd forgiven her everything. Now Zach never wanted to lay eyes on her again. He'd file for divorce and pay whatever it cost to be free of her. Since all Zenia wanted was money, she wouldn't fight if he paid enough.

What time was it?

Zach looked at his watch, confused. Had time marched backward or had he slept through to the next day? Groaning and stretching, he rose from the cot and left the tent. Where was everyone?

"Hello?" Zach called.

An African, probably an attendant, emerged from a larger tent. "Hello, sir."

"Hello. Where is the bathroom?"

The man pointed to the tent Zach slept in. Zach returned and behind the back flap found a luxurious ensuite bathroom, the toilette flushable. When he came out he asked the attendant, "Where is Ahmed?"

"Who, sir?"

"The man I was with yesterday."

"Oh Hanif! Bwana is in the village. He stayed there all night. So did his lady. May I fix your breakfast?"

Hanif? Why was he calling Ahmed by that name? Zach decided to say nothing and keep his eyes and ears open. He remembered the two men who'd been at the camp.

"And your other two guests?"

The attendant looked around. "I am not sure. They did not say where they were going, only Bwana Hanif did."

Did they really call people *bwana*? He wondered what it meant. "I was with a young girl. Have you seen her?"

"She stayed in the village all night, too, sir, but she came this morning. When she learned you were asleep, she said to tell you she is at Babu's and to come find her. She said to tell you Jess is there."

The name cut through Zach's despair and he realized it was probably the only name that could. Ariel had met Jess, the Jesus clone? He was here?

"You wouldn't have something I could eat as I walk?"

The man smiled, went into the tent and returned with a piece of bread that resembled Indian Naan. Rolled up and stuffed with something, it was half enclosed in foil wrap.

"Chapati," the man said. "Inside is Pilau. Chicken, potato, onion, rice."

Good enough. Zach took it, thanked the man, took a bite and headed into the jungle toward Udugu, being careful where he stepped and put his hands.

Chapter 32

Zenia Dunlop opened her eyes in the brick hut, sweltering beneath its tin roof. Kilomo and Koko stood by her cot, smiling. Was that how they woke people in this village?

"Habari yako, Mama Dunlop."

She yawned. "Well, habari yako to you, too. Um, I mean … nzuri, fine. I slept fine." She sat up. "What are you two darlings up to?"

They shrugged and giggled.

Cute kids. She held out her arms. "Come here."

They snuggled happily against her. "We like you, Mama Dunlop."

Zenia's eyes watered. They liked adulterers? Stupid kids.

Kilomo stood and pointed to a basin on the dresser. "We brought you water."

"Thank you very much," she said. "Shoo, now, so I can dress."

They ran out and Zenia rummaged in her Henk carry-on for toothpaste, toothbrush, a washcloth and soap, wishing she and Paul Joseph had at least finished their business because they'd certainly never have sex again. So much for Kansas. Possibly she shouldn't have said what she did, but she couldn't help it. As for Zach, she doubted he'd ever so much as be in the same room with her again.

Zenia was a realist, if nothing else.

She washed and dressed in safari wear decidedly less fetching than her jumpsuit yesterday, arranged her hair properly and stepped outside, deciding to stay in the village until a plan occurred to her, because, at present, she didn't have one. Her old life was over. Hopefully, a new one would present itself. In any case, things were out of her hands, now—something she'd never experienced. Surprisingly, she felt free.

Kilomo and Koko were playing with balloons, waiting for her. "Just a sec," she said, visited the smelly toilet and returned to them.

"What's on today's agenda, darlings?"

Giggling, they took her hands and led her through the village. As they walked it crossed Zenia's mind that she could start an orphanage. She tried to picture herself doing so, but couldn't—— not knowing what orphanage owners wore.

Everyone seemed to be gathered at Babu's compound where she'd first seen them. Once again, they sat in their sacred circle, the old man playing his thumb piano, though she knew they didn't call it that. A distinct something hung in the air around the circle, a thrilling vibration. To Zenia it almost felt like happiness itself. They looked up when she arrived.

"Welcome, lady," said the old man.

Only then did she realize he was the one who'd sat on Zach and kept him from murdering Paul Joseph. No one else in the village seemed to know what really happened in the clearing. They thought a tree fell on Paul Joseph. The old man knew it was a tree named Zach.

"Welcome," his granddaughter Suma said. She sat beside the little tart who'd been with Zach in the clearing. What did Zach see in her? She was practically an infant. Apparently, she, too, was going to pretend a tree fell in the clearing.

Suma rose, ran to her hut, picked up a bowl of something and brought it to Zenia with a bit of leaf for a spoon. "You are hungry?"

Zenia was famished. She took the bowl, the leaf, and eating as she walked, followed Suma to the tree and sat on a log beside her.

They seemed to take her arrival as an intermission because some rose from the circle and walked about, while others stayed and chatted with their neighbors.

"How are you this morning?" Maggie Johnson asked Zenia.

Gazing at Maggie Johnson's serene expression, Zenia realized she probably shouldn't have shoved her. "I'm fine," Zenia said between bites. "And you?"

"Fine. Would you like to meet my son?"

Her son, the cloned god? Why not? Zenia grinned. She hadn't gotten a good look at him the first time. "Sure."

He sat on Babu's other side. Maggie beckoned him. He rose and came to them.

After the introductions, she looked up at the boy standing in front of her and stopped eating, emotions colliding within her. He was beautiful. She wanted to kiss his feet, go where he went, strip off her clothes and screw his brains out. *No, Zenia. No. He's just a boy.*

"Um, hello Jess."

He put his hand on her head. Weird. Who did that?

He said, "You are dearly beloved of God."

Zenia dropped her bowl, put her hands in her face and burst out crying.

She heard exclamations from the group and looked up.

Through her tears she saw Zach. He was on the path to Babu's compound, coming fast. Before she could think or move, Zach reached her, grabbed her hair, dragged her to the ground, rubbed her face in the dirt, yanked her up and slapped her hard, screaming, "Bitch! You bitch!"

Some of the men pulled Zach off her. Babu went to him, speaking the same strange words that had calmed Zach yesterday.

Zenia kept crying, dirt dripping from her mouth with the saliva. Blessed and slapped in the same moment, thought abandoned her, leaving raw pain. She'd always felt and fought this pain. A poor man's daughter, a barren woman no man would want, if he knew. She'd scratched and scraped and lied herself to a respectable place in society, but the pain had never gone.

The boy kneeled in front of her, put his arms around her as she cried. Again he said, "You are dearly beloved of God."

Maggie Johnson's son must be a mental defective, Zenia thought. Couldn't he see her mouth was full of dirt?

Impassioned, she broke free of him and rose. "Look at you people!" she shouted. "Look at you! Don't you know what they're trying to do to you? How can you live like this? Taking whatever crap the world hands you? Smiling all the while? You're wearing rags! You're part of the jungle scenery everyone walks on. They're going to take your gems and poison your water! How can you smile?"

"A lot you care about Africa!" Zach cried from beneath Babu.

Zenia pointed her finger at the circle. "I'm not going to be like you! I'm not! I'm not going to let men *use* me for their pleasure," she glared at Zach, "let the *world* abuse me and just…just take it without getting anything back!"

Zach screamed. "Poor Zenia! Poor rich bitch, Zenia!"

The boy turned to Zach. "She is dearly beloved of God."

"Is she? Well, God must love sinners!" Zach shouted.

"He does. You are one, also," Babu said.

"Me? Me!"

Babu had to struggle to keep Zach down.

"I've never wronged a single soul in my whole life! Unlike some people—" he glared at Zenia—"I don't need a Bible to be a decent human being. I help people. I don't hurt them!"

Babu patted Zach's shoulder. "Paul Joseph has a concussion. Your wife has been hit in the face."

"What? You're judging me for that?"

Babu smiled. "I am only doing as you did when you judged them. They hurt your feelings. They didn't harm your body like you harmed theirs."

"Any man would do the same!"

Maggie Johnson said, "Who are you, really? You can't be that nice boy who founded OLIVE."

"Me? I'm the lucky one, that's who. Lucky all my life!"

Zenia wiped her mouth. "That's my husband. He did start OLIVE."

Jess sat on the ground beside Zach. "Without your help after my birth, I wouldn't have survived. Why were you anxious for my presence when you know I will only say: *judge not, turn the other cheek, do good unto those who despitefully use you.*"

Suddenly, everyone looked up at the sound of shouting on the path.

"Help! They're killing her!" a man yelled. Zenia recognized him as the Arab she and Paul Joseph met at the Oyster Bay Hotel. He'd said he'd come for a visit, but what was he screaming about?

"Ahmed?" Zach asked from beneath Babu.

"Zach! They're killing my love, Ajia!"

If that was the one who'd had so much mouth at the Oyster Bay's breakfast table, Zenia thought, the one who'd demanded to know why they were in her country, then it probably served her right.

Babu let Zach up and he rose, as did the others. The villagers' warm smiles had vanished. No longer full of light and happiness as when Zenia arrived, they made a human wall to separate Ahmed from Zenia, Zach, Babu, Suma, Maggie and Jess in the compound.

Babu called to Ahmed. "What is happening?"

Ahmed yelled, "They're giving her poison!"

One of the villagers gestured toward Jess with both arms. "He is Mungu." He gestured toward Ahmed. "His woman is a mchawi. She buried black magic last night."

"Jess, do something!" Maggie Johnson cried. "Don't let them poison that poor girl!"

"I cannot compel human beings, Madre. God created a world in which we must freely choose. Through each choice, good or evil, all grow."

"Zach, they're killing her!" Ahmed cried then ran back toward the village center.

Zach went to Jess and took his arm. "You're really the Jesus clone?"

Jess nodded.

"I risked my life to help you escape when you were born. Now you're just going to stand here and let a woman be killed?"

"If I must," Jess said, "but I hope it doesn't happen."

"Some fucking Christ you are!" Zach shouted, charged the line of villagers, broke through, and ran down Babu's path after Ahmed, all the village coming behind.

Chapter 33

Jess followed the villagers, feeling what they did, his heart overflowing with love for them. How nearer to God they had come in the four days he'd been here. Now their fear had returned in the form of Ajia and her spell.

All life's trouble lay in their fears and they did not see, did not know. Another day and they might have broken through. The high vibration of their meditation in sacred circle might have permanently broken through. Forever they would know to trust God at all times. To fear not, hate not, doubt not, even when in the valley of the shadow of death. It is the world's hidden science. Against such faith, nothing stands. Guns empty of their bullets and missiles their bombs. Foes desist. Poison is nectar.

If enough believed and practiced this, life on dark earth would survive. The world would fill with light.

Jess reached Watende's compound, stood aside as villagers crowded three deep around the circular compound and lined its path. He watched, feeling hearts, reading minds—Zenia Dunlop so repentant that in her soul she'd vowed never to sin again; Zach Dunlop, full of judgment, rage, violence; Maggie, his mother, pure of heart but unaware of her own virtue; the girl Ariel, a brave soul; Babu, powerful enlightened servant of God; the chief, Watende, integrity of mind, his soul frozen.

As a woman pounded the poison bark to dust and men held onto the girl, Ajia, Babu and Watende faced each other. Watende's men made a circle around them so no one else could interfere.

Babu said, "I call upon my right to examine the bark."

Watende nodded and Babu bent, picked up a sliver of unground bark, sniffed it and put it to his tongue.

Babu stood. "It is the wrong kind!"

"It is mwavi!" Watende insisted. "I am sure."

"This one has the fast poison, too violent. It makes no ordeal. It makes a murder."

Voices rose, debating what was said.

The girl, Ajia, looked exhausted as if she'd cried all night. Grief hadn't opened her heart, though. It was still full of hate. The only light was her love of the man called Ahmed. He loved her, too—was willing to abandon his soul for her. However, neither of them had true faith. Their fears consumed them—hers of death, and his of seeing her die. Neither believed God would answer, if called. Neither believed they, themselves, could move the mountain called death that loomed before them. They ignored God's kingdom within, even though in the Qur'ān Allah said, *Call on Me; I will respond to you.*

Jess could not save without faith in being saved, or heal without belief in being cured. His miracles on behalf of others in the Bible, all his intercessions, were called by the recipient's faith.

Watende consulted his chief counselor then said to Babu. "Together we seek a new bark."

No one left the compound. They knew Babu and Watende would be swift. In moments they returned, carrying a strip of bark, which Babu held high. "We agree this one is correct." They handed it to the woman who began pounding it to dust on a stone. Now, no one would object to this ancient Bantu ritual.

As he watched, Jess entered the space between the manifest and the potential world. From there, he spread his love over the gathering, ready to greet the girl's soul if her body died, ready to comfort Ahmed.

The pounding finished, the woman poured water in a cup, added two pinches of the dust and handed the cup to Watende.

Jess felt the sympathy of those gathered around the compound—most were sorry for the girl, but fear overrode their pity. Those not from the village were horrified, all except Ahmed, who was resolving to die, too, if Ajia did—and Zach, whose anger changed as he watched Ahmed and the girl.

Ajia screamed, "Subhâna-Llâh, Subhâna-Llâh" over and over, Glory to God, but beneath her sorrow the hate remained. She would not give it up, but clung on as if it would save her, though this hate had caused her doom.

Just as Watende reached the girl, Zach Dunlop pleaded, "Wait! Wait!"

Watende paused to see who called. Those in front made way for Zach.

"Isn't it ... I mean ... don't you have a way ... I mean ... give it to me. I'll drink it for her!"

Zach's wife wailed, "No! No!"

Ahmed wept. Ajia's eyes widened in shocked disbelief then she fainted in the men's grip.

Jess felt his mother's soul stir. From the place beyond death, he sent power to her.

Watende motioned to those guarding. They stepped aside and let Zach enter the compound.

Babu said, "Someone may drink for her. It is allowed."

Zach looked at his wife then at Ahmed weeping. "I'll do it," Zach said. "Just tell me the rules. What happens?"

"You must drink it all down," Watende explained through his mother. "Afterward, you may have only water. If she is innocent, you will vomit the poison. If she is guilty, you will die within twenty-four hours, but she will go free."

"Ahmed, is she innocent?" Zach called to his friend.

Ahmed rose and looked at Zach. "You have always been my friend. Praise Allah, I cannot let you die. I will drink the poison."

They gazed at each other, smiling at memories shared. In an instant Zach stepped forward, took the cup from Watende and drank it down. The men shouted. The women screamed. Zenia Dunlop, become a tigress, reached for Zach.

Zach dropped the cup and the stunned gathering grew quiet in awe. He grinned at Ahmed. "Tastes a lot better than Ninkasi I.P.A., that French piss you drink."

Then chaos erupted in the compound, Zenia Dunlop breaking through to Zach and anxiously patting his chest, frantically hugging him. "Why did you do that? Why on earth, Zach? Why on earth?"

Ahmed ran to Ajia, took her from the men, covered her nakedness with his shirt. He took her to Zach who'd saved her life, saying, "Ajia, here is an mzungu you would have killed." Supported by Zenia and Babu, Zach lowered himself to the ground then stared at the vast African sky.

Jess felt Zach Dunlop coming, felt him dying, Zach's heart pure as gold again and full of love, like before.

In all this, what surprised Jess was his mother. He felt her spirit enlarge. With determination she walked forward and, begging everyone's pardon, kneeled beside the dying Zach. She took his hands.

"Don't die, Zach," she said. "Don't leave us. A lot of people are going to be upset if you go, me included. Ask God for your life. Ask God! Really ask him. Then just have the faith of a mustard seed."

Zenia shed tears as Zach laughed. Not having cried before, she didn't expect to ever stop.

"I've never understood that line, to tell the truth," Zach said. "What kind of faith does a mustard seed have?"

Jess Johnson felt his mother reach for an answer. She found it in the realm between heaven and earth. "Even though it's tiny, a mustard seed knows it's going to grow into a huge mustard plant and nothing else. It has no doubt."

Zach choked. "Makes sense."

"Trust me, Zach. Trust my son who has returned. Trust God. Have the faith of a mustard seed. Ask for your life. If you do, only life can be the result for you, and nothing else. That's what happened to me. Jess told me I could come here without an airplane and because I had no other option, for just an instant I believed. That's all it took! One second I was in Milan, Italy's airport, the next I was under Babu's tree. I wouldn't lie to you. Ask, Zach, and it will be given. Seek and you will find."

Zach nodded, took breaths and then shouted. "God, I'm not ready to go yet! I owe Ahmed a beer!"

Everyone laughed, those who understood translating for those who didn't.

Zach laughed, too, turned on his side convulsed in merriment at his own joke, laughing his heart out as he died, nothing mattering anymore. He'd come halfway around the world in pursuit of a wife who didn't love him and now he was dying for a girl he didn't know. That Ahmed loved her was enough. He knew he'd done the right thing.

Yet it actually was hysterically funny, how little sense life often made. Zach laughed uncontrollably, heaving in mirth that vanished as he began vomiting onto the ground.

Jess left the space between heaven and earth. He joined his mother who was weeping in joy. Jess wept, too. Maggie Morelli—also known as Mary of Galilee, as Umm Nut by the Arabs, and Mater Dei by the Greeks—had remembered who she was.

Chapter 34

Felix walked past the beautiful pair of giraffe, carved of white driftwood, that guarded the front door of the hotel. Outside waited his ride to the airport—a white car with *Oyster Bay Hotel* printed on the door in gold letters against royal blue. The Tanzanian driver wore a white tunic and pants, like the rest of the male staff. Everything at the hotel was visual art and the shuttle and its driver were no exception. Led to the front seat, Felix got in and saw in the back two of the men he'd spoken with—the South African and the man he assumed was Tanzanian. The preppie one with the American accent wasn't there.

"Oh, hello," Felix said. "We're all going to the airport?"

"Eppeerently," the South African said.

"Let me introduce myself. I'm Felix Fubini."

"Kevin van Der Linden," the South African said.

Looking hesitant, the Tanzanian said, "Bahari Mahfuru."

Felix surmised that van Der Linden must be with AmerCan since it had offices in South Africa, as he'd learned while looking them up. That meant his interest in Udugu might involve mining.

"Where are you headed today?" Felix ventured.

The men looked at each other. "Just a village."

Felix smiled. "Me, too."

They rode in silence through Dar es Salaam—flowers, lawns and palms transforming to trash and dirt and palms when they left the Msasani Peninsula. Felix knew when they arrived at the airport, he'd lose his chance of influencing—or even learning more about—these men before they all reached Udugu, where his precious Ariel was.

However risky, he had to try something. He turned around. "You haven't heard anything about this Jesus business, have you?"

The men looked at each other. "JIzes?" Kevin said.

The driver reached down and held up a local paper. Its headline screamed, "MIRACLES IN VILLAGE OF UDUGU!"

What was that? Felix took the paper and, overlooking a story about earthquakes in both London and Istanbul, started reading aloud.

> Known as "Babu" or "Grandfather" in Swahili, local healer Simeon Mbeya is causing a sensation in the little village of Udugu. After five years of inactivity, Babu, a registered mganga wa pepo, emerged from retirement four days ago to resume the ancient sacred circle ritual of his ancestors. The results exceed any modern swami's dreams. See below for photographic evidence of levitation on the part of a village woman.
>
> During what appears on the surface to be a normal ngoma, replete with drumming and song, villagers sit in an unbroken circle, the sides of their feet touching, and go into trance. From this state, as many believe, traditional healings can be expected, but miracles are apparently occuring in Udugu, of which levitation may be only one.
>
> Is Babu responsible for this, or is his guest, a young man whom village gossip says appeared out of nowhere four days ago with his mother, an American?
>
> In spite of protests by the Reverend Paul Joseph, who has a mission in Udugu, villagers call the boy by three names: Mungu, Jesus, or Comforter, (Mfaraja).
>
> Villagers cite John 14 and 15 of the Bible, in which God promised to send a Comforter to abide with us forever, teach us all things and bring all things to our remembrance. 14:26 identifies him as the Holy Ghost.

Is it a coincidence that, four days ago, a rumor began in Porlezza, Italy that a boy materialized out of thin air, causing a black woman to faint. She was also an American and said to be his mother. The boy is said to have performed a miracle healing.

According to villagers, Jesus Christ and the Holy Ghost are in Udugu. Is this the Second Coming and the end of the world?

When Felix stopped reading, Kevin said, "Give me thet!" and snatched the paper. The two men read it for themselves, mouths open.

"Nobody could uv done thes but thet donder photographer, Nzuri!"

Mahfuru said, "But see the woman in the photograph."

"Some koind of trick!" Kevin said.

Felix decided to take a chance. He used a derisive tone. "Someone needs to do something!"

Kevin looked up. "Don't worry, we are!"

"Good! I'm going to Udugu myself to visit the Reverend Joseph. He must be appalled by such a thing."

Again the two men looked at each other.

"I'm a doctor," Felix said. "I can help the village."

Kevin said, "We moight be able to use yew. Yew can catch a ride with us."

"Thank you! That's very kind."

They reached the terminal of Julius Nyere Airport. The hotel shuttle stopped beneath the tall firs with needles upside down.

"What are those trees called?" Felix asked, pointing at them as they got out.

Mahfuru said proudly, "I believe they're called Ashokas."

Inside the terminal, Mahfuru presented his ID and they were led to a private door, through a corridor and out another door. On the tarmac, a jeep awaited them. Felix concluded Mahfuru must be with the government, which must favor AmerCan's mining interest in Udugu. Once in the jeep, they were sped to, and behind, a building off the shorter of the airport's two runways.

Felix's mouth dropped open when they reached the other side. Three American military transport helicopters were lined up, pilots in each cockpit. Troops began boarding them as the jeep stopped. Felix had never been to Udugu, but he guessed these three monster choppers could easily transport the entire village. Why was the U.S. government supporting the evacuation of Udugu?

"What's this?" Felix asked.

"If nobody's en Udugu, this es all over, right?" Kevin said. "Gled to ev a doctor along in case some bliksem erts imself."

Felix climbed into the first chopper along with van der Linden and Mahfuru, took a seat, and strapped himself in. Other than the three of them and the pilots, on board were a squad of troops, which still left plenty of room on the massive bird. A similar number seemed to have boarded the other choppers, creating a force of thirty to forty for the invasion of Udugu. He wasn't sure if the troops were armed, save for one with a high-powered rifle and scope.

––––––

Babu sat with Jess beneath the fig tree, calling the village with the drums. He played the big ngoma, Jess a smaller talking drum of antelope hide that Babu had shown him how to play. They spoke to each other on the wind, trading images and full-formed knowings.

Were it not for heightened awareness, they would have mistaken these exchanges for their own thoughts, but Babu knew, as Jess knew, otherwise. Many years it had been since Babu spoke so with anyone. Meeting Jess, helping with his sacred mission, was the pinnacle of Babu's life. He knew why Jess had come. When humanity spread from Africa, it left parts of its consciousness there—powers considered fearful and dark. To be whole again, like the Violet People once were, those who left must return to Africa, at least in spirit. It was no coincidence that African rhythms dominated the world's music now.

All in Babu's life had prepared him for this day. He and Jess became one with the drums, creating a frequency in the air, producing sound waves with which brainwaves could joyfully synchronize. For Babu it had always been the first step in opening to God.

To find the others, he and Jess reached out with their spirits. They saw young Ariel, her baby lost, leave Zenia Dunlop's brick hut. Zenia stopped playing with Watende's children, Kilomo and Koko, to stare at the girl, resenting her for an imagined affront.

"Zenia, thanks for your help. I'm going now. You coming?" Ariel called.

"Where are you going?"

"They're having another sacred circle at Babu's."

What Ariel didn't say, because she thought Zenia wouldn't believe her, was that as Ariel sat, feet-to-feet with the others yesterday, as she listened to Babu's drum, to his nsanza and to the singing, her consciousness had expanded and she was suddenly both here and not here at the same time. In the *not here* place, as she called it, everything came clear in an instant. Ariel knew, like Jess and Babu did, that humanity had to save itself and time was fast running out.

Zenia said, "I dunno. I'm not into this native stuff."

"Did you know Zach thinks it's the end of the world?" Ariel said.

Zenia looked sharply at her and walked over. "Sweetheart, given my situation, I'm not going to hold whatever happened between you and my husband against you, but—"

Ariel's eyes widened. "Happened?"

"Well, you were traveling together—"

"Huh? No! I mean—"

Zenia put her hand on Ariel's arm. "Dear, I'm a grown woman and—"

"Well, I'm not!" Ariel said, yanking her arm away. "I'm just a kid! I'm not even out of high school! We met on the plane! He was just being nice to me!"

Zenia exhaled loudly, folded her arms and tapped her feet,

examining Ariel. "You *are* quite the child, aren't you?"

"I'm not such a child I can't see straight. Zach helped saved the Jesus clone's life when he was born, right?"

"I'm aware of that."

"Did you know my dad's the scientist who made the clone? Somehow we're all supposed to be here. I asked Jess and he said the most important thing happening on earth right now is the sacred circle!"

"Mmm. Is that so?"

"For all we know, even one person could make the difference. Jess said so. Come help us, Zenia."

Zenia rolled her eyes.

Losing patience, Ariel grabbed Zenia's hand and yanked her toward Babu's compound.

When they reached it, people were getting into position on the ground. Helped by the drumming, some had already slipped into trance. Ariel took Zenia to the circle and demonstrated how to sit, replying when she protested, "Why not? We're just sitting. Do you want to be the one person who ends the world?"

Together, Babu and Jess bolstered Ariel's expanding soul.

Looking around and finding Suma missing, Ariel rose and went to her hut. Zach was just sitting up, helped by Ahmed and Suma.

"It's time for the circle," Ariel said.

Zach smiled at her. "What circle, little Ariel, if I may ask?"

"Jess said we need to do it or it could be the end of the world."

Zach's eyebrows rose. "Well, count me in." With Suma's help he got to his feet and went to the door, Ahmed and Ajia lingering.

Ariel turned pleading eyes on Ajia and Ahmed. "One person really could make a difference! Do you want to risk it?"

"We're Muslim," Ahmed said.

Zach turned. "If I'm not mistaken, I believe you two owe me one?"

Ajia lowered her eyes. Ahmed took her hand. All five of them left Suma's hut and sat down in the sacred circle, feet-to-feet.

So many had come they'd had to form two circles, one within the other. Except for Watende and his mother, everyone was here.

Soon the ngoma drum had done its work, and Babu picked up his nsanza, its sweet, high notes lifting hearts. He felt Ariel trying hard to return to her *not here* place, without success. Babu and Jess knew that her effort itself was the barrier. Yet the gift of her previous experience would keep Ariel on the path.

As more and more of the villagers slipped into the bliss that awaits beyond thought, Babu asked Jess the question that had plagued him all his life. How had humanity strayed so far from its source? Jess replied that the mind, once humanity's servant, had become its master. So much so that a Greek named Descartes said, *I think, therefore I am.* It was actually the reverse. *I am, therefore I think.* Humanity had forgotten its identity was consciousness itself—not mortal bodies. Faith moved mountains because of the power within, the gift of awareness given by God. Misdirected by fear, the opposite of faith, human consciousness created a world of enemies and dangers until the earth reached its present state—the brink of destruction, the planet dying, species dying, human beings daily killing each other and themselves. Of Jess's disciples, only Thomas grasped the truth and correctly reported, *the kingdom of the father is spread out upon the earth and men do not see it.*

Will we change this today? Babu asked in thought.

We two are here together for this purpose, Jess replied.

Their hearts embraced the sitting people, made ready by the music of the nsanza and the drum. In a shared unspoken thought, Jess and Babu asked the spirits of the villagers and the guests to join theirs. Instantly it was accomplished, many wondering if they were imagining the thrilling vibration that arose. Babu performed the gentle task of smiling into wondering minds as Jess set their course and direction into the sweet air, leaving abandoned bodies to slouch or lie down or rest against each other, later to be reentered by faint silver cords.

Babu quieted young Ariel, whose mind was exploding in *OhmiGods*. Zach, Zenia, Ahmed and Ajia concluded they'd fallen asleep and were dreaming. Jess's mother, Maggie, was with her son, fully aware.

Babu called on the ancestors to give the villagers courage. With no word or movement, Babu and Jess expanded the sacred circle into the jungles of Mbeya to help the people remember what they were. Happily, their energy thundered down the Jongomero River, invaded the wilds of Ruaha National Park, galloped across the game reserves, into the Ngozi Crater, along rocky outcrops and through dense bush. *The kingdom of God is within you,* Jess said in the languages of the tribes: the nearby Safwa, Malila and Sangu, elsewhere the Nyakyusa, the Nyika and Nyamwanga, the Ndali, the Bunguu and Kimbu. Babu, Jess and the sacred circle took the thrilling vibration to nearby Mbeya City in its narrow valley surrounded by high mountains, gateway to Tanzania's Southern Highlands—making the already-smiling people pause in the middle of their day and break into song, praising whatever they believed was their God.

In the blink of an eye, they'd reached all of Tanzania, its cities, its lakes, its villages, its wildlife, its people, lingering for a moment over Dar es Salaam, City of Peace. A mere thought and they'd reached the Congo to the west, Uganda and Kenya to the north then went south to Zambia, Malawi, Mozambique, and on to Zimbabwe, hovering over Victoria Falls, originally called Mosi-oa-Tuna, the smoke that thunders.

Babu felt Ariel smile at the tourists who stopped taking photos of the longest waterfall in the world and gazed up, seeing nothing, feeling bliss, their hearts opening to the vibration that reminded them what they were, burdens tumbling from their shoulders, worries flying from their minds.

From Cape Town's Table Mountain to the bustling souqs of Marrakech, across the sands of the Sahara, the world's hottest desert, and up the languid Nile, Babu and Jess led the circle, more and more of them consciously aware of why they were traveling and what was at stake, young Ariel still amazed, but making a game of it.

Then as she hovered over Egypt's Great Pyramid, Ariel heard a sound. Babu knew she resisted focusing on it. She hadn't been hearing on this voyage, only sensing—the wind, the sunlight, the hearts of people everywhere, knowing others in the sacred circle did the same on this strange journey, which by now she'd decided was the best of her life, perhaps of anyone's.

The sound grew louder and Ariel could no longer resist. Reluctantly she paid attention and recognized it as engines in the sky. Then she tumbled—through time, through space, falling, falling until she was in her body again. Opening her eyes, she saw she was back in Udugu and everyone else was, too—gasping in bliss, sighing, stretching blithely as if they'd suddenly lost weight or a lot of worry.

Around them, they heard the children, gleefully calling, "Ndege! Ndege!" and streaming into the bush toward the airstrip.

Others in the circle opened their eyes, too. Concentration broken, they rose unhappily to follow the children through the trees.

It was Jess who stopped them. Ariel felt him ask that they ignore the sounds and return to the circle. Everyone did, sitting down exactly where they'd been, not only feet-to-feet, but holding hands, creating a wall of energy.

Babu beat the ngoma drum and the sacred circle resumed, in spite of the chopping, whirring sounds that grew louder and louder. Forgetting to think, Ariel listened to the drum and suddenly was back in the *not here* place, split in two. Her normal mind wished there was a way to record it so she could prove it was really happening, but her *not here* self didn't pay the slightest attention. It was too totally beyond, too absolutely cool. This higher spirit part of her hovered there in gray aliveness, concerned about nothing, able to do or know anything, on command. How to describe it? Not even the word freedom would do, since it presupposed hindrance, something to be free of. No such thing existed in the *not here*. With one hundred percent certainty she knew it could create and destroy whole worlds. The only problem was, Ariel didn't know where the controls to *not here Ariel* were.

Then in the dimness she saw Jess coming toward her, beaming every color of light that ever was. Talk about exuding happiness. Ariel wanted to go wherever he went for the rest of her life. He reached down and took her hand as if she were a child. Only then did she remember the sacred circle. They were busily at work and she was off playing in the *not here*.

When she rejoined the circle, they'd reached Europe. They hung over Trafalgar Square, the pigeons gone crazy flying about in wild joy, the people stopped in their walking and their sitting-eating-lunch, looked up, stood up, pointed up at nothing, clapping and dancing and laughing aloud like Londoners apparently never did because she could feel their normal selves wondering what had possessed them. A second later and the circle were over Denmark's Tivoli Gardens. Her school had gone there one summer on a trip. Jugglers stopped juggling, orchestras stopped playing, actors stopped acting as the circle passed them and the flowers overhead. Next was Norway's fjords, people stopping beside the statues in Oslo's Vigeland Park and looking up, not talking about the weather, grabbing perfect strangers and very uncharacteristically hugging them. Over Greenland, Ariel could hear the Inuit speaking in Inuktitut about the happiness they suddenly felt.

Now over the Atlantic, the Americas ahead, Canada and Alaska, Ariel found she could zero in on any place she chose. She picked New York, her normal-self wanting to cry at the mountains of fear.

Then out of nowhere, Ariel felt her *not here* self inform her normal self that the sounds in the sky over Udugu had stopped.

Chapter 35

The children stayed in the grass on the perimeter of the airstrip, and didn't approach the helicopters. Bahari Mahfuru stood next to Kevin van Der Linden, the South African, looking at the children as the choppers unloaded their troops, a standoff between innocence and might.

"We must not go in without explanation," Mahfuru said.

"Well, they niver trusted you in the first place and they already don't loik me. Who's going to expIn?"

Felix did his best to hide his anxiety. "I will. Just tell me what to say."

"They don't know you at all," Kevin said.

Felix had no choice but to follow his instincts. "No, but my daughter's already there. I'm sure the village loves her. Everyone does."

Both their eyes widened and they turned to Felix. "Your daughter?"

Felix transformed himself into an irate parent and jabbed at the newspaper in his hand. "She heard about this Jesus nonsense and ran away from school!"

"Yislikes! You poor bliksem!" Kevin offered. "You've got to get her out of there."

Felix had no time to ask what yislikes meant, or wonder what a bliksem was. "Yes. Tell me what to say and I'll prepare the way for you in the process."

Kevin turned and waved at the troops who, seeing his signal, sat down on the airstrip and started talking. Apparently sensing the change in atmosphere, monkeys that looked vaguely blue emerged from the other side of the jungle and cautiously approached, examining the huge metal birds they'd never seen.

Mahfuru said, "Tell them we didn't want to panic them, but Mr.

van Der Linden is really from the World Health Organization. He's confirmed there is a dangerous disease in Udugu and we've come to save them. They'll need to leave right away and be resettled. We'll explain the details when they arrive at their destination."

"Is this true?" Felix asked, pretending surprise, "should I be worried about my daughter?"

Kevin swiveled his hands. "Well ... well ... it's true and not, ull right? True and not. Don't worry, jest do it."

Felix nodded and approached the children. Seeing him smile they ran to him, took his hands and led him toward Udugu.

Her father was here! Just outside of New York, Ariel's eyes snapped open. Again she tumbled into her body from far away, jumped to her feet, and ran toward the airstrip. Not fully her normal self yet, it was easy to avoid the snakes, them slithering, her running through the drought-diminished jungle that was still more verdant than anything at home.

In moments she'd reached him on the path and he dropped his bag as she ran, top-speed and jumped into his arms.

"Dad, I'm sorry, I'm so sorry, I'm soooo so sorry. And I'm not pregnant anymore! OhmiGod, I can't believe you're here."

He wrapped his arms around her, whispering, "Sssshh, there, there, it's all right. I'm here, Ariel. It's all right."

She let go of him and resumed standing on her feet. "We're in totally deep excrement, though, Dad."

"I know."

She grabbed his hand and yanked him forward.

They reached Babu's compound in a trot, the sacred circle unbroken except for her. "Come on, Dad, you've gotta sit with us."

"No, Ariel, I—"

"Come on, Dad," she insisted. "Trust me."

"No, no. Something's happening. Where's the chief?"

She pointed to Babu, who opened his eyes.

"They're coming for all of you," Felix called.

Beside Babu, a boy opened his eyes and Felix almost fell over.

Hadn't he seen those eyes for ten years on the shore of Italy's Lake Maggiore? Hadn't he seen that hair? Hadn't he hugged that body a thousand times?

"Good God! It's you, Jess!"

Jess rose and, navigating around the villagers now opening their eyes, went to Felix and they clasped each other.

"But you're dead! You can't be here!" Felix murmured.

"Nope he's not," Ariel said, clapping. "There he is."

"Well, I don't believe my eyes! Felix Rossi?" a woman said.

Felix and Jess let go of each other and Felix wrapped Maggie in his arms, "Maggie, if you never forgive me, I won't blame you. I was an absolute idiot!"

Maggie laughed. "You sure were." She stood back and regarded him.

Then Zach was there, extending a hand to shake Felix's. "I'm Zach Dunlop. You may not remember me. I started OLIVE. I helped you in the park."

Felix clapped his palm on Zach's, a long lost friend. "OLIVE! Our Lord in Vitro Emerging! Of course I remember you, Zach."

Felix thought of the helicopters and what he had to say, but before he could speak, a man dressed in western clothes and carrying a strange walking stick interrupted him. A woman translated for him.

"I am Watende, the chairman of Udugu. Who are you? Why are those soldiers here?"

"I came to warn you. They're going to lie and say there's a disease here when there isn't. They're going to evacuate the whole village in helicopters!"

Ariel went to Jess. "Did we finish? Did the sacred circle do enough?"

Jess shook his head, no. Babu beside him said, "It is a start."

"But we still have to be afraid of soldiers?" Ariel asked.

"Not afraid," Babu said, "only vigilant."

They heard the sound of boots tromping. Kevin hadn't waited, as promised.

A woman screamed.

Watende raised his hands to the people of his village. "Kukimbia! Run to our safe places! Run!"

The people scattered and when they'd gone Watende followed. Maggie reached for Jess, her eyes wide with terror. "Let's go with them, sweetheart. If trouble's coming, we shouldn't be here."

Jess sat on a log beside the sacred circle and gazed gently at his mother. "I will not run."

"Nor will I," Babu said, and sat beside him.

Ahmed and Zach came and stood behind Jess, Ajia with them. "I enjoyed your sacred circle. It is good," she said.

A woman Felix didn't know took Zach's hand. "Well, if you're determined to kill yourself, I'll be with you."

Ariel whispered to her father, "That's Zenia, his wife. They've had…troubles."

"We're not going to die," Zach said, and put his arm around Zenia. "At least, I hope not."

Suddenly, soldiers were everywhere—on the path to Babu's compound, in the circle, beneath the fig tree, tromping the struggling grass. Kevin van Der Linden and Mahfuru parted the soldiers and came to where Felix and the others were.

Spreading his hands, Kevin spoke to Felix. "Where'd they all go?"

"I—uh." Felix stammered.

"Bliksem en donder! Yew warned em, didn't you?"

"Of course he warned us," Ariel said, fighting the fear creeping through her, struggling to hold onto some vestige of the *not here*, as she realized the men's true target. Not her or her dad, not any of Udugu's visitors, not even Babu.

Their target was Jess.

His mother must have realized it, too, because Ariel heard her murmur, "No, please God, no," saw her grip her son, saw her kiss his cheek, saw tears run down her face.

The man with the South African accent nodded to one of the soldiers, who stepped up. As he did, Jess rose, Maggie screaming to the soldier, "What are you doing?"

Everyone crowded to protect Jess, who stepped clear of them

and joined the Kevin and soldier, the only one who seemed armed.

"Nowbody nlds to get excited. Oim jis going to talk to him," Kevin said.

Kevin pointed toward a path into the bush. Jess nodded, Maggie screaming, Ariel's dad and Zach and Ahmed struggling to reach Jess, but swiftly restrained by other soldiers.

"All koind of accidents 'appen in the jungle," Kevin van der Linden said, "but I'll we'll toik care of im."

Helpless, Ariel shuddered, watching the nicest, cutest boy she'd ever laid eyes on, march into the jungle ahead of Kevin and the soldier with the gun. How could they do this in front of so many witnesses? Then Ariel realized how. Who could seriously complain to officials about the murder of a clone of Jesus who'd died and returned to life? Would there even be a body? They'd be laughed off the planet.

Prevented from leaving, Jess's mother, Maggie, collapsed, but not Ariel. In her mind, the ngoma drum played. In her heart, she sat in the sacred circle. Once again she entered the *not here* place and, just by wishing to, followed the soldier, Kevin and Jess.

Was the Second Coming about to end the same way the first one did? In slaughter?

Kevin nodded to the soldier and turned back to Babu's compound. Silently, Jess and the soldier continued, Jess in front, the soldier behind, not watching where he stepped, his rifle pointed at Jess. Where were black mambas when you needed them?

The soldier said, "I hear you're supposed to be that clone returned from death."

Jess didn't answer.

The soldier laughed.

After a while he ordered Jess to stop. "This is far enough, dude. So, tell me, what's going to happen when I shoot you? Is the bullet going to pass through?"

Jess said nothing as the soldier laughed.

"Or are your atoms going to scatter and disappear?"

Still, Jess said nothing.

"Well, I guess we're just gonna have to find out."

The soldier raised the rifle.

Jess spoke. "Forgive him, Father, for he's utterly clueless."

Ariel smiled, knowing Jess sensed her, and had picked the words she would have used.

Visibly shaking, the soldier lowered the rifle.

"If you think you're gonna freak me out—"

"Well, not me," Jess said and pointed over the soldier's shoulder.

Whistling through the jungle, flying at terrifying speed, came a strange object. The soldier turned in time to see it catapult toward his head. It was Watende's war club. It connected and the soldier dropped, Watende ululating an ancient war cry from the planes and jungles of Mbeya, a sound his great grandfather and Chief Kalulu must once have made.

Watende emerged from the jungle and stood over the soldier.

Somehow, Ariel understood his Swahili words. "I am chief Watende. You are a guest of my village. I have protected you."

Jess looked down.

"He will live," Watende said. "Painfully, but he will live."

Jess reached out and shook Watende's hand then stepped into the bush, waving goodbye. He closed his eyes and stood in silence. From the *not here* place, Ariel heard him call his mother's spirit, which replied. Instantly she was beside him, smiling, strange winds blowing around them.

Goodbye, Ariel. Keep the sacred circle in your heart.

Then, just like the soldier guessed, their atoms scattered and they were gone.

Chapter 36

I didn't expect to arrive back in Porlezza at the snap of a finger with Jess, the sun setting on Lake Lugano's extravagant aura, amid the darkening green of Alpine hills.

On any other day, I, Maggie Johnson Duffy Morelli, would have thought I was losing my mind. I wasn't. I'd had a profound experience with my son, Jess, once known as Jesus of Nazareth, savior and Christ.

"Did we save the world, Jess?" I asked.

No sooner did I ask than Jess and I hovered over America, saw gun battles tearing it apart, saw earthquakes in unexpected places, saw people starving, others gorging, saw pieces of its shoreline break off and fall into the sea.

"We didn't save it, then?"

He didn't reply.

Instead, I saw another vision of America at its best, people living together, loving together, helping each other, children learning, innovations, clean air, clean water, families praying, meditating together, praising the divine in different religions.

Then I saw the whole world, felt it shudder on the brink, saw it fall into the abyss, only the stars still there, their glory splashed across a sky like I'd seen only in Africa.

Finally, for one moment, one staggering, silent moment, pregnant with unrisen dawns, unfallen dusks, the world stopped being itself and imagined what it could become. How I knew this was happening I couldn't explain, but I knew for sure.

I watched as over Lake Lugano the sky divided, light turning half its surface to liquid diamonds, darkness obscuring the rest. In awe I stared as the landscape split. Now there were two Lake Luganos, in two new realities, one positive and full of joy, the other negative from hate, worry and fear.

Logic told me this was impossible and not to believe my lying eyes, but I did.

"What's happened, Jess?" I cried, clinging to him as opposite winds whipped our clothes and hair.

"The sacred circle existed long enough for its energy to be felt, but some rejected the blessing. Now there are two worlds. For those in the light, things will get easier and easier. They will blossom. For those in the dark things will get more and more dangerous and dramatic, more and more depressed. In one world, only disaster. In the other, only bliss."

"I feel sorry for them," I said.

"For whom?" Jess asked.

"The people in darkness."

Jess looked on me with compassion. "The dark side is where you are, Mother."

Alarmed, I gazed on the two new worlds, and clung to Jess in fear.

"Those in the light have no need of you. They have found the kingdom within. Those in darkness need their covert messiah. They need you, mother."

"Oh, Jess! Am I like you, now?"

"Not yet. You must practice like we did at first. Meditate. Still your thoughts by following your breath. During the day, keep attention on what's right in front of you and on being in your body. Don't worry about tomorrow and yesterday." Jess smiled. "*Be here now* like the man called Ram Dass said. Do this often and you will join with me, with my Father, and with the Holy Ghost. You will become a light unto the world."

My fear vanished. I understood.

"What about our friends back in Udugu?"

The question made the village appear before us, the injured soldier being carried on a stretcher to the airstrip, Ariel saying to the others, "Trust me, Jess and his mother aren't coming back, but they're all right." Ahmed and Ajia rejoined their fly-camp. Zach and Zenia walked back through the jungle to the nearest road and caught a dala dala to Mbeya City. A day later, hungry and sleepless and scared, Kevin van der Linden could no longer keep the three military transports in Udugu. News of their presence had spread and was beginning to cause an uproar. To make sure they didn't harm the villagers, Ariel and Felix stayed in Udugu overnight and flew back to Dar es Salaam on the helicopters with Mahfuru and Kevin. The six of them, Ariel and Felix, Zenia and Zach, Ahmed and Ajia, had a joyful reunion at the Oyster Bay, prevailing upon the hotel to allow the women to share a room and the men another by adding fold-up beds because the place was, as usual, fully booked. At dinner Ahmed announced Ajia was moving to New York. He would get her a fiancé visa. She'd obtain her green card when they married there.

"What will happen to them now?" I asked.

"Ariel is in the light. She will bring her mother and father just by being around them and others, too. Babu is in the light. He will bring the rest of Udugu. Zach, Zenia, Ahmed and Ajia aren't conscious of what happened in the sacred circle. They think they dreamed. As encouragement, they'll be given gifts—problems insurmountable except by use of spirit. They will begin to remember. Then it's up to them to choose. As for the Reverend Paul Joseph, heaven has been trying to reach him a long time. His doors are closed. Yet there is hope that his wife, who is about to leave him, will reopen those doors."

"I wish Adamo and Peter could know about this."

Jess let go of me. "It is up to you to show them the light. For them, you've only been gone a few hours."

He put his lips to my forehead, raised my hands and kissed them. "Ti voglio bene, Mamma. I always will."

It's what we said to each other in Italy, practically every day.

"I will never leave you, my mother."

"I know, sweetheart. Me, too. Forever and ever. Ti voglio bene."

Jess smiled, turned and, his curls blowing, walked between the two new worlds.

I knew Jess wouldn't die. He couldn't. Nothing dies, nothing is born where he is. I knew I'd come from there myself and would return. Everyone would.

I watched until I couldn't see him anymore then with a grateful heart turned from Lake Lugano to find a taxi to the ferry that would take me back to Lake Como and home. There I'd tell everyone to be happy, have faith, don't doubt, don't judge, love everybody, fear not, turn all problems over to Elohim, Yahweh, Jehovah, Allah, Hu, Brahma, Vishnu, Waheguru, God, the Universe, so they can be solved.

It is time. The kingdom comes.

THE END

ACKNOWLEDGMENTS

I first owe a debt of gratitude to several gems of anthropological research on Tanzania, but especially to Dr. Jessica Erdtsieck's extensive research into East African medicine and healing. Her papers and her thesis, *In the Spirit of Uganga*, were superbly informative. Any inaccuracies created in pursuit of a novel's drama are entirely mine.

Much appreciation to two of my earliest fans who read along as I wrote *The Covert Messiah*: Debbie Norris and Chuck Schwager. Thanks also to NovelPro's Gloria Piper-Martinez and Joyce Moore who read and commented on the first and second drafts, respectively, in full. Vanitha Sankaran and Albert Verrill, also of NovelPro, gave me feedback and I thank them. Special thanks to Engin Süren, Turkish translator of *The Jesus Thief* series, for reality-checking my Muslim characters in this novel. Any remaining errors in this regard are not his.

There are no words to express my gratitude to Frank Lankford, virtual husband and BFF, no matter what. You are a novelist's dream companion—encourager and devoted believer, provider of computers, builder of bookshelves and fanciful cabinets, carver of nameplates, taker of photographs, manifester of book cover ideas upon request, and listener as I read aloud each night to test the sound of the day's words. Ultimately, this novel is about selfless love. You're a living example.

Many books informed my spiritual understanding over the years. Thanks to them, I was able to relax my logical electrical engineer's mind enough to experience Ariel's "not here place" and write about it.

To list a few: *The Holy Bible*, *The Torah*, *The Noble Qur'ān*, the *Tao Te Ching*, the *Bhagavad-Gita*, *The World's Religions* by Huston Smith, *The Five Gospels* and *The Acts of Jesus* by Robert W. Funk and The Jesus Seminar, *A New Earth* and *The Power of Now* by Eckhart Tolle, *I Am That* by Sri Nisargadata Maharaj, *The Miracle of Mindfulness* by Thich Nhat Hanh, *The Untethered Soul* by Michael Singer, *The Way of the Peaceful Warrior* by Dan Millman, *The Message of a Master* by John McDonald, *Conversations with God, Book 1* by Neale Donald Walsch, novels by Carlos Castaneda and Richard Bach, *Siddhartha* by Herman Hesse, the Seth books by Jane Roberts and—pivotal for me on the science side—*Asimov's Chronology of Science & Discovery* by Isaac Asimov, *Coming of Age in the Milky Way* by Timothy Ferris, *Chaos* by James Gleick, the incomparable *Biocentrism* by Robert Lanza, and the groundbreaking *A New Kind of Science* by Stephen Wolfram.

ABOUT THE AUTHOR

In her former career in international electrical standards, J R Lankford traveled the world, falling in love with its people, cultures and beliefs, which she now depicts in novels. She lives in Texas, not far from her BFF. Presently she is at work on Book 5 of *The Jesus Thief* series: *The Enemy Apostle.*

MESSAGE FROM JESS

The kingdom of God is within you.

CPSIA information can be obtained at www.ICGtesting.com
Printed in the USA
LVOW06s1214260713

344471LV00001B/1/P

9 780971 869486